LOVESONG

The Boston tryout of a Broadway-bound show was always a scary time—but for Jenny and Patrick, it was especially so.

For it meant they were alone together, far from Tony, Jenny's handsome businessman husband, and Meredith, Patrick's beautiful singing star wife.

Now Jenny and Patrick sat facing each other, glasses of chilled white wine in their hands.

Patrick raised his glass and looked into Jenny's eyes.

"No one but you," he said.

"No one but you," she answered.

If only that were so . . .

Great Reading from SIGNET

No One But You

by

Justine Valenti

A SIGNET BOOK

NEW AMERICAN LIBRARY

NAL BOOKS ARE AVAILABLE AT QUANTITY DISCOUNTS
WHEN USED TO PROMOTE PRODUCTS OR SERVICES.
FOR INFORMATION PLEASE WRITE TO
PREMIUM MARKETING DIVISION
NEW AMERICAN LIBRARY, 1633 BROADWAY,
NEW YORK, NEW YORK 10019.

SIGNET, SIGNET CLASSIC, MENTOR, PLUME, MERIDAN and
NAL BOOKS are published by New American Library,
1633 Broadway, New York, New York 10019

First Printing, January, 1985

1 2 3 4 5 6 7 8 9

PRINTED IN THE UNITED STATES OF AMERICA

they had moved to New York and continued to work together until her hasty departure.

Eventually the physical distance between them had resulted in an emotional distancing, and in a silence that had remained unbroken until yesterday.

When her phone rang in the late afternoon she expected it to be a woman friend. Instead, she heard a shockingly familiar male voice. "Jenny Ryland. How wonderful to talk to you after all this time. This is Patrick Lattimore."

As if she could ever have mistaken him for anyone else.

Clutching the phone to her ear, she lowered herself into the nearest chair, feeling electrical charges radiate from inside and spread to her fingertips and toes.

Patrick's way of speaking, in a rush of words, gave her a painful nostalgic twinge. Somehow she managed to get his drift. He had seen *Yesterday Morning*, the Off-Off Broadway showcase musical for which she had written the lyrics. He wanted to meet, talk.

Although he wasn't more specific, she recognized from the barely suppressed excitement in his voice that he must be composing music for a new show. Could he possibly want her to collaborate with him again?

She was too flustered to ask what had happened to his last collaborator or how he had gotten hold of her phone number. Besides, he was calling from a phone booth, his quarter had dropped, and he was on the run.

"Jenny, meet me for coffee tomorrow at three."

"Well . . . yes, all right."

They didn't need to say where. "Coffee" meant

the Café Borgia, and eight years telescoped into
eight days.

Although she tried to treat his call with the casual-
ness it deserved, she couldn't quite manage it. In
fact, she thought of little else during the next twenty-
four hours. How perfectly idiotic. She had no intention of working with him again. She wasn't even sure
why she had agreed to meet him. There had been no
time to refuse. Anyway, she supposed that she was
curious to hear what he had to say. And curious to
see him again, he who had once meant so much to
her.

Jennifer had met Patrick through Meredith O'Neill,
her roommate during her senior year at Yale.

For three years Jennifer had been steeping herself
in poetry and literary criticism but she had begun to
doubt that she was sufficiently interested in the aca-
demic life to teach. The prospect of going on for a
master's degree and then a doctorate depressed her.
When her monastic quiet was suddenly shattered by
her new roommate's records of musical comedies,
she welcomed the change. Meredith, a music and
drama major, was as vivacious and outgoing as Jennifer was soft-spoken and wryly humorous. Yet the
two became good friends.

If appearance was important to a career in musical comedy, Meredith, Jennifer thought, would succeed brilliantly. A cascade of red hair framed her
oval face, with its thick-lashed teal-blue eyes, pert
nose, full, well-shaped mouth, and flawless skin that
needed no cosmetics. Meredith dressed in bright
blues, greens, and purples, colors that reminded Jennifer of a child's paintbox.

She could admire her friend's beauty without jealousy, feeling quite comfortable with her own un-flamboyant appearance. So what if her face was a little narrow, her eyes catlike and teasing, her nose slightly pointed, her mouth a touch too wide? It all accurately reflected the person she was: informal, verbally adroit, and quick to see the humor in any situation.

When Meredith introduced Jennifer to Patrick, he was sitting at a relic of a piano in the sprawling downstairs room of his fraternity house. He nodded to her to acknowledge the meeting and continued to play.

Meredith had told her that he was composing music for a show they were creating, one with an anti-war theme. Although they weren't particularly political, they were against the Vietnam war, as was their librettist/lyricist.

"Trouble with the guy writing our stuff is that he's so dogmatic," Meredith whispered to Jennifer. "We want a comedy, not a polemic. You're the ideal one to write the show, Jenny, I know you are."

"That's more than I know," she whispered back. "But I agree that Patrick's music is really something."

While she listened, Jennifer looked Patrick over carefully, amused by the way his tangle of sandy brown hair kept falling onto his forehead and almost obscuring his eyes.

In her clear, tuneful voice she sang, "Let's make love instead of war/That's what you and I are for," and grinned at him.

Patrick stopped playing then, and really looked at her, a warm smile animating his attractive face. "Hm. What else have you written?"

"Well, nothing much really. Those who can,

write. Those who can't, plan to teach writing. At one point I thought of myself as a minor poet. Not minor enough, according to my teachers. They assured me I'm too frivolous for serious poetry. Ergo, I stick to doggerel."

"For example," Patrick challenged, studying her with twinkling gray eyes.

"Oh, Jenny," Meredith said, "give him the takeoff you did on Elizabeth Barrett what's-her-face. You know, a feminist's reaction to a proposal, à la Germaine Greer."

Jennifer oblingingly recited her parody, and Patrick laughed. "That's funny, but remind me not to propose to you in the near future."

"Propose anytime you like. If I turn you down it won't be for the reasons stated above. But I've always found the original poem such a bore, I couldn't resist."

Patrick's appreciation of her efforts encouraged her to render her "Ode on a Grecian Burn," about overexposure to the sun in the Aegean, and then her "Hip Haiku":

A handful of seeds
For growing flowers? No, man
Grass to smoke. Groovy

"Didn't I tell you Jenny was great? Much better than your stuffy old friend Pete. I think you need her, Patrick," Meredith assured him.

"I think you're right." He smiled at Jennifer with increasing interest. "What did you say your last name was?"

"Ryland."

He played a witty flourish on the keys. "Ta ta.

Lattimore and Ryland present *Make Love, Not War*, starring Meredith O'Neill. Now all we need is a plot."

Intrigued by the challenge of writing a musical comedy, Jennifer began working on it immediately. Involvement in the theater reminded her poignantly of her early days with her parents. Her father had been an actor, her mother a costume designer.

Within a few days Jennifer had come up with the idea of using Aristophanes' *Lysistrata*, changing the setting from ancient Greece to America during the Civil War.

Enthusiastically, she outlined the original story to Patrick and Meredith. Lysistrata, tired of her husband endlessly going off to battle, barricades herself in the Acropolis with other wives of both sides, and they refuse their husbands' conjugal rights until they promise to stop fighting.

"Our Lysistrata will be Northern Lizzie, who enlists the support of Southern Suzie. They hole up in Fort Whatever, in a town that keeps changing hands. You'll be Lizzie, of course, Meredith, and we'll find an alto to sing Suzie. There'll be a duet showing your different points of view, only done in fun. Lizzie will sing, 'All the slaves should be set free,' while Suzie sings, 'I need *some* slaves to bring my tea.' Then you put your arms around each other and sing something like, 'It's wonderful how women can agree.' In other words, women can manage to set aside their differences peacefully, but men prefer to slug it out—"

"Jenny, you're a genius!" Patrick interrupted.

They began to work on the spot. Meredith tried to follow their train of thought and especially their jokes, but she didn't quite get it all. Finally she concentrated on singing what they wrote, and criticizing the results from a performer's point of view, which proved helpful.

Jennifer so enjoyed collaborating on the show that it gave her a new slant on work altogether—namely, that it could be fun. Part of it, of course, was that Patrick's sense of humor and way of thinking were close to her own. With every passing day she liked him more; in fact, she began to find him extremely attractive.

One afternoon, when she happened to see him on campus with his arm around another pretty coed, she was struck by a strong pang of jealousy. She followed the couple, feeling stupid and wondering how she was going to deal with this new and disturbing development. Although she dated frequently and had had a couple of good-natured, unimportant affairs, they hadn't affected her deeply. But Patrick was special, a kindred spirit.

She maneuvered herself into a position to see his face. It was animated, not to say seductive. Dammit, he looked at her the same way. Why, then, did he never put his arm around her or ask her out?

Later, she casually mentioned to Meredith that she had seen Patrick with a new girl.

"Are you surprised? Hell, he's worked his way through all the attractive coeds—except thee and me. We're family," Meredith told her breezily.

Jennifer didn't trust herself to say more, but she wondered about the "family" stuff. She and Patrick joked so much that it was difficult to tell what he thought about her. Certainly they were friends and had, at odd moments, shared personal confidences. She had told him of her sadness over the early death of her parents, of her closeness with her grandfather. Patrick had told her about his childhood in the Midwest and how his father wanted him to have the career in serious music he had failed to have himself. His parents were disappointed because he preferred musical comedy.

Jennifer searched her memory for the smallest sign that Patrick had any romantic interest in her, but she could come up with nothing. It seemed more likely that he would be after the beautiful Meredith. Except that Meredith dated only professors and New Haven businessmen. Her mother was pushing her to marry rich as a backup to a stage career. Patrick, the son of piano teachers and attending Yale on a music scholarship, would hardly qualify. Would he be interested if Meredith were receptive?

Jennifer didn't see how she could find the answers without giving herself away. Not only was she a lousy actress, she always began to tremble when she wanted to appear cool. Before the end of the semester, Jennifer changed her mind about going on for an advanced degree. She didn't want to teach, she wanted to write musical comedy—with Patrick.

Her secret daydream was that their show would be a hit, move to Broadway, and make them rich and famous. Suddenly Patrick would realize that they were meant for each other as mates as well as collaborators. She even devised a lyric to cover that eventuality: "So This Is the You I Never Knew."

Since Patrick was now the only man who remotely interested her, Jennifer stopped dating altogether. She preferred to immerse herself in her work. For hours she studied the relationship of the words to the music of such oldies as "My Funny Valentine," "This Can't Be Love," "I Get a Kick Out of You." She learned by heart all the numbers of her favorite shows: *Kiss Me Kate, My Fair Lady, Candide, West Side Story, Guys and Dolls.*

Any biographical material she could dig up on female lyricists such as Dorothy Fields and Betty Comden fascinated her. And she read about such successful collaborations as the Gershwins, Rodgers and Hart, Rodgers and Hammerstein, Lerner and Loewe, and the new, exciting team of Andrew Lloyd Webber and Tim Rice. Nor did she neglect such brilliant one-man shows as Noel Coward, Cole Porter, and Stephen Sondheim.

When *Make Love, Not War* was staged at Yale, it was very well received. Her libretto, Jennifer learned, was considered especially clever and appealing. Feminists felt that the show presented their point of view. Male viewers, on the other hand, were convinced that the story was old-fashioned and sweet because the soldiers were expected to stop fighting and return to their wives rather than avail themselves of the services of camp followers. Some saw the show as antiwar; others found the humor and tunes appealing and didn't care about the politics.

Suddenly Jennifer became a big deal on campus, and her new popularity was quite exhilarating. Meeting Meredith and Patrick had been the best thing ever to happen to her.

The three planned to go to New York to try their luck after graduation in June. A scary move because only Meredith had a mother who would be able to help her financially. Jennifer's grandfather deplored her interest in the theater and wanted her to come back to San Francisco, something she couldn't bring herself to do. But neither could she ask him for money.

Then the trio was given the best graduation present they could have imagined. A savvy young New York producer, Sharon McEwell, saw the Yale show and offered to produce it Off Broadway.

Their first month in New York, Lattimore, Ryland, and O'Neill went a little wild, subletting a small three-room apartment in the Village they couldn't really afford, and seeing every musical in town in spite of the exorbitant ticket prices.

Neither Jennifer nor Patrick could take on jobs, even part-time, because they were working full-time expanding the show. They needed a blues number to be sung by a slave woman mourning her man, and they were adding a scene for the camp followers, which meant a couple of new songs.

After their initial binge as tourists, they were almost broke. So Meredith paid the rent and bought the groceries, assuring her friends that they could reimburse her when the show began to make money. At the time, they received only a token draw from the front money put up by investors.

That was when the three newcomers discovered that for the price of a single cup of exotic coffee they could hang out at the Café Borgia for hours. When the weather grew warmer they sat at a table outside, behind a wrought-iron grille, speaking fractured French and pretending they were in Paris.

Two days before their show was to open, they went for coffee at the Borgia to talk about rehearsal.

Jennifer was so preoccupied that she took a gulp of very hot liquid and burned her mouth.

"Careful, Jenny," Patrick admonished, handing her a glass of water and looking at her with such concern that it almost made her discomfort worth his attention.

"Wow, that *is* hot," Meredith said, sipping from her cup carefully. "Good thing I didn't do that. All I need is a burned-out throat."

"Not even liquid fire could quench your flames," Patrick assured her.

"True," Jennifer confirmed. "Once you let loose, watch out Streisand."

"Right on. And you're a lot better to look at, too," Patrick added.

On opening night Patrick and Jennifer sat in the last row of the Village theater, their fingers crossed, mouthing the dialogue, the words of every song, agonizing every minute with each performer, worrying over the lighting, the staging, the orchestration, the choreography.

In spite of a fit of hysterics just before the performance, Meredith sang like an angel, charming the audience with her rendition in the first act of the haunting ballad "Let Me Love You," then stopping the show in the second with her rousing performance of "The Only Arms You Need Are Mine."

After the show the company gathered at a party Sharon McEwell gave for them at her SoHo loft. They all drank innumerable glasses of punch and smoked pot while waiting for the reviews. Sharon, who knew everyone everywhere, learned the results over the phone. The *Daily News* critic was extravagant in his praise. And even the more cautious *Times* characterized Lattimore and Ryland as having "a pure, fresh talent and serious promise." Meredith's performance was called "the exciting debut of a singer headed for stardom."

After the initial uproar subsided, the three took themselves off to a corner to discuss the future.

"This is only the beginning," Meredith promised.

"With you two writing starring vehicles for me, nobody's going to be able to stop us. We're unique."

"Just imagine if they make a movie of our musical," Jennifer mused, "while we work on a sequel—"

"*Daughter of Make Love, Not War,*" Patrick interrupted.

"Exactly," Jennifer breathed, feeling a familiar surge of love for him.

"Then we'll do a sequel to the sequel," he continued.

"*Make Love, Not War Three,*" Jennifer supplied.

"Terrific." He laughed and rewarded her with a kiss, making her hands tremble.

Of course they were only fooling around, but Meredith looked puzzled.

"It means the third in the series, of course," Patrick explained, "but it could also mean 'make love, not World War Three.' Don't you get it?"

"Well, sure," Meredith snapped, "but what's so terrific about that?" Before they could answer, she walked away.

"She's right, it isn't that terrific," Jennifer said. "We really shouldn't tease her."

Patrick shrugged. "She ought to be able to take it by now." But he looked dismayed, especially when he saw Meredith smiling at a stocky man with a fringe of white hair round his dome.

"Oh, isn't that the producer who brought a couple of English plays to Broadway? She's leaving with him, Patrick."

"So what, who cares?" he said sharply.

"Sounds as if you do." Jennifer studied his sullen expression.

"I don't. It's just that he's old enough to be her

grandfather and frankly, I think that's disgusting. Anyway, to hell with them. I'm getting hungry."

"Me too. How about going to Chinatown?"

"Great idea. Let's sneak out without the gang."

She could have asked for nothing better.

It was a balmy October night, perfect for a walk. While they waited to cross East Broadway, they hummed random snatches from their show. Other people waiting with them looked up curiously.

For their benefit, Patrick said loudly, in his best Midwestern drawl, "If there's one thing I expect when I spend my hard-earned money for a musical—"

"It's to come out humming a tune," Jennifer finished, and they both burst into the chorus of the finale.

In Chinatown, Jennifer and Patrick chose an unpretentious storefront restaurant with Formica tables because the only diners were Chinese. She dubbed the place "The Greasy Chopstick." He insisted on ordering two dishes from Column A, three from Column B.

"We can't eat all that, Patrick, we're going to be wading in sesame noodles."

"And why not? We're entitled to oodles of noodles. How about some beer to wash it all down?"

The waiter shook his head. The restaurant had no liquor license. He offered them tea and soft drinks, drawing mock outrage from Patrick. "Tea? On the greatest night of our lives?"

"Our musical comedy opened tonight, to raves," Jennifer told the waiter, who continued to shake his head.

Patrick suddenly reached for her hand. "The truth is that this lovely young lady has just consented to be my wife." He fixed a suitably lovesick smile on his face and kissed her hand reverently. "So you can't expect us to celebrate with *tea*."

The waiter smiled with new understanding. "You wait."

Jennifer felt her heart doing a somersault and she looked at Patrick quickly.

He grinned. "Musical, schmusical, all the world loves a lover. Did you see how quickly the waiter changed his tune?"

She managed a weak smile and then did a rat-tat-tat on her cup with chopsticks to cover the way her hands were shaking.

The waiter returned with a teapot. "Special tea," he said, winking as he poured.

Patrick solemnly lifted his cup. "To Making Love."

She smiled at the double meaning and took a big gulp, hoping it would calm her.

"Mm. Some sort of rice wine, wouldn't you say, Jenny?"

"I'll say anything you like. Do anything you like," she replied in a whisper that he didn't hear. But he did see the way she looked at him, and for a moment their eyes locked. Her breathing was becoming ragged, and it didn't help when he gently ran his finger down her cheek.

She stopped breathing altogether at that point, and the only thing that kept her from making an absolute fool of herself was the arrival of the food.

With admirable control, she rhapsodized over it instead of him, and he jumped right into the spirit. They fed each other, making a mess of the table, and winding up dueling with their chopsticks.

The doggie bag Patrick requested turned out to be big enough to hold a week's worth of groceries.

"For our kennel of Russian wolfhounds," a straight -faced Jennifer assured the waiter.

"Yes. I understand. Honeymoon." He winked.

By the time they found themselves on the sidewalk, they were limp with laughter.

"That Chinese firewater has some kick," Patrick said, lurching into the street. He waved wildly at a taxi flashing its off-duty sign. As it sped by, Jennifer shouted "Derelection of duty!" after it.

When they found a taxi, they were forced to hold on to the seat as the driver shot through the empty streets like a rocket. Jennifer's handbag fell on the floor and opened, spilling out her comb, lipstick, notebook, several pens, and a handful of change.

The two bumped heads trying to retrieve her stuff.

"Our cabbie thinks we're into something kinky," Patrick whispered loudly, making Jennifer laugh and feel weak at the same time.

The driver looked at them through his mirror. "Gimme a break, huh?"

In front of their building, the driver turned off the meter, cursing while they scrambled up from the floor. Patrick felt so good, he tipped him a dollar on a two-fifty ride.

Their night doorman was startled out of his snooze when Patrick dropped their bag into his lap. "Chinese breakfast. Enjoy."

Laughing so hard she could hardly fit her key into the lock, Jennifer opened the door, then went to the bedroom she shared with Meredith; it was empty.

There was a loud thump from the living room. "Jenny, I need some help with this damn sofa. It keeps walking away from me," Patrick called.

The two struggled to open it, getting in each other's way and laughing until they were exhausted.

He flopped on top of the covers, pulling her down next to him. "Stay awhile. Let's talk."

What words were exchanged, if any, she would never know because she fell asleep instantly.

An hour later she awoke and turned to look at Patrick beside her. He looked so vulnerable, so sweet. Should she kiss him? No, she should gently remove his shoes and get the hell out of there. Yet, she hesitated. His best, his only tie was twisted behind his shoulder. Surely she could just undo it carefully . . . His hands suddenly shot out and grabbed her around the waist.

"Come here," he commanded in a whisper. Insistently he pulled her onto his chest so he could kiss her mouth.

Her body pulsated with desire. Without further coaxing she glued her lips to his and wound her arms tightly around him.

When they broke apart they were breathing heavily. Without a word they tore off their clothes.

Patrick, I love you. Did she dare to say the words? No. His silence dictated hers. Although she responded to his ardor, she bit back her moans when she had an orgasm, very quickly, and another when she felt him reaching his.

"Oh, baby," he groaned, his lips against her hair.

She kissed his earlobe. "Patrick, I . . . oh, Patrick!" Snuggling into his arms, she felt him brush her forehead with his lips.

Just as she was drifting back to sleep he stirred beside her. "Jenny? What if Meredith comes home?"

What difference did that make? A curtain over the doorway prevented anyone from seeing into the room. But if he was embarrassed to have her in his bed, she couldn't very well insist.

Regretfully she began to gather her clothes. How she would have loved to sleep in his arms, to make love again, to hold him and be held.

"I can't find my unmentionables," she muttered.

He fished under the covers and came up with a crumpled garment.

"Yours," she identified it.

Rummaging further, he scooped up a bra from under the pillow. "Yours."

They laughed. Finally she located her panties rolled into a ball under the sofa.

She kissed him once more, then went to her room.

It was noon before she awakened, feeling marvelous in spite of a hangover. Meredith's bed hadn't been slept in.

Jennifer jumped into the shower, softly singing to an original tune of questionable merit, "So This Is the You I Never Knew." She threw on her jeans and shirt, and brewed coffee.

"Good afternoon," she said to Patrick, presenting him with a mug. He was still in bed.

His eyes widened and he raised himself on one elbow. "Is it that late already? God, my head." He grimaced and moved it slowly from side to side.

Her smile faded when she saw his face alter as the memory of their lovemaking registered. What she read in his eyes was faint embarrassment.

A chill worked its way down her spine. "I . . . I'll get breakfast started," she mumbled, fleeing into the kitchen. With unsteady hands she dumped bacon into the frying pan.

Last night had meant nothing to him! The pain she felt was a new experience for her. In the past, the man of the moment had been so full of compliments, of assurances that it had been wonderful. But not Patrick. For him, apparently, the earth had stood still.

God, she felt like such an idiot. At least she hadn't been so stupid as to tell him she loved him.

The hurt suddenly became acute, and her whole body shook with silent sobs. She had to lean against the sink to steady herself.

Never before had she felt such love. Such passion. Such despair. Up to now, she had been able to make excuses for Patrick's indifference. He considered her only a colleague, a pal. Okay. That was because he had never seen her at her best or realized how loving she could be. She had secretly hoped that when she took off her clothes it would be like the girl in the old film taking off her glasses. Why, Miss Ryland, you're beautiful.

A dream turned nightmare.

Furiously she rubbed at her eyes with her fists. Then wound up washing her face with cold water. She was damned if she would let him know how hurt she was.

When she heard the shower going, she put bread in the toaster and scrambled the eggs.

He came into the kitchen, glanced at her, and quickly kissed her cheek. "You said you'd start breakfast, and in fact you've done it all. You really are sweet, Jenny."

Sweet. But not lovable. Not sexy. Not desirable. She poured the coffee so ferociously that hot droplets bounced dangerously off the sides of their cups.

Sitting facing him, she felt faintly sick and could do little more than push the egg around her plate.

"I'll bet that our roommate, wherever the hell she got to, isn't tucking into such a delicious breakfast," he said between mouthfuls. Then he glanced up and saw that Jennifer wasn't eating. Compressing his lips, he put down his fork and looked guiltily at her. "Jenny, I'm sorry. Christ, I don't know what to say—"

"Don't say anything," she broke in softly, attempting a feeble smile. As she felt her throat closing, she forced some coffee down.

His expression was contrite. "It's all my fault. I must have been dreaming. When you took off my shoes and started on my tie, I assumed . . . Oh, shit. You were only trying to make me more comfortable, weren't you?"

"Probably." She had to force the word past the lump in her throat.

Looking at her ruefully, he patted her hand. "Please forgive me. You know how much I like you."

"Sure. I like you, too. I'm a big girl. I could have stopped you, but I didn't. So forget it. It just . . . happened, that's all. No harm done." She jumped up to get more coffee.

Plenty of harm done. He "liked" her. Terrific. His "like" was to her "love" as ice is to flame.

But by the time she sat down again she had willed herself to feel more positive. To give it more time. He might not love her—yet—but they had had a marvelous time in Chinatown, and he *had* wanted her to some extent. She would have to be patient until he realized just how right she was for him.

During the following week she and Patrick kicked around a few new plot ideas that sank without a trace. Her determination to hold back her love for him, she suspected, was causing her to hold back creatively as well. She felt uninspired, heavy, like a caterpillar inching its way, waiting to become a butterfly so it could soar.

Although Patrick never referred to their intimacy—indeed, seemed to have forgotten it had happened—Jennifer could think of almost nothing else.

I kissed his temple, right in that spot, she would remember, sneaking a look at him when he was too absorbed to notice. Those slender, sensitive fingers playing the piano had caressed her body, those lips had kissed hers. She and he had been as physically close as two people could be. How could it have meant so little to him?

At night she lay in bed tortured by the nearness of him, asleep in the living room. And yet he might as well have been on the moon.

One of the dancers in the show was looking for a roommate, and Jennifer was tempted to move in with her. If she did, maybe Patrick would wonder why. Maybe he would begin to take her seriously.

She couldn't decide what to do. Getting used to a new roommate didn't appeal to her. Besides, if she moved she would see less of Patrick. Would absence make his heart grow fonder? Or would it be a case of out of sight, out of mind? She laughed at herself, wondering which cliché would apply.

While she mulled the pros and cons of moving, she had a call from her grandfather. At the sound of his voice guilt flooded through her. She hadn't called him in a while, partly because he always lectured her on the evils of the theater. He had opposed his only daughter's marriage to an older actor. When his son-in-law died onstage of a heart attack, and his daughter of cancer a few years later, he was more sure than ever that the theater was bad luck.

"When are you coming home, girl?" her grandfather asked. "I'm anxious for a look at you while I still see out of these old eyes." He was trying to keep his tone light, but she heard a shakiness in his voice she hadn't noticed before. A sudden premonition that all was not well with him frightened her. He was past eighty, and although he had seemed spry and vigorous enough when she had seen him last, a change could occur at any time.

To her guarded question about his activities, he replied, "I've been keeping busy tending to financial matters, seeing some old friends, going to the opera. Jenny, how long am I going to have to wait to see you?"

"I can't say for sure, Gramps. Our show's going to be running longer than anyone thought, and some of the actors have other commitments. So cast changes mean other changes, and I have to be here for that."

What she was saying was legitimate, but she knew she was also stalling.

"How are you for funds?"

"Fine. We're sold out every night, and I'm earning some pretty good money."

Her grandfather grunted, and she said again that she would come home as soon as she could.

When she hung up she felt dishonest because "home" to her was now New York, not San Francisco.

Patrick stuck his head out of the living room. "Meredith asked us to come to the theater tonight. Says she always does better knowing we're there cheering."

Jennifer agreed to go, although the prospect of spending the evening with him was a mixed blessing.

She gave all her conscious attention to the perfor-

mance—Meredith was especially good that night—
while being excruciatingly aware of Patrick sitting
beside her. Of his hand lightly brushing hers. Of his
strong thigh only inches away from her own. Every
time he turned to smile at her or whisper something
in her ear, she thought she would die from the effort
to keep herself from jumping into his arms.

Afterward the three friends went out for a drink,
and on the spur of the moment, splurged on a bottle
of champagne. Patrick was bright-eyed, sparkling,
even wittier than usual. Jennifer, her spirits soaring,
bantered with him, while Meredith, for once not
making an attempt to keep up, just sipped her champagne, her smile so dazzling that it drew many
admiring glances.

When they got home, Patrick suddenly put his
arm around Jennifer's waist and whispered in her
ear, "I'm rushing out tomorrow at the crack of
dawn. Possible assignment to do a tune for a radio
commercial. But I have to speak to you. Meet me for
coffee in the afternoon—say, two-thirty."

She nodded, transfixed, feeling pinpricks of heat
stippling her skin while she tried to digest the meaning of this new secrecy. Had he finally come to his romantic senses about her?

All night long she dozed for what seemed only moments at a time, waking with a start. She replayed
an imaginary love scene between them so many
times in her head that her body was on fire with desire for him.

Patrick was gone by the time the two women had
breakfast. Jennifer, utterly unable to concentrate on
what Meredith was saying, broke a glass, almost
poked her eye out applying mascara—something she
seldom wore—and was in such a state of anticipation

that she felt quite giddy. Lunch was out of the question.

Her imagination, always extravagant, ran wild. She would take him to meet her grandfather, who would give them his blessing once he heard Patrick's wonderful music. They would call their first daughter Melissa, after the *character in Lawrence Durrell's Alexandria Quartet*, which she and Patrick had loved when they read it at Yale.

Worked up to a level of such excitement that she could barely stand it, Jennifer got to the Borgia half an hour early. She drank double espressos, which only agitated her further.

Patrick was forty minutes late. He slid into his seat and grinned at her sheepishly. "You probably think I'm behaving like an idiot, but I had to see you alone today and ask you something. I know we're planning to celebrate Meredith's birthday the day after tomorrow with dinner and a cake, but I want to buy something really special for her to . . . well . . . I mean . . ." He stopped and looked at Jennifer guiltily. "Jenny, did you tell her about . . . about us, opening night?"

Slowly she shook her head, swallowing hard to hide her devastation.

"Of course Meredith's very ambitious," Patrick continued, "and she's been brainwashed to marry rich. But we're all going to be rich. It will be Broadway next time for sure, and I just can't wait. I want her to know how I feel, so that if she really doesn't care for those old guys she dates . . . Tell me honestly, Jenny, if you think I'm kidding myself."

She forced herself to look him in the eye. She must have been blind. How could she have missed it? Patrick loved Meredith.

"I can't imagine she won't return your feeling," Jennifer said generously at last.

He smiled. "Thanks, Jenny. You're a pal. You know, you're so cool, if you ever fall in love you'll have to put it in writing, preferably in verse, or the guy will have no way of knowing."

A spark of anger darkened her eyes. He could be pretty damn stupid about some things. "If the man is right for me, he'll know," she answered crisply.

Quickly she averted her glance. "A present for Meredith . . . let's see, something romantic, under the circumstances. Jewelry, I suppose, expensive—"

"I'll buy it, no matter what," he declared.

Feeling like a fool, she let him persuade her to help him choose, and he settled on a gold locket, heart-shaped, which cost him two weeks' royalties.

Wearily Jennifer dragged herself home and took a good look in the mirror. What she saw was a pleasant but unremarkable face, nothing to compare with Meredith's shimmering beauty.

Jennifer critically regarded her broad shoulders, firm, average-size breasts, slender waist, slim, rounded hips, and straight, strong legs. She looked like a tennis player, whereas Meredith, all pink and white, with voluptuous breasts and flaring hips, was a modern version of a Renoir.

Glumly slipping into jeans and a shirt, Jennifer went for a walk. Patrick was no better than most men. She had been naive to expect his other perceptions to be as acute as his musical sensibilities.

Maybe he had a Pygmalion complex. It wasn't uncommon for composers and filmmakers to fall in love with their singers/leading ladies, because they had, so they imagined, created them. Maybe Jennifer was too smart, too independent in her thinking. "So This

Is You, the Same Old You." At least she was able to laugh at herself—a little.

If Meredith and Patrick, her best friends, were going to be lovers, she would damn well have to get used to it.

Meredith wore the locket at her birthday dinner, but from her casual behavior and Patrick's look of disappointment, Jennifer gathered that it was a case of unrequited love. Later, he glumly confided to her that Meredith thought of him like a brother.

Jennifer's hopes revived slightly but she made a joke of them, composing a little verse called "Triangle" to amuse herself and try to ease the ache in her heart.

However, the pain got worse instead of better. Jennifer just didn't know what to do about her living arrangements. She found it unbearable to continue to watch Patrick watching Meredith. Not only would she have to move, she wondered how she could continue the collaboration when every moment spent with him had become a torment to her.

She lost her appetite for food and began to subsist on sweets, especially chocolate. Her sleep was disturbed by nightmarish dreams she couldn't recall but which left her irritable and drained.

Another week crept by slowly, while she agonized. Finally deciding she simply had to make a move, and to hell with how she'd explain it, Jennifer called the dancer who had wanted a roommate. She was too late: a new roommate had been found.

Jennifer was annoyed with herself for having waited, and it put her in a bad mood.

When she got back to the apartment she found the bedroom in a mess. Meredith had strewn clothes all over, including on Jennifer's bed.

Furious, she began to gather up the garments, just as her roommate walked in.

Jennifer whirled. "Do you have to be so goddam sloppy? It's bad enough messing up your own bed, but stay away from mine, okay?"

"What are you so bitchy about?" Meredith yelled, her temper flaring. "I only ran down to the drugstore. I was planning to put the stuff away. It's not as if you were going to bed at five in the afternoon—"

"That's not the point. We each have a space here and you're always encroaching on mine. You put your stuff in *my* drawers, your makeup on *my* side of the dresser, your clothes in *my* spot in the closet—"

"Yeah, and I paid *your* share of the rent and food when you were down to your last dollar a couple of months ago."

Jennifer felt a wave of remorse. "You're right. I am being bitchy. I'm sorry, Meredith."

"Yeah, okay, forget it," she mumbled. She had a quick temper but was quick to get over it.

Jennifer, ashamed of her outburst, helped Meredith to put away her things. What she had really been saying, with all that yours-and-mine stuff, was that Meredith had won the affections of *her* Patrick.

Maybe she needed to get out of town altogether and give herself time to get over Patrick.

The following Saturday, Jennifer moped around the apartment all day. It was raining, Meredith was out shopping, and Patrick was in the living room with the curtain drawn while he did some work on his radio assignment.

Meredith returned only in time to change and rush to the theater for the early performance. Then Patrick went out to meet someone for a drink, leaving Jennifer feeling especially forlorn. The three of them were going to have coffee at the Borgia between performances, but that prospect didn't cheer her up very much.

What the hell am I doing here? she asked herself repeatedly. Nothing much, came the answer.

When the phone rang she almost didn't bother to answer it. She wasn't in the mood for a conversation, for forcing herself to be cheerful when she felt rotten. But after the fifth ring she decided it could be Patrick or Meredith, and she answered.

It was her grandfather's lawyer, telling her that her grandfather had suffered a stroke while at a luncheon and had been rushed to the hospital.

Her knees went rubbery. She had waited too long, and now she might never see her grandfather again. Frantically she phoned an airline and reserved a seat for an evening flight.

She packed in a rush and with her suitcase in her hand, left the apartment and went directly to the Borgia.

Patrick was already there, early for once. He stared at her suitcase and then at her. "Jenny, my God, what's wrong?"

As she tried to tell him, she burst into tears.

He got up from his seat and enfolded her in his arms, stroking her hair and murmuring soothing words. That only made her more hysterical.

She hated the irony of being in his arms, where she had so longed to be, for such a grim reason. The more he tried to comfort her, the harder she cried. She felt like an impostor as well as an idiot because she was crying for him, too.

Patrick insisted that she sit down for a moment

and that she have a cup of coffee. He offered to get her a taxi and to go with her to the airport.

"No, thanks," she sniffed, ashamed of having made such a spectacle of herself.

"You're sure?"

"I'm sure. Stay and tell Meredith. I'll be in touch as soon as I can."

Carrying her suitcase, Patrick insisted on waiting with her for a taxi. It was pouring once again, and he was getting wet. God, she felt like such a fool.

When a taxi finally stopped, Patrick gave her a last damp hug. "Good luck, Jenny. Let us know if there's anything we can do."

As the cab pulled away, she turned in her seat.

Her last sight of him was through the rain-streaked rear window. She had the sad feeling that she wouldn't see him again for a long time.

Eight years.

Jennifer glanced at her watch. Patrick was late. Wiping her moist palms on a tissue, she willed her heartbeat to approach to a normal rhythm. It was ridiculous to feel so nervous. Her abortive romance with him was long ago and far away. And Meredith had married him after all.

The coffeehouse began to fill up with noisy students from NYU. A decade ago Jennifer had been exuberant like them, believing anything was possible. Not anymore. She was thirty, and she had lived through an unforgettable tragedy. But if she was no longer wildly optimistic, at least she had learned to enjoy fully all pleasures that came her way.

Jenny Ryland had been unrealistic, wanting a love

she could never have. But Jennifer De Palma knew what love really was.

Suddenly Patrick was standing in front of her, smiling and holding out his hands—warm, strong hands whose touch she had not forgotten.

2

Patrick pulled her to her feet. "Jenny, for God's sake, how the hell are you?" After kissing her cheek he stood back, looking at her with undisguised pleasure.

She smiled idiotically while her heart worked like a hydraulic pump. "Fine," she finally got out in a voice that was almost inaudible. Feeling a weakness in her knees, she gripped the table, staring as hard at him as he was at her.

"You look smashing, Jenny, and not a day older. Your hair's different. I like it. God, it's been ages," he finished grinning at her.

"Yes," she murmured, her smile a little stiff as she felt drops of moisture gathering in her eyes. Embarrassed, she averted her gaze, hoping he hadn't noticed.

He looked wonderfully, achingly the way she remembered him. His hair, almost the same color as hers, was shorter than in the past and fell casually around his strong-jawed face. He was youthful still, with only the merest traces of lines in the corners of his mouth and eyes. He hadn't put any weight on his solid, broad-shouldered frame. Somehow he seemed taller than she remembered, in his gray herringbone-tweed jacket, dark gray trousers, and black wool turtleneck. He wore no coat, only a familiar muted plaid scarf that she recognized as a Christmas present from her years ago. He probably didn't even remember.

"Shall we stay?" she teased, sitting down quickly.

"By all means." He grinned and took a seat. As he tucked his feet under the table she noticed that he was wearing a pair of De Palma loafers, with their distinctive buckle across the top. She smiled, remembering that Meredith had always felt shoes and accessories were the most important items of a person's wardrobe.

"How's Meredith?"

"Very well. She sends her love and is looking forward to seeing you. And . . . your husband." Patrick smiled and touched Jennifer's wedding band with his finger. "Congratulations."

She was aware of moving her hand away more abruptly than she intended. "Thanks. I'm not exactly on my honeymoon. I've been married for seven years. To Tony De Palma. You know, leather?"

Patrick continued to look interested but unenlightened.

She laughed, and it helped her to relax. "I don't suppose you've ever heard of the De Palma boutiques? Even though you're wearing De Palma shoes?"

"I am?" Patrick stuck his foot out comically, regarded it, and laughed with her. "I guess I am, if you say so. I still have no clothes sense. Meredith drags me shopping when I'm so down-at-heel that she can't stand it anymore. We pay more for our shoes, I think, than the rest of our gear put together. As long as they're comfortable. These are great, in fact. So you're married to that De Palma. Happily, I gather, judging by how wonderful you look."

"Yes, very happily," she echoed, aware that her enthusiasm was slightly forced. She stifled a sigh, ashamed of her stupid inability to let go of the past. *Of course* she was happily married, and to the most loving man in the world.

"How long have you been in New York, Jenny?"

"About two years, I guess—"

"Two years! And you never called!"

Surprised at how hurt he sounded, she quickly said, "I always meant to, Patrick, but the time seems to go by so fast. I've traveled quite a lot with Tony. And the longer I postponed getting in touch, the harder it was somehow," she finished lamely.

He studied her soberly. "I thought you might be here only on a visit, for the duration of the showcase production. Well, never mind. I've found you again and this time I won't let you go. Neither will Meredith. Or Lissa, when she meets you. She's almost seven, a real delight, if you'll forgive a father's prejudice. I never thought much about kids until she came along. Suddenly I began to notice, and to understand why people have 'em and go through all that mess to bring 'em up. What's the matter?"

"Her . . . her name is Lissa?"

"Melissa. Meredith shortened it. How about you, Jenny? Any children?"

She felt her throat closing. All she could do was shake her head mutely and let the pain wash over her.

Noticing her distress, he smoothly changed the subject. "It's just marvelous to drink cappuccino together the way we used to. But dammit, Jenny, I need something stronger to celebrate our reunion. Like a Scotch."

She nodded, feeling she needed a drink at least as much as he.

When the waiter brought their drinks, Patrick lifted his glass. "To old friends."

"To old friends," she repeated, unable to tear her eyes away from his for a long moment.

She sipped her drink nervously. "What are you and Meredith doing these days?"

He shrugged. "Nothing much for about a year, not since *Cameo*. Our first show on Broadway, but it ran for only a couple of months. If you were traveling or something, maybe you didn't even know about it."

She concentrated on an ice cube melting in her glass. "I saw *Cameo*."

"I see. And never thought of coming backstage?"

"I did think of it but I . . . I just didn't."

"You hated it that much, huh?"

"Of course I didn't hate it. I thought Meredith was terrific—"

"But the show stank, and so did my music," he said in a tone of disgust, looking at her steadily.

She met his glance. "No, your music didn't stink, though I'll agree you can do better. The rest of the show, well . . ."

He nodded and smiled ruefully. "Dear Jenny, still honest, still true blue. In fact, *Cameo* had a longer run than it deserved. The lyricist was all wrong, the book was hopeless . . ."

As he talked on, she was a little ashamed of feeling vindicated. He was implying what she had been sure of for the past eight years: that she had been the ideal lyricist for him.

"I could say the same thing about your showcase, *Yesterday Morning*. The music was so derivative, in fact, that *Songs of Yesteryear* would have been a better title. That composer carried eclecticism to ridiculous lengths. Hell, he was all over the place."

"Absolutely," she agreed. "He mixed a little Porter with a little Dick Rodgers—"

"Added some Bernstein and Sondheim, stirred it up with—"

"A dollop of Andrew Lloyd Webber—"

"And wound up with a mess. Yet you managed to find just the right words for each musical idiom. That's what I admire so much about you, among other things."

As Patrick smiled sadly at her, her hands began to shake. Idiot, she lectured herself, clasping them in her lap. The other things he surely meant would not cause tremors in any sensible woman.

"You're still cool, Jenny, and so elegant. The Contessa De Palma," he joked.

As waves of heat coursed through her she reflected angrily on how wrong he was, and abruptly said, "Did you call this meeting with something specific in mind?" She winced as her question came out sounding stiff and businesslike, then decided it was exactly the right tone to adopt.

"Yes," he said, looking at her intently. "I want you back, Ryland. Lattimore and Novack aren't worth a damn. Neither were Lattimore and Thomas. The same would hold true, I suspect, for Lattimore and You-Name-It."

Although she had many times imagined him saying such words, they came as a shock all the same.

"Before *Cameo*, Jenny, there was *Me, Tarzan*. God, the high hopes we had for that one, even if it had to be Off Broadway. Except it only ran for seventy-seven performances."

She knew. She had followed the show's progress from California, wanting it to fall on its face, yet not enough of a killer to really mean it.

"Meredith had to carry the whole show. I won't bore you with all the disasters, such as losing our original Tarzan the second week. He literally broke a leg." Patrick sighed. "Still, the main problem, as one critic so caustically and, I'm afraid, accurately, put it, was that my music couldn't rise above the banal lyrics."

Her heart hammered unevenly against her ribs. "I assume Tarzan was the idea you had when . . . when last we talked on the phone way back then?"

He nodded. "If only you had worked with me on Tarzan, what a different fate it would have had. I always thought we were perfect together," he added softly, looking at her with a flicker of resentment.

Her face grew hot. He could say that now!

"Why did you stay in San Francisco after your grandfather died?"

She looked at him sharply, wondering how he dared to ask her such a question. Yet, he seemed serious.

Swallowing, she waited until she was sure she could control her voice. "Well, you had taken on another collaborator, so I decided—"

"What? What the devil are you talking about?" He sounded genuinely astonished. "I was waiting for *you* to come back. It was only after I found out you weren't that I had to find someone else."

She held her breath. That wasn't at all the way she remembered it. But she realized that there was no way for her to say so without . . . without complicating an already difficult discussion. Exhaling slowly, she decided she had to let it drop for the moment, although her mind was racing wildly.

"Oh, damn, Jenny," he said, suddenly apologetic. "You must already have met De Palma, hadn't you?"

"Yes."

"And his business was out there?"

She nodded.

Patrick studied her and traced the rim of his glass with a long, slender finger. "I can understand that you got married. I can even see why you felt you had to give up our collaboration. But what I don't understand—and neither does Meredith—is why you sent us a wedding gift and then dropped out of sight. I tried to call you a couple of times, but the phone number had been changed. We wondered if you'd moved. Then I wrote, thinking the letter would be forwarded. We never heard from you again. And you've been back for two years. Why, Jenny?"

She couldn't look him in the eye. Couldn't tell him that she had been furious with him, not for marrying Meredith but for finding a new collaborator without even checking with her first. At least, that was what she had believed until just now. In fact, she had torn up his letter because by the time it arrived she had thrown herself into her new life with Tony. She had convinced herself that Patrick wasn't the only composer in the world, that she, too, would find another partner. And she had, but nobody to compare with him.

"All those years I've been wondering if you really gave up wanting to be the best on Broadway."

She swallowed. She never had given it up, but a lot of youthful enthusiasm had gone out of her because of what he had done—or she had thought. And afterward, there was Melissa. Her Melissa, hers and Tony's.

Licking her lips, which had suddenly grown dry, she spoke softly. "We had a daughter. She . . . died in an accident when she was only two. And afterward I simply couldn't work. Words wouldn't come, not lighthearted words, anyway. It happened four years ago but I'm still not over it." She stopped speaking as two large tears formed and rolled down her cheeks.

"Jenny, my God! I'm so sorry." Patrick's voice was pained. He pressed her hand for a moment while she used her other to dab at her face with a tissue.

She was grateful for his understanding that further words wouldn't help, and that she did not want pity.

Both were silent for a few minutes. Then he gently said, "When I noticed in the paper that the lyrics of *Yesterday Morning* were by Jennifer Ryland, I rushed to see it. It only confirmed what I already knew: that your talent is uniquely suited to me."

If only he had said so to her on the phone all those years ago. He would never know how much that would have meant then. But before she could speak he began to hum softly.

With a shock, she recognized his incomparable way of weaving a melody that was original and complex, yet simple enough to be catchy.

"I've been playing around with a few tunes. Like that one?"

"I do, but—"

He put a finger on her lips for a moment, sending a tremor down her backbone. "*Helen of Troy*," he said simply.

Jennifer frowned. "Wasn't there a show a while back, *Golden Apples*, something like that?"

"*The Golden Apple*, yes. But that was different, set in the U.S. in the early 1900s. Besides, it was as much about Ulysses and Penelope as Helen."

"As I remember, some of the songs were nice."

"They were. Still, the idea was a little cornball, mythology updated for the mass audience. I find the original story more exciting, and I'd take it right through the Trojan War."

"Hm. Not a bad idea, depending on how it's handled."

"With you doing the book and lyrics, and Meredith playing Helen, it'll be terrific. We need you, Jenny."

She looked quickly at him. "Does Meredith think so?"

He hesitated only a fraction of a second before answering, "Of course. And I want a hit for her. God knows she deserves it. Think of the challenge, Jenny. The Trojan Horse onstage. The costumes, the chorus . . ."

She listened with burgeoning excitement, forgetting who and where she was as he drew her into his vision and hummed snatches of music to tempt her further.

His music was so compelling, so upbeat. It made her feel so happy. "Helen, Helen, luscious melon/ Kidnapped by a Trojan felon," she sang playfully.

Patrick's eyes lit up. "There's our title: *Helen, Helen!* Jenny, we've begun. No, shut up and listen to this. Aphrodite's tune when she first tells Paris about Helen." He hummed and then stopped. "I'm stuck. Help me."

"Again."

As he la-la-ed, Jennifer visualized the scene, under a pale blue sky in summer. From her visit to Greece she remembered the wondrous light, a light that could magically be reproduced.

An opening line popped into her head, and while he experimented with the rest of the tune, she began mentally shaping the verse.

"I see from your face that you've got something. Shoot."

She laughed. "Never mind my face. 'Wait till you see Helen's glorious face/ It's much too—something —for that Spartan place.'"

While Jennifer scribbled on a paper napkin, Patrick altered the tune to coincide with the lyric, then sang it back to her.

She frowned and repeated the notes of the last two lines. "That's a little off, lacks punch, somehow."

"Mm. Yeah, I see what you mean. Okay. Okay. How about this?" He sang the change.

"Much better. Oh, I like that."

They worked back and forth. Then together they sang the verse softly, and the years simply fell away. It was as if they were back at college, collaborating at the old upright.

When they finished, both said at the same time: "We're on the right track, but it needs a helluva lot of work."

They laughed and exchanged a look of nostalgic recognition.

"We're going to write one helluva show, Jenny," he said, his voice low with emotion.

Suddenly uneasy, she blinked her way back to the present. "I . . . I really have to think about it, Patrick. I mean . . ." she stalled desperately. "I have to discuss it with Tony. The show would occupy so much of my time, and I've been involved with my husband's business, entertaining clients," she rushed ahead, "seeing to a million details—"

"Bullshit!" Patrick interrupted so vehemently that she jumped. "You've been running away from your talent. He can hire a hostess and a secretary to do all that. Jenny, listen. I can imagine the agony you went through when you lost your child. I know how I would feel if anything happened to Lissa. But time has passed, and even if the hurt never goes away, it sort of moves over and lets other things in. You're ready to work again—the lyrics of *Yesterday Morning* prove it. What we're doing right now proves it. Jenny, you've got the right stuff—we've got the right stuff, all three of us—to make *Helen, Helen!* the best musical on Broadway a year from now. We can knock their socks off, we can!" He grabbed her shoulders, every muscle in his face alive with his vision.

Jennifer felt his excitment physically transmitted.

"God, I've just got it! Listen!" He hummed a phrase, wrote feverishly, then hummed it again. It was hauntingly romantic, in a minor key.

"Paris has just seen Helen," she guessed.

"Exactly! Jenny, I love you."

His words were shattering. Those particular words— words that people said all the time to mean all sorts of things—on *his* lips reminded her that this collaboration could be dangerous.

"We've got to get started on this, Jenny, while we're both so hot. Inspiration has to be respected or it vanishes."

"I don't know, Patrick. It's so sudden. I really have to think it out."

"Dammit, if you don't come in on the project, it will be killed. I had this idea months ago and have been kicking it around. But the tunes that came to

mind weren't right. I was floundering, until I saw
that showcase. Then I came up with what you heard
today. Don't you see—you inspire me. And I inspire
you. Look at all the successful shows of the past few
years. In every instance the collaboration was exactly right. Take *Chorus Line*, for example—"

"You take it, I couldn't, except for the dancing.
Thin music, trite lyrics, embarrassing string of con-
fessions—"

He smiled and held up his hands. "Okay, maybe
that one's not the best example. *Annie* would be better."

"Much. Strouse and Charmin did a good job on
Annie, I think."

"Isn't it nice how former collaborators can agree?"
he sang softly, paraphrasing a song from *Make Love,
Not War*.

It was nice, but they could also disagree, both
talking at once, arguing about some points, seeing
eye to eye and ear to ear on others. With a mixture of
admiration and envy they evaluated other shows—
Cats, *Evita*, *Dreamgirls*, *My One and Only*.

"Goddammit, it's time for Lattimore and Ryland," Patrick declared, fixing her with his compelling gaze. "Jenny, you're as keen as I am. Talk to
your husband. Hell, I'll talk to him. Do anything he
wants. Skin hides, tan leather, whip masochists and
kick 'em with De Palma boots—"

"Patrick, stop it, please." She was speaking as
much to herself as to him, laughing more than she
had in ages. In fact, she was verging on hysteria. It
was cowardly of her to imply that Tony would stand
in her way when she knew he would not.

"Seriously," she said, when she had regained her

control, "let me think about it. I'll call you next week, I promise."

"Make it Monday or I'll park myself on your doorstep, I swear I will."

She couldn't look at him. "Stop threatening me and just give me your phone number. And how did you get mine, by the way ?"

"I've always had your number, kid," he joked. "Okay, from Renee Smith," he admitted, naming the costume designer for *Yesterday Morning*. "She's an old friend, and I pried your secret loose by threatening to steal her designs for her next show. Hey, what time is it? I have a four-thirty appointment. Damn. I'm late."

Jennifer was astonished to realize that they had been together for two hours.

Patrick, helping her on with her coat, suddenly turned her around and hugged her. "I've missed you, Jenny."

She stood transfixed for a moment, her cheek against the rough tweed of his jacket, feeling his heart beat faintly before it was drowned out by the pounding of hers.

He was the first to break away and smile at her. That smile had once haunted her dreams.

"If I haven't heard from you by Monday I don't know what I'll do, but it will be something desperate. And the four of us must get together. Five. I want you to share Lissa with us."

"Thank you," Jennifer murmured, looking at him with eyes that threatened to brim over. "I'll call you Monday. 'Bye."

She turned and fled out of the door, then stood numbly on the corner, not knowing what to do next.

Patrick came out, slung his arm around her shoul-

der, and waved to a taxi. "If you're going in my direction, I'll be glad to drop you—"

She thanked him but declined.

It was already dark and much colder. Shivering
slightly, she drew her down coat tightly around her.
Would her fur have been warmer? Tony often teased
her about walking around in duck feathers while her
mink hung in the closet. Well, she felt overdressed in
mink when she wasn't with her husband. Especially
today. Patrick had been used to her in her ratty old
cloth coat.

Patrick. Tony. Jennifer's emotions were in a jumble as she began walking blindly north.

She was more excited by his new show than she
had been about anything in years. Every professional bone in her body told her it was right for her.

She had had a taste this afternoon of what it was
like to work with such intensity again, of becoming so absorbed that she forgot everything but the
words, the music.

While she had been with Patrick she had thought
of Melissa only when the subject came up. For the
first time in ages there hadn't been that constant dull
ache in the pit of her stomach that felt like chronic
emotional indigestion.

All of her repressed ambition was ready to burst
out of her. However, she was afraid that working
with Patrick would be impossible. For one thing, it
would inevitably mean bringing them all together.
Would she and Meredith be able to repair their
friendship? Would she really be able to bear seeing
them so happy with *their* Melissa? And how would
Tony fit in?

But those were not the most important doubts, she
admitted to herself. The big question mark was Pat-

rick. All those hours they would spend together, the mutually inspiring moments they would share, the realization of how much alike they thought—everything would bring them closer together. Maybe none of it would affect Patrick, but it sure as hell would affect her. It already had.

She walked until her feet wouldn't carry her a step farther, and her legs in her boots felt hot. Only then did she see that she had gone from Bleecker Street all the way up to Park Avenue and Thirty-fourth.

She found a taxi, willing her brain to make some sense, to stop reeling with uncertainty.

She loved Tony and had enjoyed a fine marriage for seven years. Why, then, had seeing Patrick today so shaken her? If she agreed to collaborate with him, could she be absolutely certain her old feelings for him wouldn't return?

3

Merdith O'Neill Lattimore, laden with purchases from Bendel's, fidgeted impatiently as the old freight elevator took forever to rise to the sixth floor. She entered the loft and flung her packages on the unmade double bed in the only part of the sprawling area—with the exception of the bathroom—that had walls and a door.

As she began to unpack her new clothes, she regretted having bought quite so much. Well, everything had been on sale. Besides, if she got the role she had just been told about . . .

God, what a day it had been. All she had expected of it was the usual irritation she felt whenever she went to the studio to tape a voice-over. For more than a year, voice-overs for radio and TV commercials had been her only work. She found it demeaning and hated to see the finished TV commercial. There would be this gorgeous babe in her twenties demonstrating the product while Meredith's voice, eerily disembodied, sang the sales pitch.

It was after three, and Lissa would be home any minute. Meredith began to panic as she realized that she had a big decision to make and very little time in which to do so. Decisions had always been a problem. One reason she loved being onstage was that her role was fixed and the plot had to be worked out by the end of the performance. Interpreting the role was fun, especially since there was a director and a musical director to guide her. When she was acting and singing she felt at home, so attuned to the audience that she knew intuitively what to do. It was the only time she ever felt sure of herself.

Real life was a pain in the ass, with its conflicts and choices. Today's pain had started early, at the breakfast table, when Patrick had dropped his little bombshell moments after she had sent Lissa off to school with Bridget, their housekeeper.

Meredith had been dawdling over her coffee, wishing she could cancel her taping session, when Patrick suddenly said, "I'm having coffee with an old friend this afternoon. You'll never guess who. Jenny Ryland."

"Oh, no!" It had come out just that way before she could stop herself.

"Hey, don't look like that. How long can you hold a grudge anyway? Okay, so we were hurt at the way she vanished from our lives. That was years ago. The point is that she's in New York now—"

"How did you find out?" Meredith interrupted. "Did she call you?"

"Nope. I called her. After I saw a showcase musical that had her lyrics—"

"You saw it without me? Never even said a word?" Meredith broke in accusingly.

"I'm sorry, love. It's because I knew how bad you've felt about Jenny. First I wanted to catch the showcase and see if she still had her old touch. Then I was going to ask her to collaborate with me again. If she said no, I wasn't even going to mention her to you. But if she said yes . . . I'm only telling you now because I hate to see you wasting your voice on commercials, and I feel sort of responsible. It's taking me so damn long to come up with a new show."

Meredith suddenly experienced the left-out feeling she had suffered long ago when Jenny Ryland was around. What was the real reason her husband hadn't told her about Jenny's showcase? She hated being treated like a child that had to be humored.

But she sighed and didn't express what she was feeling, fearful of saying too much.

Anyway, Meredith did want a hit for Patrick. In which she, too, could shine. The years hadn't dimmed her faith in his talent. If only he had found another compatible lyricist. Unfortunately, his biggest success had been the show with Jenny's libretto and lyrics.

What was Jenny like now, after all this time? Was she fatter? Married? Did she have children? Meredith wished she could satisfy her curiosity without involving Patrick.

She tried to discourage him from attaching too much importance to the meeting. "If she were interested, she would have found us, darling, you know she would. We're in the phone book."

"Maybe, but does it matter? I really want her to work on *Helen*. In that showcase, Jenny's lyrics stand out a mile. They're funny, clever, romantic in all the right spots. If she had done *Tarzan* with me it would have been brilliant—"

"Well, she hasn't made it big with anyone else. Maybe the showcase is a fluke. Maybe she'll only be in New York a couple of weeks."

"Hey, stop trying to spoil it, okay? I never knew you to carry a grudge for so long."

"It's not a grudge."

"No? What is it, then?"

"Nothing. It's nothing. Look, darling, I want you to have a hit, and if Jenny can make it happen, of course I'll be thrilled."

As she said the words, Meredith knew she wouldn't be thrilled at all.

Patrick went out, and she lingered over another cup of coffee, trying to talk herself out of her funk. Surely he was right in thinking that enough years had passed for any hard feelings to have evaporated. The three of them had been separated and had lost touch, something that happened all the time.

But the knowledge of the meeting between Those Two bothered her all day.

Her taping session turned out to be as irritating as she had anticipated, and she consoled herself an hour later by buying out Bendel's.

After her shopping spree she called her agent on the chance he might be free for lunch. He wasn't, but he had been trying to reach her all morning. She was being considered for a leading role in a new musical opposite Raul Julia.

"Don't tell me you're not interested," her agent bellowed into the phone. "Christ, you haven't worked in over a year—"

"I didn't say I wasn't interested, only that I can't possibly audition for a few days," she fibbed, stalling until her quarter ran out.

Sheer terror gripped her. She didn't know why she was suddenly so frightened, but the fear was palpable. She had always assumed she and Patrick would make it together. The possibility that she might be offered a role in another Broadway show hadn't seriously occurred to her. Dare she consider it?

Really, she was too dependent on her husband. Yes, he was working on an idea with her in mind for the lead, but what if *Helen* never got further than his piano? This new show was ready for casting, and she could be in it. Starring with Raul Julia—her mind boggled. He was a big name on Broadway, big enough to keep a show running even if it didn't get ecstatic reviews.

She visualized her name on the marquee night after night, advertised on TV, the radio, in newspapers.

Dammit, timing was everything in this business. Why did it have to be feast or famine? If this offer had come along after *Cameo* closed, wouldn't she have grabbed it? She wasn't afraid of the role, surely, only of hurting Patrick.

Stop thinking about it. Thinking gave her a headache.

Standing in front of her full-length mirror, she absentmindedly tried on the plum-colored jumpsuit, wondering why she had bought it. It didn't do a thing for her except make her look big in the beam. Well, she could wear it around the house, though it was ridiculously expensive for a lounging outfit.

Three-thirty. Where was Lissa? Suddenly Meredith imagined her child under the wheels of a car, or being mugged by a knife-wielding thug.

Ever since they had first moved to Twenty-sixth Street and Sixth Avenue she had complained to Patrick that the neighborhood wasn't safe. Too many disreputable-looking types worked there loading and unloading merchandise for the small manufacturing companies and warehouses in nearby buildings. Often the men just hung around, smoking pot and blaring music from big radios, looking insolently at Meredith as she walked by. Only a few lofts on the block had been converted to residential use.

Although Meredith didn't doubt that her Dublin-born housekeeper was as tough as old boots, Bridget still would be no match for an armed New York mugger.

Meredith phoned the school but got no answer. Surely Lissa would be home any minute. Maybe she wanted to stop for a milkshake; maybe Bridget was doing some shopping.

Meredith went through this worry daily. Yet, she had not allowed herself to get into the habit of bringing Lissa to school and taking her home, or allowing Patrick to do so either. If they happened to have a meeting or a rehearsal, their daughter would be too disappointed.

In the kitchen Meredith cursed angrily. The refrigerator was almost bare. Damn that woman, she hadn't bought a thing for dinner. What the hell did she do all morning, after delivering Lissa to school? The loft was a mess, stuff strewn all over the place. Even when it was clean, it never looked really neat.

How she wished they could have a conventional apartment with identifiable rooms and some order in their lives. They had rented this place temporarily six years ago when Lissa was an infant. Patrick knew the owner, who had promised to sell it to them as soon as they could afford to buy. Well, that turned out to be a joke. Loft prices had gone through the skylight, and they hadn't a hope of a down payment, unless they had a hit show. In the meantime they didn't dare to make any alterations, such as enclosing the kitchen or Lissa's sleeping space or Patrick's so-called studio. And as lofts went, it was on the small side.

Anyway, Meredith didn't want to remain in the neighborhood. Lissa had no local children to play with, so she had to invite her school friends up from the Village. That meant a long visit, at least one meal, lots of noise, and often a sleep-over.

By a quarter to four Meredith was ready to call the police. If only Bridget had phoned to say they'd be late, as she had been instructed to do. Didn't Meredith have enough on her mind without this too? She paid Bridget a fortune so she wouldn't have to worry about her daughter.

Standing in front of the phone, she tried to quell her panic. She would wait until four. It was unlikely that anything had happened. Bridget might be an indifferent housecleaner but she truly cared about Lissa. Besides, she always arrived at school at least ten minutes ahead of time, and in fact met the child inside the building. Maybe thay had gotten stuck in a cab or on a bus; maybe traffic was tied up.

If only it weren't already so dark.

Just as she was reaching for the phone, she remembered that it was Thursday. Lissa had ballet class today instead of Wednesday. She wouldn't be home until after five.

Meredith exhaled slowly. She simply had to stop worrying so much about Lissa. Her own mother had worried obsessively about her, and she had hated it.

After a shower she put on a lavender mohair sweater and navy culottes. God, the pants were tight. Had they shrunk at the cleaners? Or had she put on a couple of pounds? She really had to cut down on the calories, do some exercises regularly.

The sound of the doorbell made her jump. She opened the door only after Mel Fox, a TV producer, had identified himself. He had an appointment with Patrick. Automatically Meredith smiled brightly at him, turning on the charm, gratified by the appreciative way he looked at her.

She led Mel through the clutter to Patrick's corner, which contained his desk, some chairs, file cabinets, stereo system, and a piano. After making Mel a drink, she left him thumbing through *The New Yorker*.

Meredith began to fret over how late Patick would be today, remembering his sessions with Jenny years ago, when they would get so caught up in what they were doing that they forgot there was a world out there. If their meeting had gone well, what should she do? Assume that the collaboration would go ahead quickly and she'd soon be starring in their show? Or should she tell Patrick what her agent had said and let him advise her?

What did she want, anyway? Raul Julia and Meredith O'Neill? It sounded terrific, but scary. And she would be second in the billing. In Patrick's show she'd be first, the top of the marquee.

That wasn't it, though. The plain truth was that she was scared to death to be out on her own, to work in a show with people unknown to her—producer, director, musical director, librettist, lyricist, composer. Would they care about her? Would they make allowances?

Not even Patrick knew the extent of her performance anxiety. Her mother hadn't either. From earliest childhood Meredith had been pushed toward musical comedy by her ambitious mother. Meredith had always hidden the awful stage fright she experienced before any sort of performance, whether it was acting in the grade-school play or singing in front of the neighbors. It wasn't unusual for her to vomit secretly just before the curtain went up.

In her husband's shows she felt protected. In some ways Patrick was like a father (hers had deserted her when she was a child, never to be heard from again), encouraging and supportive.

The thing sticking in her craw at the moment was Lattimore and Ryland, that interlocking mutual-admiration society where she was always standing on the outside looking in. With Those Two, Meredith felt intellectually and verbally inadequate.

When Patrick walked in the door, she saw at a glance that he was elated.

He kissed her lightly. "Hello, baby. Is Mel here yet?"

"He is," she confirmed, taking her husband's scarf. "You're half an hour late."

"True, but it may be the most important half-hour I've spent in years."

So it had gone well with Jenny. Thoughtfully Meredith put the scarf in the closet and made her decision. Or rather, it made itself. No way would she be able to keep her mind on another role, another show, when Lattimore and Ryland were working cheek to cheek, mind to mind. She wanted to be there, all the way. And she would, too. Good-bye Raul Julia; welcome back, Jenny Ryland.

When Lissa came home with Bridget, Meredith was relieved to see that the woman had done some shopping after all. But the next moment all thoughts of dinner vanished.

"Lissa, you're limping."

"I know. I twisted my ankle. Jill—she's the biggest show-off in the class—took up all the room at the barre, and I lost my balance."

Patrick, trying to concentrate on what Mel was

saying, was irritated by the commotion coming from the other end of the loft. He needed silence in order to work, and got it only when his family was out. How the devil could he demonstrate his musical idea for a mini-series with all that background noise?

"Sorry, Mel, bear with it this once, please. I'm in the process of renting a studio. In fact, I saw a place only today."

After Patrick had ushered Mel out, he stopped in the kitchen.

Lissa, perched on the counter, flanked by several half-peeled potatoes and a bunch of broccoli, was holding out her foot while her mother bent over it. Meanwhile, Bridget was standing with her hands on her hips, evidently disapproving.

Lissa was a sturdy child with her mother's teal-blue eyes but not her hair, unfortunately. Hers was sandy and straight like his. He didn't think she would ever have Meredith's beauty, but she would be pretty enough. More important, she was bright, charming, and sweet, as well as graceful, with a lovely singing voice.

Spotting him, the child smiled and held out her arms for a hug. "Hi, Daddy. I twisted my ankle," she said importantly.

He kissed her. "Poor baby, does it hurt?"

"A little."

While she told him the details, he felt her foot gently. "Nothing to worry about," he assured her, "but let's put a cold compress on it, just in case."

"You think a cold compress? Wouldn't heat be better?" Meredith questioned anxiously.

"Like Mr. Lattimore said, cold," Bridget insisted.

"Thanks, you can go home now, Bridget," Patrick told her. "We'll manage."

"Oh, yes. I'm so sorry, Bridget. Didn't realize the time," Meredith apologized.

Patrick shook ice cubes into the ice pack and applied it to Lissa's ankle. He had spent more time than Meredith in caring for their daughter because of rehearsals and matinees during the runs of their shows.

"I just hope the ankle doesn't swell," Meredith muttered, drawing an anxious frown from Lissa.

"It won't swell, it's nothing," Patrick assured his wife, trying to sound neutral. Last week Lissa had scraped her knee, and the week before it had been a cut lip. She seemed to be accident-prone lately, and he wondered if Meredith's anxiety could be the cause.

After he bandaged the ankle he hoisted his daughter down. "How about setting the table, sweets? I'll get the plates down for you."

"But her ankle—"

"Meredith, stop making her into a hypochondriac," he murmured, while Lissa carried plates to the dining area. "If it really hurt, she'd be complaining."

"I guess you're right."

He felt more than ever that the sooner his wife was busy with a show, the happier she would be. It still surprised him sometimes that the same woman who could belt out two hours of songs in front of an audience night after night, captivating her listeners with her authoritative delivery and fantastic vocal range, could be such a nervous wreck as a mother. Of course, Meredith's own mother had coddled her, too, and Lissa had been premature.

Meredith took up the vegetable parer while Patrick made the salad and cut up the broccoli.

They both looked up and asked at the same time, "How was your day?"

"Singing stars first," he said, making a gallant gesture.

"Well, it was . . . mixed," Meredith answered truthfully. "The ad was for a sugar-free soda. At least I didn't have to drink it. The actress took a mouthful, but it hadn't gone flat enough and she burped right on camera." Meredith talked on, a little nervously, postponing the moment that she would hear about Jenny. "There, that takes care of the potatoes. Enough for you two. None for me. Not till I drop some of this lard."

"You, lard? Nah. You look pretty good to me," Patrick said, patting her backside affectionately.

"Anyway, the jingle I had to sing was really ghastly. You know, a rock beat, with repetitions, just to make sure it gets the viewers and that they can't stop humming it."

"Never mind, love, you'll be doing better things soon. I had that meeting with Jenny and it was . . . well, just great to see her again." He put the steaks in the broiler.

"What did she say about me?"

"Asked how you were, of course. I told her you were fine and looking forward to seeing her again—"

"And what was her reaction?"

He looked at his wife curiously. "She said she'd like that very much. What's the matter with you anyway?"

"Nothing." She smiled too brightly. "How does she look?"

"Terrific. Very much the same, I guess. You know, like our Jenny."

"She's here on a visit? Or staying, or what?"

"She's living here. Has been for two years. She's married, to De Palma, that Italian who deals in leather, as in my shoes."

Meredith's mouth fell open. She stared at her husband, digesting what he had said.

The potatoes began to boil over. "Oh, my God!" She rushed to the stove.

Patrick shook his head fondly at his wife, who could never quite manage to talk and do something else at the same time. "Don't scald yourself. Easy. Here, let me."

He used a potholder to move the lid and uncover the pot halfway, while he turned down the flame.

"I can't believe that Jenny is married to the owner of the De Palma boutiques. I always thought she'd marry someone literary, intellectual." Meredith searched her memory. She had seen photos of De Palma, and somehow recalled an older, dashing Italian.

"Well, I can understand why she didn't call us, Patrick. She must be rolling in money and living a very different life-style. De Palma shops are all over the place. What was she wearing?"

Patrick's eyebrows shot up and he shrugged. "Let's see, a blue something, I think. Oh, her hair's different, sort of fluffy."

"Is she fatter? Older-looking?"

"Not that I could tell. Hell, I wasn't judging her for a beauty contest. I told her about the show."

While Meredith leaned her elbows on the counter and listened, he turned the steaks and mixed the salad dressing.

"I set the table," Lissa said proudly, joining them.

"Thanks, honey. Why don't you sit down at the

table now, Princess Lissa. Your mother and I will wait on you in a moment."

Lowering his voice, Patrick told Meredith about Jennifer's child.

"Oh, how horrible." Meredith shuddered. If anything ever happened to Lissa, she wouldn't be able to go on. Losing a child was the worst thing she could imagine. "Poor Jenny. What happened?"

"I couldn't ask. Mostly we talked about the show. And it was just like the old days. As I hummed, she was spouting lyrics off the top of her head."

"Did she actually say why she never got in touch with us?"

"Not really. But you can imagine why. She was busy, new husband, and then the grief over her daughter. I don't think it was deliberate. Maybe De Palma doesn't want her to work. I feel she's itching to collaborate but has to convince him first."

"How soon will you know?" Meredith tried to keep her tone casual.

"By Monday. Keep your fingers crossed."

As Meredith helped Patrick dish out the food, she reflected. If Patrick thought Jenny was right for his show, then she was. The more he elaborated, the more enthusiatic Meredith became.

They reminisced about Jenny over dinner, telling Lissa how they had written their first show. She begged to hear some of the songs, even though she had listened to the record many times. Clapping her hands with delight, Lissa joined in the singing.

Meredith ate some potatoes after all, and then a little ice cream. Hadn't Patrick said she looked fine?

After dinner, Patrick went to his piano with an idea for a song. He felt good. He had communicated

his excitement to Meredith, and she had stopped
being so negative about Jenny. Moreover, she hadn't
said another word about Lissa's ankle.

As he experimented on the piano, he thought
about his meeting with Jenny at the Borgia. He had
forgotten what fun it was to work with her, how perfectly attuned they were to one another. He saw
with new clarity the reasons his other collaborations
had been failures, more or less. The lyricists had
been too serious, too petty, in a way, even competitive, fighting his music instead of working with it.
And maybe he had been just as bad, having to force
tunes to fit uninspired words.

Whereas with Jenny—had he told Meredith that
Jenny looked the same? He realized, startled, that in
fact she had changed, though he wasn't quite sure
how.

Curious, Patrick got up and rummaged in his
bookcase for his album of press clippings and publicity releases. He found an eight-by-ten glossy color
still of the three of them, taken shortly after the
opening in New York of *Make Love, Not War.*

Studying the photo, he dismissed himself, so young
and raw, with too-long hair. He smiled at the picture of Meredith, who looked the same to him.

Jenny's likeness confirmed that she hadn't aged,
though she certainly had looked less sophisticated
back then. Her hair had been a little wild, her
clothes undistinguished and casual. But her eyes!
Had they always been that vivid green? And had the
expression in them been so . . . so promising?
Funny. He had always thought of her teasing as intellectual, humorous, rather than sexy.

Patrick snapped the book shut and went back to

the piano, feeling uneasy without quite knowing why.

Trying to shake the moodiness overtaking him, he scanned his musical notations and played through a section several times, making alterations. But dammit, it wasn't coming right. Something was nagging at him.

Besides, his wife and daughter were making so much noise that he couldn't think straight. He would have to take that little place on Houston Street even if it was an extra expense. He simply had to have a quiet studio in which to work with Jenny.

Abstracted, Patrick drummed his fingers soundlessly on the piano keys.

It suddenly came to him with a shock that he and Jenny had once made love. He had forgotten about it years ago, probably out of guilt. In those days, while hoping to win Meredith, he had taken advantage of any opportunity for a sexual adventure with an attractive woman. But Jenny—that had been different, a mistake. Jenny had been Meredith's friend and roommate as well as his collaborator.

Although the night vaguely came back to him— the tension of the opening, the celebration at Sharon's loft, the foray into Chinatown with Jenny—the actual sexual encounter was pretty much a blank.

"Oh, Christ," he murmured to himself, growing warm with shame as he realized what he had done. Because Meredith had gone off with an older, wealthy man, Patrick had been angry and jealous and he had used Jenny in a totally selfish manner. Jesus, he had behaved like such a bastard.

But Jenny . . . she had been simply wonderful. Generous enough to give him what he wanted and

No One But You

needed, mature enough to forgive him and never refer to it again.

Did Meredith know? She had been behaving so strangely about Jenny, almost as if she were jealous. Well, it was completely without reason, he quickly told himself. He was steadfast in his love for his family. And even if his marriage had turned out to be somewhat different from what he had expected, he would never do anything to hurt his wife or daughter.

A picture of Jenny suddenly flashed before him, Jenny as she had looked this afternoon. He now was able to recall her outfit in detail, a lovely blue-green clinging knit dress with black slashes and dots— terrific-looking.

He remembered the feel of Jenny's firm flesh when he had held her for a moment in an affectionate hug. And the fresh smell of her shiny hair, the subtle fragrance of her expensive perfume. A streak of desire for her flared momentarily, leaving him stunned. *Jenny hadn't changed at all; he had.* Suddenly he saw in her what he had missed in the past.

Jesus! Well, it was too late now. He was married, and she was too. To a rich Italian.

Patrick banged aimlessly on the keys for a few minutes, but he was getting nowhere. Finally he leaned forward on the keyboard and rested his head on his folded arms. With his eyes shut, he let his mind float freely while musical phrases bounced off his imagination.

After a while, notes that had been eluding him for the past two hours came to him. He played them over and over, correcting and perfecting. When he was satisfied with the number, he played it through several times.

Looking up from the piano, he saw his daughter leaning against his desk, rubbing her eyes. "I can't sleep, Daddy," she said grumpily.

"I'm sorry, sweetie. I didn't mean to wake you up." He lifted her in his arms and carried her back to bed. It was almost eleven.

"Now you get to be tucked in a second time."

"But it's only the first time you're tucking me in."

"True. When you're right, you're right," he said, making her smile.

As he pulled the blanket up around her, a strong feeling of love made him want to hug the breath out of her. But he gave her only a gentle kiss on her forehead and smoothed her hair on the pillow. He felt so lucky to have her.

"Go back to sleep, sweetie. I love you."

She smiled with her eyes closed.

When Patrick went to bed, he saw that Meredith was still awake. "God, I've been disturbing everyone tonight, it seems."

"I'm not disturbed." Meredith snuggled against him. "I just sleep better when you're here. You'll always be here, won't you?"

"Of course." He kissed her cheek and thought involuntarily of Jenny.

Within moments Meredith was asleep, curled up in his arms.

Patrick sighed and forced himself to put Jenny out of his thoughts. Just as he was falling asleep, however, a memory surfaced—of Jenny lying with him on his lumpy sofa bed in their old living room. Her long hair swirled around her face, a face that was alive and intense with passion. He could feel again her silky skin next to his body, her inadvertent quivering as she moved beneath him.

Patrick experienced a strong feeling of arousal, and he sat up in bed, touching his hot face with both hands.

He thought of their meeting today, and the way they had joked and worked. Talked and drank coffee. Looked into each other's eyes.

He imagined them having dinner together, walking through the city, arms around one another, not feeling the cold because of the warmth between them.

Then he saw them in their old Village apartment, only this time he wouldn't be so impatient. He would kiss Jenny very gently at first. Nip at her earlobes, nuzzle her neck, caress her breasts. Use his tongue and his fingers to excite her, little by little. And she would kiss him back, her hair brushing his skin, and stroke him until . . .

Shutting his eyes, Patrick shuddered and lay back in bed. He simply had to curb his imagination. Jenny was an inspiration, yes, but only musically speaking. Anything else was unthinkable.

But he thought it just the same, and he dreamed it all that night.

4

"Good afternoon, Mrs. De Palma," the concierge greeted Jennifer as she came into the East Fifty-sixth Street entrance of the Trump Tower. Momentarily startled, Jennifer Ryland, lyricist, snapped into her other identity and returned the greeting.

She spoke of the weather with the elevator operator and got out on the sixtieth floor. She and Tony had moved there only a month before. Their previous apartment on the Upper East Side had been elaborate enough for her, but Tony wanted to be closer to his newly relocated boutique on Fifth Avenue. When he showed her the blueprint of the apartment, he was so excited that she couldn't bring herself to dampen his pleasure by objecting to the move.

In addition to three bedrooms and as many baths, the apartment had a formal dining room and a thirty-two-foot living room, with floor-to-ceiling and wall-to-wall windows. They were double-thermal and shut out noises, making the apartment seem disconnected from the rest of the world.

"Tony?" Jennifer called from the foyer.

"Ah, you're home, *cara*, wonderful." As he rose from his chair in the living room and came toward her, she was struck anew by how handsome her husband was, with an unmistakably Continental sophistication that had always made her think of Vittorio

De Sica. Tony would age handsomely, too. He already was beginning to look his thirty-seven years, as his luxuriant black hair showed increasing streaks of gray. It was expertly cut and just reached the collar of his shirt. Seductive, velvety dark eyes and a brilliant smile suffused his face with warmth.

His suits, beautifully hand-tailored in Italy, gave breadth and stature to his narrow frame. He carried himself proudly, with the merest swagger, a little macho, perhaps, but endearingly so, she thought.

Jennifer and Tony kissed.

While he opened champagne, she crossed the room to the window. The apartment had been decorated to combine Italian antiques with custom-made modern pieces. A seventeenth-century inlaid commode, topped by a gilt-framed mirror, served as a backdrop for a curved modular white leather sofa. Ultramodern gray suede chairs, amid low glass tables, preserved a feeling of space and airiness. There was a large Sandro Chia painting on one pale beige wall, and a small Giacometti sculpture stood near a huge ficus tree in front of the windows.

Jennifer watched the lights on the Queensboro Bridge glitter in the clear, icy air as a steady procession of cars inched over the roadways. Directly south, the illuminated Chrysler Building showed off the dazzling lines of its Jazz Deco crown, but its beauty only heightened her sadness. She took several deep, troubled breaths in the eerie silence, which was finally broken by the gentle popping of the champagne cork.

January was the worst month of the year for Jennifer because the twenty-fifth was the birthday of Melissa Frances Giovanna De Palma, the beautiful, wonderful child she and Tony had so adored.

No matter where they had lived after Melissa's death, Jennifer had always felt the silence to be an accusation. How she missed the happy laughter of her little girl, the sounds of her toys, her motions in play.

"Your drink, cara," Tony said, coming up behind her.

She accepted the tulip glass and returned her husband's sad smile. They clinked glasses wordlessly, remembering their child. It was a daily ritual that brought them as much comfort as it could.

"I hope you have nothing too complicated planned for the next few days," Tony said, "because we're going to be entertaining Herr Schlamme and his assistant. They're coming to talk about the final stages before we open the Vienna boutique. Not only that, Marta Sond is here, and I've hired her. She'll go to Vienna and help to promote the opening."

"That's wonderful," Jennifer exclaimed, knowing that having the internationally famous model at the opening of the boutique would be good publicity. "Is she as gorgeous in the flesh as she is in photographs?"

"She would be, if she had any flesh to speak of, poor girl. Arms like sticks. Nothing to get hold of." Tony smiled and playfully squeezed his wife's arm to illustrate the contrast.

It was their private little joke. When Jennifer had been pregnant and feeling like a blimp, she had stayed at home toward the end instead of traveling with Tony. Once she had expressed concern at all the svelte models he met, and he had assured her that to him they appeared merely undernourished.

Tony talked on, and she listened attentively, as always, admiring her husband's business acumen.

From the day he had opened the doors of his first

boutique, a few months after their marriage, Tony had been successful. An advertisement in the San Francisco *Chronicle* had heralded his new venture, showing a photo of a well-dressed woman holding gloves and a handbag, and the simple phrase "De Palma—we're in your hands."

Tony knew how to hire the most effective managers and salespeople and how to choose the best Italian designers. Most important, he had learned all about leather in his family's tanning business in Florence.

From the start, De Palma leathers had had their own distinctive character, one that had quickly made them competitive with Gucci products.

Gradually the De Palma boutique had expanded to include belts, shoes, and luggage. Branches had been opened, and new lines added, until finally the shops were selling women's clothes, jewelry, and perfume.

Although Tony believed in putting profits back into the business, he always kept something aside for diversification. In the seven years they had been married, his timing had been perfect. He invested in oil just before the world crisis, and in Sun Belt real estate preceding the boom. He had made millions, and Jennifer was terribly proud of him.

In the beginning, she helped him in his boutique because he needed her; later, she traveled with him and entertained his clients and colleagues because she enjoyed it. But had Patrick been right in suggesting that she had been running away from her career?

She snapped back to what Tony was saying. "Tomorrow? They're arriving in New York tomorrow, Friday? Oh, Tony, that means we'll have to entertain them for the weekend, and I haven't planned a thing—"

"Never mind, *cara*, you'll come through. You always do." He smiled encouragingly at her. "I'm sorry to give you such short notice. I wasn't sure myself until today. I thought Marta was going to Vienna from Paris and I would join them all. But when I learned earlier that she is in New York, it seemed easier to bring Schlamme here and save myself an extra trip. They'll stay at the Plaza. Let's plan to see a show, something entertaining, a musical. You're the best judge of that, naturally."

She nodded, a dull pain suddenly gnawing at her. What was she going to do about Patrick? She would discuss their meeting with Tony, of course, but not now, when he was so engrossed in his important new venture and she had so much to do.

As they sat on their sofa, side by side, sipping champagne, Jennifer planned the weekend. "Tickets for *Cats*, I think, or if they've seen it, *My One and Only*. Lunch at Le Cirque, so Marta can be seen, dinner at La Côte Basque—"

"Later," Tony whispered, putting his arm around her shoulders. He nuzzled her neck with his soft lips, then drew her close to him, putting the champagne glasses on the coffee table, and kissed her. She opened her lips to receive his gently probing tongue, her nipples stiffening as he caressed her breasts. When she unbuttoned his shirt to touch the curling hair on his chest, she felt his quickening heartbeat.

They moved languidly, without urgency or tension. A little later, arm in arm, they went to their bedroom and their enormous oval bed, covered with scented silk sheets. He lit a candle and turned on the tape, so that soft Vivaldi music filled the room.

She was touched by Tony's romanticism, as well as by his rather old-fashioned shyness. Rarely were they fully nude above the sheets. He had told her, smiling, when they first became lovers, that they must always leave something to the imagination.

As she lay on her back, he lightly kissed her neck and shoulders. She stroked the small of his back, making him shudder. He moved his head to her breasts, then to her belly, while gently holding her hips. Moaning softly, she fondled the insides of his elbows.

Tony's motions were gentle, graceful, and fluid, and she adjusted herself to his body in bed as she did on the dance floor. Over the years they had perfected their timing so that they could climax together.

Afterward they showered and slipped into lounging clothes: for him an elegant crimson silk smoking jacket that set off his dark good looks; for her a two-piece peach-colored satin ensemble with a long skirt. The outfit, designed by Laura Biagiotti, was a gift from Tony. He was forever buying her clothes, and scarcely a week went by without her finding something new and enticing in her closet. It had become a game.

At the beginning she had felt a little strange in the silks and satins and velvets he bought for her; however, she had become accustomed to dressing up for him in such sensuous fabrics.

She was fortunate, she thought, to have such an attentive husband, one who brought her flowers, who preferred to live mostly by candlelight, who still treated her like a cherished bride. If the formality they observed kept the romance in their marriage, she would certainly not question it.

The housekeeper had prepared their meal before

she left for the day. Jennifer had only to serve it in the dining room, something she knew Tony liked her to do on the evenings they dined alone at home.

Sitting across the dinner table from his wife, Tony regarded her with satisfaction. She was a good companion, always interested and interesting. She knew when to speak and when to listen. She had never exerted her will to oppose his, as so many American women did with their men, who foolishly permitted it.

He knew that Jennifer always put him first, and it was rare for them to argue. Only after *la tragedia* had their marriage faced a crisis. It still chilled him to remember their marital difficulties when they lost their daughter, the worst blow of his life.

After a year of intensive mourning for Melissa they had discussed having another child, both clinging to the hope that it would come soon. But gradually, when nothing happened, they had stopped speaking of it.

He had been inventive in trying to rouse his wife from her depression: taking her traveling with him, encouraging her to become more involved with his boutiques, especially since she had shown no interest in writing musical comedy again, even when they moved to New York.

Last year someone who remembered her work had asked her to rewrite the lyrics for a showcase production. Tony was glad that she had agreed, glad that she was working once more. He enjoyed the show; in fact, he took some clients to see it, pointing with pride to the program: *with words by his wife*, explaining that she felt it necessary to retain Ryland as her professional name.

* * *

After dinner, Jennifer and Tony watched the news on television, read the paper, and decided to have an early night.

In bed he kissed her cheek. "I love you, *cara.*"

"I love you, too," she said. Nevertheless, a sharp stab of disloyalty shot through her as the image of Patrick intruded.

Idiotic. That was something else altogether. It had nothing to do with her feeling for Tony, with the companionable life they shared, which had everything she wanted—except children.

For no reason that the doctors could find, she simply didn't conceive. But the years were passing and she was worried. Several times she had gently broached the subject of adoption to Tony, and he had just as gently put her off, saying there was plenty of time.

As she lay next to him and listened to his steady breathing, she wondered if it wouldn't be better to turn Patrick down. Not that the situation really held any danger, she quickly assured herself.

The point really was how much she wanted the collaboration. Did she want it enough to possibly put temptation in her way?

5

"Okay, hon, a little to the right. That's it," the photographer said, snapping his shutter expertly. "Now, walk toward me, stop—that's it—point your toe. Smile. That's it. Hold it. Beautiful."

Debra Dillon followed the photographer's instructions mechanically, annoyed about the smiling. He wasn't supposed to be interested in her anatomy above the waist, because what she was modeling was lace panty hose, stockings, and fancy underpants for a glossy magazine ad.

She had come to today's assignment with her honey-blond hair tousled, wearing no eye makeup, and with only a dab of blusher on her cheeks, a smear of lip gloss across her pouting mouth. Her head was splitting, and she was not in a smiling mood. Everthing was made worse by the noise and the commotion. The photographer was being hassled by both the art director from the ad agency and the account exec.

Debra did her best to ignore her throbbing temples and block out everything but the photographer's commands. She was a leg and foot model and hated the work. If she wasn't prancing up and down, she was sitting or lying on her back with her legs stretched into contorted positions until they ached.

Often she had the weird feeling that the camera was really aimed at her crotch.

Still, at three hundred dollars an hour, Debra knew she could be earning a bundle if she could bring herself to take on more assignments. Then she would hardly miss the money she sent her sister every month.

"Okay, break for lunch."

Debra reached for her wool wraparound skirt, tucked in her blouse, and slipped into a pair of soft boots and a coat. Declining the account exec's invitation to lunch, she left the studio hastily, swallowed two aspirin without water, and lit a cigarette as soon as she was in the street.

She tried to avoid the midday crush by choosing a dinky diner where she could sit at the counter surrounded by stock clerks and gum-chewing salesgirls. There Debra coud be herself and not give a damn what anybody thought. She needed to relax for an hour.

Ordering a container of yogurt and a piece of melon, she sat with her hands in her lap, twisting her engagement ring with her thumb and looking forward to the day that she could quit modeling forever.

Although Debra was only twenty-one, she had none of her generation's ambitions for a career. Hers had been forced on her by circumstances.

Debra was the youngest of seven children, all of them grown and scattered by the time she was old enough to be aware of her surroundings: a dusty gas station on a lonely Arkansas road in the middle of nowhere. Her parents drank and fought a lot. They had little interest in their last child.

The only one of their offspring still occasionally in

touch was their daughter Charlene, who lived in West Palm Beach, Florida, with her husband and year-old son. When Debra was seven, her parents sent her to her sister for a visit.

Charlene, at twenty, was as plain as Debra was pretty, and she took a real liking to her little sister. Debra loved being fussed over for a change, and she also felt very important being in charge of her nephew.

When, months later, Debra's parents asked if she was coming home, she said she wasn't. And that was that.

Unfortunately, when Charlene got pregnant again, her husband, Bud Milgram, began to drink and neglect his job as a gardener on a Palm Beach estate. He lost several jobs because of drunkeness.

By the time Debra was nine, she disliked Bud intensely, and feared him, too. He always looked at her in a funny way, especially when he had a bellyful of whiskey. One night she woke up with a feeling of terror. Her brother-in-law was sitting on her bed, leaning over her. With one hand he was stroking her tiny bumps of breasts, with the other, trying to get between her legs. Fighting him off, Debra began to scream for her sister. She hit her brother-in-law so hard she broke two fingers in her right hand.

Charlene burst into the room and pushed her drunken husband onto the floor. Furious, she kicked him out the next morning. He disappeared, leaving her with two small boys, a shabby house, and no money.

She was forced to support all four of them by working days as a supermarket checker and evenings as a carhop.

From that time Debra knew that the one thing

keeping her sister going was the hope that her prettiness would help them escape from their squalid life.

"Honey, with that face and figure, you're going to make a fortune," Charlene kept promising.

Every Sunday she dressed Debra and the boys in their best clothes. Then she would pile them into her old Chevy and drive to her favorite place of worship, Palm Beach.

As soon as they went over the drawbridge, Debra felt as if they had entered heaven. Slowly they would cruise North Ocean Boulevard or North County Road. While the boys played or fought in the backseat, Charlene, a cigarette dangling from her lips, pointed out the elaborate mansions partially hidden behind tall hedges. As Debra inhaled the wonderful fragance of the carefully tended gardens, she imagined the exotic life within the pastel-hued palaces of the rich.

"One day, Debbie, you're gonna live in one of them houses," Charlene promised.

After a while they would park downtown and stroll up Worth Avenue, looking into the elegant shops. The clothes displayed there made Debra feel tacky even in her Sunday best, and she became as obsessed as her sister with the longing to wallow in luxury.

By careful scrimping, Charlene managed to send Debra to a local modeling school when she was thirteen. Tall for her age, and skinny, Debra had silky blond hair, china-blue eyes, and a lovely skin blessedly free of acne. Dutifully she learned how to walk and sit and preen. Although she disliked being on display, she felt she owed it to her sister. After all, Charlene had come to her rescue and broken up her marriage because of her. Debra was grateful and guilty at the same time, and the responsibility sat heavily on her.

For years she suffered from a recurrent nightmare of that terrible time when her brother-in-law had forced his way into her bed, nauseating her with his alcoholic breath. Even awake, she remembered Bud Milgram every time she looked at her slightly disfigured right hand, on which the broken fingers had healed imperfectly.

Although Debra's height stabilized at five-foot-ten, her hips widened and her bosom developed to a thirty-six C when she was only fourteen. She was told at modeling school that she would never make it in fashion unless she went into "parts."

Unfortunately, her heart-shaped face and undefined cheekbones did not project the right look for the late seventies. Since one hand was ruined, and she refused to model bras, only legs and feet were left, and hers were flawless. But it was necessary for her to lift weights in a special way and to do toe exercises. Dancing with a partner was out because someone might step on her feet. So were high-heeled shoes and walking barefoot. Debra petulantly submitted to the discipline; she had no choice.

She got her first real job with a large agency in Los Angeles, where she had to work very hard, hating every minute. How she longed to meet a man who would take possession of all her parts and make her into a whole woman, namely his wife. But not just anyone would do.

"Don't make the mistake I made," Charlene always said. "I didn't have your looks. You've gotta go for the big bucks; then, when it turns sour, at least you can get out lookin' good and with enough money to buy yourself anything or anyone you want. Let's

face it, kid, all men are bastards—only there are two
kinds: rich and poor."

Keeping her sister's maxim in mind, Debra rarely
dated, contemptuously brushing off the young men
who were struggling to make it themselves. She was
after much bigger game.

When she was sent out of town on a modeling assignment, she thought she had found Mr. Rich, and
at seventeen she lost her virginity as well as her heart
in San Francisco. Unfortunately, the pigeon turned
out to be a fox. Her inexperience and naiveté proved
very costly.

Sighing now, Debra finished her lunch, lit a cigarette, and went back to work.

Her afternoon was grueling. She had to parade
back and forth, sit with her legs crossed and re-
crossed, and even lie on an ermine rug in a bathtub,
her legs in the air, while the photographer snapped
away.

Finished at last, Debra splurged on a taxi to the
Carlyle Hotel, where her fiancé lived. They were
meeting for a drink before dinner.

Her first sight of Arnold Brody was always a
shock. Two inches shorter than she, he wore dark
three-piece pin-stripe suits that only emphasized his
painful skinniness. His gray hair was thinning, and
the perpetual scowl on his face didn't soften his sharp
features. He looked more like fifty-five than forty-
five.

Sighing, Debra forced herself to remember that
Arnold Brody was a multimillionaire. She smiled co-
quettishly at him and pursed her lips for his kiss.

"I only have time for a quick drink," Arnold said
briskly in his slightly nasal voice redolent of his

lower-middle-class Brooklyn beginnings. "Important meeting in half an hour."

"Oh, Arnold, we were supposed to have dinner," Debra pouted. "And then go back to my place for a 'fashion show,' " she finished, throwing him her most seductive look. He loved her to dress in black mesh stockings and black-and-red underwear and model for him. Most of his sexual experience, she gathered, had been with high-priced call girls.

Arnold smiled at her suggestion. "It'll have to wait, babe."

"I don't see why we can't have dinner. You have to eat in any case—"

"It's a business dinner. You don't make money unless you put yourself where the bucks are, even if it's inconvenient. I didn't inherit a penny, you know that. Everything I've got I had to earn the hard way—"

"Yes, I know," she said quickly, to forestall the story of his self-made millions, which she had heard countless times.

Business was always getting in the way of her social life. Well, that was part of the package. Once she was married, she would have more friends, maybe even bring her sister up to New York.

Still, Debra left the Carlyle feeling resentful and out of sorts. It was too late for her massage, so she went directly home to her lushly furnished one-bedroom apartment on East Fifty-seventh Street. She had thought it important to have a good address and to pretend that the last thing in the world she was after was a rich man. The only reason Debra was still modeling was that she didn't want Arnold to think marrying him was her way out. On the contrary, she maneuvered it so that it was he who was insisting she stop working when they got married.

She relaxed in a hot bath, looking with dismay at her feet. Her chiropodist would scream when he saw the discolorations and tenderness from her latest workout.

After her bath she soaked her feet for twenty minutes in a whirlpool foot bath. Then she creamed them gently, patted them with silky dusting powder, and put on white socks.

Finally she collapsed in front of the television with a salad she had ordered from the corner deli. While she ate she thumbed idly through the New York *Post*.

Suddenly she sat up straight as a photograph caught her eye. The caption noted that the group of five had gone to Regine's after having attended a performance of *Cats*. Tony De Palma and his wife were shown with two men and Marta Sond, who was helping to launch a De Palma boutique in Vienna.

Debra nervously smoked one cigarette after another as she studied the photo under her magnifying glass, quickly glossing over the willowy Marta, with her enviable cheekbones. More interesting to Debra was the shot of Jennifer Ryland De Palma, looking very attractive and stunningly dressed in a Karl Lagerfeld beaded gown and a mink cape.

Grimly Debra clipped out the photo and added it to her file on Tony De Palma.

On an impulse she went through the whole file, growing more depressed by the moment.

But there wasn't much point in thinking about Tony now, when within a month she was going to become Mrs. Arnold Brody. Arnold was richer than

Tony; therefore, it followed that she would be happier than Mrs. Tony De Palma.

And yet, when Debra compared her unprepossessing fiancé with the handsome, dashing Tony, she experienced a pang of anguish. Quickly she forced herself back to reality.

She was not the wide-eyed innocent she had been once. She had lived and learned.

Debra was keeping Tony De Palma on a back burner for the time being, but she would never forget him. And if it ever became necessary, she would see to it that he never forgot her.

6

The weekend went well, Jennifer thought. She prepared for bed on Sunday, hoping a good night's sleep would clear her brain. Tony was sometimes on the phone to Europe for half the night. He could easily get by on four hours' sleep, something she greatly envied, since she needed at least seven to function normally.

Just as she was drifting off, she felt her husband get into bed, and she moved closer.

He kissed her cheek. "Thank you, *cara*, for making the weekend so perfect."

"Mm. It was fun for me, too," she murmured sleepily, pleased that he never took her efforts for granted.

She fell asleep with her head touching his shoulder.

Hours later she awoke shivering with excitement. Patrick's music was filling her ears, and snatches of words were coming to her to match the tunes.

Glancing at Tony asleep beside her, Jennifer carefully got out of bed and reached for a pad and a pen fitted with a pocket flashlight. Quickly she scribbled the verse fragments she had dreamed.

Afterward she lay back, listening to her pounding heart. Long ago she had learned to trust her instincts. She knew very well that if she had been dreaming of *Helen, Helen!* to the extent of dredging up lyrics in her sleep, it was a sign that she should agree to the collaboration.

But if the prospect of the work was exhilarating, the thought of Patrick was still troubling.

What agonies she had gone through seven years previously in San Francisco. It was a few weeks after her grandfather had died, and she was wondering whether she should stay and marry Tony or return to New York and the collaboration. She couldn't have both, because Tony was planning to open his boutique there.

Meredith had phoned to announce that she was marrying Patrick.

Jennifer, feeling as if she had been punched in the stomach, had offered her congratulations.

Then Meredith had dropped her second bombshell. "If you've got something going out there, Jenny, you'd better stick with it. Patrick's found a new collaborator."

Jennifer now tossed restlessly in bed. Had Patrick forgotten the sequence of events? Or had Meredith lied?

Tony stirred, opened his eyes, and looked at his wife. "You're awake, *cara*. Why? What's bothering you?"

"Nothing, really. I'm sorry my restlessness awoke you. It's so late. I'll tell you in the morning."

"Tell me now or I won't be able to sleep either."

"Well, it's Patrick. Lattimore. You remember, my old collaborator?" Although trying to keep her tone casual, she could feel the excitement creeping into her voice. "He wants us to try it again."

Tony sat up, propping the pillows behind his head, and listened intently.

"I . . . I haven't quite decided what to do. He wants us all to get together, socially, I mean. They have a daughter too. She's almost seven . . ." Jennifer stopped and looked pained.

Tony had heard the "too." He drew his wife close and kissed her hair. "I would like to meet your friends. And I think it would be a wonderful idea for you to collaborate with Patrick. That's what you always wanted, isn't it?"

She had never discussed the hurt over Patrick she had felt at the time. Tony believed she had put her career on hold because she loved him. Then, of course, there had been Melissa.

"I . . . I want the collaboration in a way, Tony, but I also want another child. And it doesn't look as if it's going to happen—"

"Of course it will, my sweet one. We must give it time. There's nothing wrong. The doctors have all said so."

"I know." She sighed. Unfortunately, fertility drugs had bad side effects for her.

"Couldn't we adopt, Tony?" she asked wistfully.

"I've told you before, *cara*, there's plenty of time. Maybe you're trying too hard."

"Maybe. I wonder if there could also be an unconscious reason. Maybe I see another child as being disloyal to Melissa's memory."

Tony kissed Jennifer's forehead. "The best thing you could do now is work. Were you writing before? I was half-asleep, but I felt you getting up."

She admitted to having had a dream about *Helen*.

"You see? Your dreams are telling you what you must do. You have only to listen. You know, *cara*, I dreamed of you often before I asked you to marry me. Now, tell me more about the show. It would star Patrick's wife?"

Jennifer gave him the details she knew and sang a bit of a song for him. He was so delighted with it that her enthusiam increased.

She realized that she had been talking for half an hour. "God, now I won't be able to sleep because I'm so excited."

"Could you possibly spare a little of that for me?" He smiled seductively and ran his fingertips over her bare arm.

Jennifer threw herself into their lovemaking even more than usual, and it relaxed her as nothing else could.

Her decision made, she fell asleep feeling happy and very much loved.

Tony quietly rose, slipped into a robe, and went to the living room to pour himself a brandy. Looking out of the window, he sipped his drink slowly.

He hadn't wanted to upset his wife by revealing that in fact he was deeply concerned over her inability to conceive another child. For the past two years he had secretly consulted doctors and experimented with drugs designed to increase his sperm count. In addition, he carefully monitored his wife's periods so that he would know her most fertile times.

Reviewing what she had said regarding a hidden reluctance to have a child annoyed him. All that psychobabble. Meaningless.

His wife was the most creative person he had ever known. Maybe it was a blessing that her old collaborator had turned up out of the blue with a project to get her juices flowing again. Perhaps the jump from creative to procreative was smaller than anyone believed.

Tony was sure his wife would become pregnant any day. She had conceived the first time almost on their honeymoon, which proved it was possible.

His three brothers and two sisters were all married, all with several children of their own. It was unimaginable that he alone would not succeed in producing a son or daughter. Adoption was simply not the same thing.

Sighing heavily, Tony drained his snifter. However much he might have sinned, he had atoned. Was still atoning.

Surely God would not be so vengeful as to deny him fatherhood.

7

"It's only a cubbyhole, but it has everything I need," Patrick said, showing Jennifer around his new studio. The windows looked out on attractive gardens, rapidly becoming covered with snow.

The studio was actually an old-fashioned tenement apartment consisting of two rooms, about ten by twelve, separated by a kitchen.

"I raided a thrift shop for the furniture, such as it is," Patrick continued, indicating the chipped white Formica table with two wooden chairs in the kitchen.

One room had a futon and an old chest of drawers. The other held the piano, a battered parsons table covered with sheet music, a chair, an old bookcase, and a portable stereo and tape deck.

"That piano looks familiar," Jennifer observed, amused. "It's almost a duplicate of the old upright in New Haven."

He grinned at her. "Looks like and sounds like. I really had to scrounge it up." He played an arpeggio. "Remember how thrilled we were the first time we heard our stuff played on a decent piano? When my music satisfies me on this old clinker, I know I've got something."

Old piano or not, the tunes for *Helen* came alive as he played them.

Jennifer had written a first draft of the libretto, which they were polishing as they went along, picking up some of the dialogue for song lyrics.

But somehow neither of them seemed to be completely in the spirit this afternoon. For one thing, the place was cold. Even with boots, wool pants, and a couple of sweaters, Jennifer kept shivering, while Patrick had to stop playing every few minutes to rub his hands together. "I'll talk to the super about more heat. Trouble is, we face north, so the sun doesn't do us much good."

His use of "we" and "us" startled her. They hadn't been a "we" in a long time.

They looked at each other and smiled nervously.

"I feel a little like a cat," Jennifer said. "You know—having to nose out every corner of a new place in order to feel at home."

"Why don't you? No use trying to force it. I'll run down and get some coffee—"

"Why don't we both go out and have coffee at the Borgia." She suddenly needed to escape from that small room. After only an hour, she was feeling very closed in. It was almost as if they were inhaling each other's breath.

Several inches of snow now blanketed everything. While Patrick was speaking to the super in the basement, Jennifer looked at Houston Street, admiring the wide expanse transformed from urban gray to country white. The vehicles crawling forward looked like mechanized polar bears.

From nowhere a song title came into her head, and she traced it in the snow on the windshield of a parked car.

Something gently hit her back. She turned to see that Patrick had tossed a snowball at her.

"Okay, you asked for it," she cried, scooping up snow in both hands and throwing two snowballs back at him.

"Hey," he laughed, ducking. "You're ambidextrous. No fair."

Without thinking, she she shot back, "All's fair in love and war," and then felt her face growing hot.

"In that case I'd better retreat," he replied.

However, as she was bending to make more snowballs, he suddenly ran up and grabbed her arms, twisting them behind her back. "Gotcha."

"Okay, I give up," she murmured, feeling a dangerous frisson at the way he had overpowered her. "You win. Let go, please."

He tightened his hold for a moment before releasing her.

Nervously brushing the snow from her hair, she stole a glance at his face and saw that it was ruddy. From the cold no doubt.

He looked beyond her, at what she had written on the car windshield, and read aloud, "You're Divine, Be Mine." The intense look he shot her took her breath away.

Trembling, she managed to get out, "Song . . . Paris . . . Helen."

"I gathered as much," he responded wryly. "I like it. And it would make a nice refrain, too."

Taking her arm firmly in his, he steered her toward the Borgia, talking calmly about the verse.

His matter-of-fact gesture was reassuring. She was being an idiot, seeing innuendos where none were meant.

They didn't linger long over their coffee. Inspiration came rushing at them, and it seemed silly to re-

main at the café when they could go back to the
studio and work with greater efficiency.

The rest of the afternoon sped by, and by the time
they had finished, it was after seven.

As Jennifer trudged toward Astor Place, her
breath steaming, she felt terrific. Once Lattimore
and Ryland had started rolling, everything had been
fine. Working with Patrick was the delight it had always been.

Several times before reaching the subway, words
came to her, and she stopped in the middle of the
street, in spite of the snow coming down, to make
quick notations in her book.

She ran down the subway steps, euphoric with her
own power. What she had felt for Patrick in the past
had been no more than a silly schoolgirl crush. Definitely old stuff.

Patrick prowled the studio restlessly, inhaling a
lingering scent of Jenny's perfume, very subtle and
yet powerfully evocative.

It had been difficult as hell. Seeing her with new
eyes, yet having to ignore the sight, and the disturbing feelings she called forth in him. Staying cool.
Light. Easy. But there had been so many dangerous
moments.

Watching her wonderfully animated face out-
doors when the snow had grayed her hair prema-
turely.

Those dancing, teasing green eyes, promising so
much. A promise once delivered, only he had been
too stupid to realize what a gift she had given him.

The snowball fight. Grabbing her arms, and the
electric sparks shooting through him. He had wanted
to turn her around and kiss her breath away.

You're Divine, Be Mine. Jenny had laughingly rubbed the words off the windshield with her hand, but they were still etched in his heart.

Oblivious of the strong wind blowing gusts of snow in his face, Patrick started home on foot.

The Lattimores and the De Palmas must get together, the sooner the better. Two couples. Unshakable.

That would knock some sense into him. It had better.

"Jenny, it's good to see you." Meredith stepped aside so Jennifer could enter the loft. She kept staring at the visitor, a smile on her face.

Jennifer smiled back, hesitated, and lurched forward to hug her old friend.

"Is Tony parking the car?" Meredith asked.

"No, I'm afraid he couldn't make it. I'm terribly sorry. And he sends his apologies. We were just about to leave when a call came from Vienna. Some trouble with a zoning permit for his new shop. He had to get there as soon as possible," she explained truthfully.

In spite of her reservations about seeing Meredith again, Jennifer was now glad. Once a friend, always a friend. "Meredith, you look wonderful. I love your purple jumpsuit."

"Thanks. I'm afraid the place is a mess," Meredith apologized, showing her guest through the loft and explaining how hard it was to keep it organized when rooms, as such, didn't exist.

A little girl wearing a tutu and ballet slippers danced forward until she was right in front of Jennifer. Then she rose on her toes and did a graceful plié.

"How beautiful," Jennifer exclaimed. "Thank you. You must be Lissa."

"Yes. You must be Jenny." The child smiled, showing a gap where she was missing a tooth. "I've heard all about you."

"Have you? Well, I've heard about you, too."

Lissa danced alongside Jennifer as she followed Meredith to the couch and accepted a drink.

"Patrick's cooking," Meredith said. "He's more domesticated than in the old days."

Jennifer smiled, remembering that Patrick's interest in food had been confined to eating it.

"Daddy's teaching me to cook," Lissa confided, sitting next to Jennifer. Just as quickly, the child jumped up. "Oh, I'm supposed to be helping." On her toes, she ran toward the kitchen.

Jennifer, watching her go, turned to smile at Meredith. "She's absolutely darling. And so graceful."

"Yes, she is, isn't she. Right now she's really interested in ballet. She sings, too. We're not pushing her, though. I want her to be what she wants to be. I didn't have that choice as a child, and I resented it for years."

Meredith examined Jennifer closely. "Funny. The girl who never cared what she put on her back. Look at you now. Anne Klein, right?"

Jennifer laughed. "Right, but I don't see how you can tell from such a simple dress. It's Tony's influence." Self-consciously she smoothed the skirt of her white wool.

The two women continued their desultory chatter, moving from clothes to the advantages of living in New York versus San Francisco.

"Of course, if you can afford the Trump Tower . . ."

Meredith trailed off as Patrick walked in, followed by Lissa. She was holding a tray of cheese and crackers, and with an air of self-importance, she offered them to Jennifer.

"Put it on the coffee table, sweetie, so she can get at it," Patrick suggested, setting down his tray of raw vegetables surrounding an avocado dip. He gave Jennifer a peck on the cheek. "Tony not here?"

She shook her head and explained, noting that her host was dressed in a denim shirt and jeans. Tony, in his suit and tie, would probably have felt out of place. Although she very much wanted him to meet the Lattimores, she now thought it was just as well for her to reestablish the friendship first.

Meredith was friendly enough but a little distant. It was almost as if the two women had been the merest acquaintances instead of roommates, borrowing each other's clothes, almost as close as sisters.

Lissa, used to being around grown-ups, was fascinated by adult conversation, and it was Jennifer who kept bringing the talk back to her, wanting to know about her ballet classes, her school, her friends.

Dinner was excellent, a veal roast prepared by Patrick, with help from his daughter.

"I'm not much into cooking," Meredith said. "Anyway, I had a voice-over to do this afternoon."

Lissa was allowed to sit up for a while after dinner, then directed to get ready for bed.

Tonight was Patrick's turn to read her a story. Lissa kissed her mother and then came to say good night to Jennifer.

As the little girl stood there in her red flannels, clutching a panda, her charming gap-toothed smile made Jennifer think poignantly of Melissa. Who would, at six, also be losing her baby teeth.

"G'night, Jenny," Lissa said, kissing her on the cheek.

The child's spontaneous show of affection caused Jennifer a burning shaft of pain. Overcome with emotion, she pulled Lissa close to her, partly to hide the anguish she was feeling. "Good night, Lissa," she murmured in the best voice she could muster. "It was a pleasure to meet you."

As Jennifer quickly lowered her head and fumbled in her purse for a tissue, she could feel the compassionate eyes of her friends on her.

After Patrick led his daughter away, Jennifer looked up at Meredith. "Sorry for being so emotional. It's just that Lissa made me think of my daughter. . . . I don't know if Patrick told you—"

"Yes, he did. I'm awfully sorry, Jenny. It must have been terrible for you." Meredith moved closer and put her arm around Jennifer's shoulders in the first warmth she had shown all evening.

Jennifer dabbed at her eyes, willing herself not to be so maudlin. No doubt it was the alcohol.

Meredith was looking at her expectantly.

"I'll tell you about it—sometime," Jennifer promised.

"Of course. I understand. But I'd love to hear about Tony. How you met, everything."

"Well, we met at a club where I was writing skits and songs for the North Beach Players. A nice bunch of very talented performers. Tony liked the show and offered to buy me a drink. He looked so interesting that I accepted."

Patrick joined them, and Jennifer continued her story of Tony's courtship, keeping her tone light and sticking to the superficial facts.

"Even though he hadn't been in San Francisco

long, Tony had met lots of people in the retail business. And he had contacts in Florence. He knew everything there was to know about leather, and from opening day the boutique did fabulously." Jennifer's voice was filled with pride.

"You mean," Meredith questioned, "when you married Tony he hadn't yet started his business?"

"No, but he had it all planned, down to the smallest detail. He loves his work, and he's always encouraged me in mine. He's really delighted about this show—"

"So am I," Meredith interrupted, "but so far I've hardly heard about it. Patrick's being so secretive."

He glanced sharply at his wife. "Not really. We were just waiting to get enough material before we let you in on it."

Jennifer, hearing the "we" and feeling a slight strain between husband and wife, quickly said, "Now would be a perfect time, Patrick."

"So be it," he agreed. "Shall we adjourn to what is laughingly called the music room?"

He played Meredith a couple of *Helen*'s songs, which she sang once, then a second time, while Patrick and Jennifer saw things that needed correcting.

After a third rendition, Meredith said, "The more I sing the songs, the better I like them. They sort of grow on you."

"That's the way I feel," Jennifer said. "Patrick's music gets better with every hearing."

"Hear, hear," he chimed in, making Jennifer smile.

Meredith wanted to be in on the rest of what they had done, and they showed her what they felt was reasonably ready.

"It's really wonderful," Meredith exclaimed. "Until now it's just been an idea to me. Although I've heard Patrick playing with notes, he also works on TV themes and I wasn't sure which was which."

"Or what was what," Patrick added, smiling playfully at her.

Jennifer was glad that husband and wife were in harmony again.

Meredith's enthusiasm grew, and she predicted that *Helen* was going to be a hit. "It even has a plot, something librettists have completely forgotten about lately."

Jennifer smiled at her hosts. "I'm so glad we're all together again."

When she saw that it was twelve-thirty, she was amazed.

Meredith and Jennifer embraced warmly, promising to meet again soon, with Tony.

Patrick insisted on accompanying Jennifer to the street, and she couldn't help remembering the last time he had put her in a taxi, eight years ago.

Better not to think of it. Better to forget the past and look forward to the wonderful future.

"Good night, Patrick, and thanks. It was super. The dinner, seeing Meredith again, meeting your daughter—everything."

They exchanged a peck on the cheek, and then he was gone.

Jennifer rode home feeling that the evening had been a success.

"Jenny really lucked out with De Palma," Meredith said as she helped Patrick clean up. "But I don't know that I believe her story about tonight."

Patrick glanced at his wife reflectively. "What makes you think it wasn't true?"

"Instinct. He's from a different world. Maybe he didn't want to spend time with theater folk who hardly have a dime to their names."

Patrick soaped a dish without replying.

"In fact, that marriage seems a little suspect altogether. I mean, Tony marrying her before he started his business but after her grandfather died and left her his money."

"Don't you think you're jumping to conclusions?"

"Maybe. Anyway, clothes certainly make the woman. Jenny's better-looking than ever before. Her hair, makeup—everything was exactly right. Don't you find her much more attractive?"

"Yes, I guess so," he answered, his eyes on the roasting pan he was scrubbing.

"Still," Meredith went on, "not even money can buy happiness. It can't bring back her child. Did you see her face when Lissa kissed her?"

He had, and it had pained him greatly. "I'm glad Lissa and Jenny like each other."

"I wonder why she doesn't have another child. They can afford it," Meredith mused.

Patrick compressed his lips, uneasy at thinking of Jenny trying to become pregnant, and not succeeding. He felt uncomfortable, too, at the way his wife kept harping on their lack of money. She had chosen him over all the rich men she could have had, and it weighed on him. He wanted Meredith to be able to afford the clothes, a nice apartment, and all the other things she craved.

Wiping his hands on a towel, he put his arms around her and rested his chin on the top of her head. "Don't despair, love. You saw tonight what a show we're writing. Next year at this time you'll be looking out at New York from the highest penthouse in town."

Meredith smiled up at him and kissed his lips tightly. "You bet I will. I didn't mean to sound envious of Jenny. After all, I have Lissa and I also have you."

As she snuggled against him, he held her tightly, but a vision of Jenny flickered behind his closed eyes for a moment too long.

8

Jennifer sat on the rug in her living room, a large yellow pad on her knees, writing. Books and papers were all around her and on the coffee table. It was dark, except for one lamp, and it was silent. She was absorbed in her second draft of the libretto. This was the way she worked best. A habit left over from her adolescence, when she had liked to do her homework on the living-room floor while her grandfather sat reading or dozing.

Jennifer felt happy as she worked, and only a little uneasy. She never spread herself out this way when Tony was at home, knowing how particular he was that everything in the living room be in its place.

He was on one of his frequent trips to Vienna, and she was glad he hadn't insisted that she go with him, because she was so busy working.

"I shall miss you, of course," he had said before leaving a week earlier.

"If you need me, Tony, just phone and I'll get on the next plane."

He smiled. "Good. And the same holds true for you, my sweet. If you get lonely, just come. Working on that libretto hour after hour by yourself—"

"But I'm not by myself. I'm with Helen and Menelaus and Paris and Cassandra. All the characters

103

come alive for me. They'd better or they won't be believable to the audience."

"I suppose so. But I can't imagine how you do it."

"And I can't imagine how you get everything together to open a store that looks so beautiful and runs
so smoothly. And makes money, too."

They had both smiled and bowed at each other, in
recognition of their different talents.

When the phone rang after eleven, Jennifer was
surprised. It couldn't be Tony. It was the middle of
the night in Europe.

It was Patrick. "I didn't wake you up, I hope,
Jenny."

She could hardly hear him over the pounding of
her heart.

"No. I was working."

"Me too. I'm glad I'm not the only nut of this two-
some."

He was phoning to talk about a refrain they had
been having trouble with.

Jennifer tried to concentrate on what he was saying, but mostly what registered was a husky murmur
right into her ear. Disturbingly intimate. She could
almost feel his hot breath tickling her earlobe.

Quickly she grabbed a sheet of paper and made
some notations. "Uh, let me think about it, Patrick,
okay? I'm into something else right now, a section of
the libretto," she babbled, promising to get back to
him in the morning.

She thought he sounded a little hurt at the way she
cut him off, but she didn't care. When she hung up
she was trembling.

What was the matter with her, anyway?

She jumped as the antique Swiss clock in the foyer
gently struck the quarter-hour.

Then, total silence, except for her breathing. That must be it: the silence, the lateness of the hour, the fear, whenever the phone rang at night and Tony was away, that something had happened to him.

Nothing to do with Patrick. She was just being silly.

She turned on the television, immediately comforted by the cheerful voice of the newscaster reporting on the weather.

Jennifer went to the bathroom to wash her face.

On her way back to the living room, she saw Tony. "Oh!" she exclaimed, startled.

"Sorry if I frightened you, *cara.*" He smiled and held out his arms. "I didn't know I was coming home until the last minute, so I thought I'd surprise you."

As he drew her to him, she hugged him tightly, terribly glad to see him.

"How I have missed you," he breathed, holding her close. Then he looked behind her to the disarray in the living room. "So this is the way the mice play when the cat's away. Why aren't you working in the den?" His tone held a tinge of disapproval.

Jennifer was embarrassed at having been caught. She explained, but not fully. The den, in her mind, was meant to be a child's room, and working there made her too sad.

While Tony poured them drinks, she gathered up her books and papers and put them out of sight.

He told her how his European trip had gone, and she made an effort to listen attentively. Yet, half of her was still hearing the echo of Patrick's husky voice in her ear.

Tony's talk was sprinkled with the names of buyers, models, window dressers—almost all of them women.

She looked at him speculatively. He was so attractive to women. And had the money, the opportunity for an affair. . . .

"I suppose you had lots of female company at lunch . . . and maybe even dinner."

He smiled. "Yes, of course. I always do. But surely you don't think . . ." He stopped, surprised. "My dear, why do you ask such a question now? I have never known you to be jealous of my business associates."

Jennifer flushed. "I'm not. Forget it."

"Believe me, you are the only woman in my life and I love you. Now, come to bed, *cara*."

"Listen, guys, I'll give it to you straight," Sharon McEwell told Lattimore and Ryland over drinks. "We're into another era now. Getting a musical on Broadway costs four, five million bucks."

The producer of *Make Love, Not War* was now in her late thirties, thin and intense. Her jet black hair was cut short on the sides and back, dipping into a wave on top, and she was modishly dressed.

Although Sharon was glad that the songwriting team was together again, she expressed more caution than enthusiasm.

"Backers are scared to lose their shirts. When a show like *Dance a Little Closer* can close after one performance, nobody knows what to expect anymore."

The example she had mentioned was every producer's nightmare. The musical, based on Robert Sherwood's *Idiot's Delight*, had had a book and lyrics by Alan Jay Lerner and music by Charles Strouse. But it had flopped anyway after poor reviews.

Lattimore and Ryland didn't have the clout of

Lerner and Strouse. What they did have, they believed, was a dynamite show, but they would have to convince a lot of people in order to get it produced.

"It's impossible for me to take on a property without co-producers, and it's damned hard to find independents. I don't want to be involved with a giant like Paramount or Warner's," Sharon continued. "They like to have first refusal on media rights. That means cable, feature film, video cassette, and I can't work like that. Blows the control. It's got to be my baby or I'm not interested."

Sharon talked of spiraling costs for everything— wardrobes, scenery, advertising, theater rental, union contracts, royalties. "Just keep in mind, you guys, that a musical has to take in more than two hundred thou a week just to break even. Yeah, I thought that would choke you up. It sure sticks in my throat."

Sharon was a worrier, but she was also a terrific producer, with mostly successes to her credit and a reputation for repaying her backers.

Patrick had warned Jennifer that this wouldn't be easy. Although Sharon had produced his *Me, Tarzan*, she had refused *Cameo*. Still, the collaborators had absolute faith in their show.

Within four months they had produced a workable libretto and almost all the songs they would need for the production.

It had been a happy period for Jennifer. She was delighted to be able to work with such concentration again, and her worry over the personal aspects of the collaboration had proved unfounded. Patrick hadn't called her at home again. In fact, he had been totally businesslike at all times.

Somehow the Lattimores and the De Palmas never

had gotten around to meeting socially, mostly because Tony was so busy negotiating the opening of his Vienna boutique. Once it was launched, Jennifer was sure they would finally get together.

Meredith had dropped in to the studio several times, claiming she had to talk to Patrick—there was no phone—and, of course, stayed to hear the songs. At times she did somewhat break the creative flow between Lattimore and Ryland. Naturally Jennifer couldn't say so to Patrick. It wasn't like the old days. Meredith was his wife.

Patrick said nothing to Jennifer either, but he did install a phone. Several times she overheard him dealing with Meredith's questions and tactfully discouraging her from appearing at the studio at an unpropitious moment.

Jennifer snapped back to the present when she realized that Sharon had talked herself out.

"We get the picture, Sharon, my love," Patrick said. "Now, how about listening to an impromptu audition?"

Sharon smiled. "I doubt the 'impromptu' part, but sure, let's hear what you've got."

They summarized the story and sang a few songs. The producer listened impassively, making a few notes now and again. When the demonstration was over, she sighed. "A few years ago it would have been a piece of cake. I have some co-producers in mind, but it won't be easy to convince them that a couple of Yalies who had a hit Off Broadway a decade ago can do it again on Broadway."

"Sharon, what are you really saying?" Patrick began.

"That you don't like it?" Jennifer finished.

"Hell, no. I love it. I really love it. I see all sorts of possibilities. It's just going to be tough, that's all."

While Sharon went on moaning, Lattimore and Ryland grinned at each other.

"You do your stuff, Sharon," Patrick said happily, "and we'll do ours."

Debra Dillon sat on the edge of her bed chain-smoking, her television tuned in to a soap. But nothing was registering. The twists and turns of fiction were paltry compared with what happened in real life.

She was still dressed in her dark suit, her mink flung around her shoulders, feeling too numb even to take off her boots. The snow was melting into a gray puddle on her expensive white carpet, and she stared at it, mesmerized, until ashes from her cigarette dropped and fizzled in the wetness.

Born under an unlucky star, that's what she was. Doomed to be unhappy. Why? What had she done to deserve everything going wrong, time after time?

Arnold Brody had come home from a trip to the Middle East more glum than she had ever seen him. True, he wasn't ever a bundle of laughs—just as long as he was a bundle of bucks. What was bothering him, she didn't find out. He never talked much about himself or his business.

She only knew that something was wrong. First, he postponed the wedding and refused to give her an explanation. Second, he lost interest in sex.

Debra became desperate. Sex was the main hold she had over him, and as the days turned into weeks, she tried everything she could think of to revive his interest, including pornographic videotapes.

Occasionally that worked, but Arnold seemed to need new and more bizarre material.

With a combination of wheedling and pouting, Debra finally got Arnold to agree to get married at the beginning of May. "But it's not going to be a fancy affair," he cautioned. "City Hall, and that's it. And your sister can stay where she is. If you start spreading the word, it's all off."

Debra bit back her anger, afraid to antagonize him. Especially as he continued to behave strangely. Whatever meager affection she had felt for him had diminished. Still, she had made an investment and she was going to stick with it. Afterward she could get divorced—for a price.

At the end of April Debra's relationship with Arnold sank to its lowest point when, one night in bed, he became rough with her, slapping her until she was a mass of bruises. Only then was he able to get sexual relief.

The next afternoon she went to a modeling job, annoyed that it was snowing unseasonably. At least this would be the last time she would have to display her legs for anyone but her husband.

Every bone and muscle in her body ached, and working was torture. For three hours she went through painful contortions modeling her legs for a body-cream ad.

After the session she took a taxi home, bathed and dressed, and waited for Arnold. When he failed to appear, she phoned him at the Carlyle.

The telephone operator, sounding strange, said Mr. Brody couldn't take any calls.

"He'll take this call," Debra snapped. "I'm his fiancée."

The operator hesitated, then told her there had been an accident.

In a panic, Debra rushed to the hotel and found it crawling with cops.

Arnold Brody had hanged himself in his room.

As the newspapers later reported his death, he had invested heavily in certain oil ventures, prices had plummeted, and he had lost several million dollars of his clients' money. Although he still was personally wealthy, the disgrace of having been so mistaken in his judgment was too much for him.

Debra had immediately consulted an attorney, but there was nothing he could do. Apparently Arnold had told nobody but Debra of his intention to marry her. He had been a loner, and she had been a fool.

Today she and her attorney had been to a reading of the will. An old one. Everything was left to Arnold's mother, now deceased, and would revert to a cousin living in Ohio.

Debra was left with her mink coat and several thousand dollars' worth of jewels. Pathetic fripperies compared with his millions.

Her body still ached from the bruises he had inflicted. The selfish bastard. How had he dared to kill himself without marrying her first? Without at least making some provision for her?

Debra came out of her trance when she began to feel hot in her street clothes. And she was out of cigarettes.

She decided to go south and stay with her sister for a week or two while she considered her next move.

Dammit, she had wasted almost a year. When she thought of all the boring evenings she had endured with Arnold, she wanted to scream.

All in vain. She was back to square one. A little older, much more disillusioned, and still with no way of quitting modeling and settling down to the luxurious life she deserved.

9

While Jennifer and Tony were returning from Vienna after his successful opening, she told him of the backers' audition Lattimore and Ryland were going to hold for *Helen, Helen!*

"The main purpose is for Sharon to interest co-producers and get some money for the production. So Patrick and I will put together about an hour's presentation, and sing the songs ourselves. That's the way it's usually done." She went on to explain that the more that was left to the audience's imagination at this point, the better.

Tony suggested that they become backers, but Jennifer pointed out that it was inadvisable for people to put their own money in a show one of them was involved with.

"I see. Well, how about having the audition at the apartment? I can also invite some of my contacts."

Jennifer hugged him. "That would be wonderful."

When Sharon saw Tony's invitation list, she was greatly impressed with the prominent fashion names—Lagerfeld, Ungaro, and Valentino, among other.

"That looks terrific," Sharon said, "but keep your fingers crossed. All we're selling at the moment is an illusion. Sure, people love the idea of having a piece of the Broadway action, but it's hard to get them to shell out four and a half million bucks. It's up to you and Patrick to make them want to do that."

At the end of May the audition was held in the living room of the De Palma apartment, rearranged to accommodate the concert grand piano and enough chairs for the one-hundred-plus people invited to attend.

A caterer had been engaged to provide champagne and caviar, to be dispensed by a staff of six.

Jennifer decided to wear her simplest evening dress—a Ralph Lauren black cashmere knit with one bare shoulder. The dress clung subtly to her form, and she wore no jewelry except diamond-and-emerald earrings.

"Beautiful," Tony pronounced, looking at her critically. "You could use a touch more jewelry, though."

"I'd rather not. I'll be leaning on the piano and walking around. I don't want to be jingling all over the place."

"I see." Tony kissed her forehead. "Don't be nervous. You'll do very well, I'm sure of it."

Patrick and Meredith arrived early. She was wearing a Lagerfeld dress of pale blue lace which revealed her lush pink shoulders and arms and delineated her bosom while being generally slenderizing. Although she had shuddered at the cost, Meredith had felt she must have the dress for tonight, and Patrick had agreed.

"You look gorgeous," Jennifer exclaimed, embracing Meredith lightly.

As Tony was introduced, he kissed Meredith's cheeks, Italian style. "At long last." Smiling at her with appreciation, he murmured, "You're even more beautiful than I had pictured."

Meredith felt herself blushing. *And you, Tony De Palma, are much handsomer and sexier than I had pictured.*

Tony and Patrick gripped hands, quickly assessing one another with a shrewd exchange of glances and smiles.

"I'm sorry it's taken us so long to meet," Tony said easily, taking each Lattimore by the arm as if he had known them for ages, and showing them around the apartment.

Jennifer was reassured when she saw Tony behaving to her friends in his most relaxed and charming manner. It had been foolish of her to wonder if they would hit it off.

Patrick moved to the piano to limber up his fingers. He didn't appear too happy in his tuxedo, although it suited him very well, Jennifer thought.

He glanced up at her as she leaned against the piano. "You look smashing, Jenny. If the audience doesn't like the songs, they can at least enjoy watching you. Sexist get-ups, tuxedos," he continued, only half-teasing. "I wish I could show a bare shoulder."

She laughed. "You look very good in full regalia, if that's any comfort. And I agree that looking good is important for tonight's crowd. How's the piano?"

"Fantastic. To go with the surroundings and the view." He smiled at her. "I'm so damn nervous."

"Me too. As long as we don't show it."

Meredith , glancing at the two at the piano, had to admit that Jenny looked lovely. Her figure was so beautifully yet elegantly revealed in that clinging dress.

Quickly scanning the room, Meredith took in the antiques deftly mixed with the modern made-to-order pieces. Tony De Palma had exquisite taste in everything.

As other guests began to arrive, Meredith watched her host being charming to everyone, and she wondered how Jenny continued to hold his attention. A man like that could have had any woman he wanted. In fact, he had greeted Meredith so warmly, made her feel so desirable, that she almost had a crush on him herself.

Meredith tried not to be envious. Anyway, some of the De Palma good fortune was going to rub off on the Lattimores. First, having the audition in such a place was impressive. Money went to money, success to success. That the De Palmas actually lived here had to be a plus. And that Tony De Palma was who he was, likewise.

Sharon McEwell swept in, dramatic in a flowing kimonolike striped black-and-white satin dress. She greeted other guests effusively, trailed by her husband, a theatrical lawyer in glasses, as drab as Sharon was flamboyant. The attraction of opposites, Meredith thought. Was it the same between the De Palmas?

Her excitement increased as more and more glitzy people arrived. She recognized several of the designers and personally knew a number of Broadway angels. Soon she was in the thick of the crowd, feeling she belonged in this stunning assemblage. Carefully she limited her intake of champagne and ate no caviar. She couldn't afford an attack of nerves tonight because she was going to sing one important number. Although it was unusual, Sharon had decided that as long as Meredith was the star, one song would give the audience a taste of the real thing.

During a moment alone with her husband, Meredith couldn't resist murmuring, "Can you believe all this? Jenny, the simple kid who didn't notice if she was living in a crate, has lucked into millions. I'm not begrudging her, understand, I'm just observing."

"Uh-huh." Patrick grinned at her. "We're ready to begin."

"Break a leg, darling," she said, kissing his cheek. "You too."

Jennifer and Patrick began their performance with the overture and then a summary of the plot, getting the laughs they had been counting on.

Both had good, serviceable voices and the flair for putting over a song. They sounded especially nice in the duets because her voice came across as light, airy, while his was low and husky.

One of their favorite numbers, a duet sung by Helen and Paris, "Do I Love Him?/Do I Love Her!" was funny, poignant, and romantic at the same time. The audience was silent for a moment after it ended, then broke into applause.

After the Spartans win the Trojan War, and Paris is slain, Menelaus sails for home with his wife. Helen, always pragmatic, decides she's once more in love with her husband and sings "First Love, Last Love."

This was Meredith's number, and she put it over so brilliantly that she brought the audience to its feet.

After the finale, people applauded enthusiastically. Lattimore and Ryland were elated but trying not to go overboard. The important thing was if the listeners would put their money where their applause was.

Jennifer, Meredith, and Patrick stood together as the others thronged around them telling them how much they had enjoyed the performance.

Meredith's agent, Conrad Black, was there and congratulated her warmly. On his way out a little later, the agent passed Patrick and pumped his hand. "Brilliant. Absolutely tops. No wonder Meredith turned up her nose at a role opposite Raul Julia. She never breathed a word, of course, but I figured she had something else going."

Before Patrick could digest that information, Sharon grabbed his hand, her other pulling Jennifer. She led them to two men who had agreed to co-produce. One, Nat Fenway, owned a record company which would record the show. The other, Ed Zinn, had been involved with several successful Broadway properties in recent years.

"I'm over the moon," Sharon told Patrick and Jennifer a little later. "Those two French manufacturers Tony invited are looking for big American investments, thanks to their socialist government's restrictions, and they simply adored the show. I've never been so excited by a property. We're gonna do it, guys. Oh, I love you both." She kissed them and floated away.

Finally, only the De Palmas and Lattimores remained.

Meredith grabbed Patrick and Jennifer, and the three did a spirited dance around the room, snaking between the chairs and singing one of the rousing numbers from the show, "The Gods Are on Our Side." They tried to get Tony to join in, but he held back with an apologetic smile.

Breathless, the three came up to Tony.

Patrick touched his host's arm. "Thanks for tonight, Tony. The ambience was just perfect, and I think it made all the difference."

"It was my pleasure," Tony replied. "You know, I hadn't heard any of the music before. I wanted to be surprised. In fact, I'm astonished. It was wonderful, Patrick. Now I know why my wife has always wanted to work with you. And you, my dear," Tony continued, turning to Meredith, "sang so exquisitely it gave me chills down my back."

Meredith, thrilled by his words, impulsively hugged him and pecked him on the lips.

Tony pecked her back, careful of how he encircled her lush body. She was one gorgeous woman, and he felt in his bones that the show was going to be a hit if for no other reason than that she was the star.

"Ryland, you're terrific," Patrick murmured, draping his arm across Jennifer's shoulders. He squeezed her for a moment, then lightly kissed her cheek.

"Ditto, Lattimore." Jennifer kissed him back and immediately moved away. Taking her husband's hand, she smiled at him, feeling elated.

Later, in bed, Jennifer nestled happily in Tony's arms. Everything had worked out so perfectly. She had made the right decision to collaborate with Patrick. She was lucky, too, in having a wonderful husband whose support had helped make the evening possible.

Patrick lay awake waiting for the aspirin to take away his headache. Too much champagne, mixed with euphoria, had practically lifted his head off his shoulders.

What a hell of an evening. The heights and the depths. About the show he felt exhilarated, his optimism confirmed by the audience's reaction. It had been a glorious evening that had fulfilled its purpose—and done a little more, unfortunately. Tonight had marked a disturbing breakthrough in his feelings about his collaborator.

When Lattimore and Ryland rehearsed, they hadn't actually acted out the parts. But during the performance—especially in the love duets—they had looked at each other and tried to imbue the songs with feeling.

After the performance, wherever he had been standing, his eyes had followed his collaborator, his curiosity piqued. What was she really thinking? Feeling?

Then, when he had touched her bare shoulder without thinking, he had been stunned. Her skin was so soft, so velvety, yet warm, strong, real. Such waves of feeling had flooded through him that he still didn't understand how he had managed to kiss her lightly and release her.

At the same time that he was upset by his new feelings about her, he felt awed by Meredith's loyalty to him. She had turned down Raul Julia even before she knew for sure that *Helen* would be staged. Dear, loyal, talented Meredith. Always believing in him. Never letting him down.

Except perhaps in one respect. Whenever they made love, he suspected that Meredith faked her pleasure. In the beginning, he had been so dazzled by her he hadn't realized. Later, he had tried to broach the subject gently, at an appropriate moment, hoping she would help him to understand what really aroused her. But she had never admitted that every experience was less than perfect.

Well, he couldn't very well accuse her of lying. Especially since he might be wrong.

However, when he had made love to Meredith tonight, her faking—if that's what it was—hadn't been any worse than his. Because the demons within had tantalized him with visions of Jennifer.

Patrick sighed and pushed his damp hair back from his forehead, trying not to awaken his wife.

It was a good thing Tony De Palma was so handsome. So sophisticated and smooth. So goddamn rich. A good thing his wife obviously adored him. Otherwise . . .

The way Jennifer had looked at Tony!

The jealousy Patrick had felt!

The idiocy of all this!

Yet, the terrible truth remained: clever, funny, warm, delightful Jenny Ryland had merged with the beautiful, sensual, exotic woman whose bare shoulder had pulsated for a fraction of a second beneath his fingers.

She could never be Jenny to him again. She had become Jennifer, and he knew that he was in love with her.

10

"I don't get this," Raf Garcia said, stopping in the middle of a song. "I don't know what the hell I'm singing."

"If you bothered to read the libretto, you'd know perfectly well," Meredith snapped to her leading man. "For God's sake, stop being such a prima donna."

"Hey, lady, maybe you'd like to sing my part too."

The two began to shout at each other until the walls of the rehearsal hall reverberated with their angry voices.

"Raf, Meredith, please, you guys, be reasonable," the director, Milo Braden, pleaded.

Jennifer, leaning on the piano, exchanged a rueful look with Patrick. He played a few attention-getting chords that effectively stopped the shouting match.

Jennifer moved over to Raf. "The point of the lyrics in every song is to carry the action forward."

"Right," Milo confirmed. "You can't expect every song you sing to sound like a hit right off the bat. This is a joint effort, not a one-man show. And the songs follow the plot—"

"Bullshit. *Dreamgirls* doesn't have a plot, and *Cats* doesn't either—"

"Then go and work in them," Meredith shouted. "This isn't that kind of musical—"

"Listen, you, shut up, huh? I don't have to take this shit from you—"

Sharon intervened, and with Milo's help succeeded in calming Raf.

Later, over a postrehearsal drink, Milo discussed the problem with Sharon, Jennifer, Meredith, and Patrick. "Raf isn't a quick study. The music has twists and turns he's just not used to—"

"Then why cast him in the role?" Meredith inquired. "He's a pain in the ass to work with. Everyone on Broadway knows that."

"I'm not arguing that point," Milo said smoothly. "But the fact is he's perfect to play Paris. Looks the part. Has the voice for it. When he gets to the romantic numbers he'll have the women in the audience swooning. There's a Valentino-like quality about Raf."

"That's right, mixed with a little John Travolta. Try to humor Raf a little, Meredith," Sharon said.

After Milo and Sharon had gone, Meredith was still not pacified. "I've come across temperament, but that guy is off the wall."

"He'll settle down eventually," Patrick said. "Probably just nervous at having to learn new stuff—"

"But there's always new stuff," Meredith pointed out angrily. "Songs come and go, you know that. Especially during tryouts. If he keeps on that way, I'll be in the loony bin before we even get to Boston."

"Ironically," Jennifer said, "Raf is ideal for the role of Paris exactly because he's so vain and selfish, as well as handsome. Paris to a tee."

"I agree," Patrick chimed in. "And in Raf's culture, men take the lead, literally, in everything. The fact that he's got second billing rankles him to start with. Then, when you shout at him, Meredith, it only makes him more defensive and it becomes a macho thing for him—"

"Oh, I see. He won't put up with my shit, but I have to put up with his, right?"

"No, dear, not at all," Patrick soothed her. "Just don't attack him directly, okay? Tell Milo. That's what he's there for. It's his job to keep Raf in line, not yours."

Patrick went on to remind Meredith that the show was capitalized at more than four million dollars. If Raf quit, they would be in trouble.

A few days later, Raf was complaining again. "How can I sing 'sweet' on that high note? That 'ee' sound closes up my larynx like a trapdoor—"

"Oh, for Christ's sake," Meredith muttered under her breath. To her annoyance, Jenny sided with Raf.

"Oh. I see what you mean. My fault. I'll fix it." She consulted with Patrick, and they went over the line, then the entire refrain.

"Instead of rewriting the whole verse, let me play with the tune," Patrick suggested. "It doesn't have to end with a sustained note."

He smiled at Jennifer, and she smiled back. As they la-la-ed and bantered, the good humor between them was transmitted to the cast.

Patrick made the change. Raf sang it and said, "Yeah, that's a lot better." He actually smiled himself.

Meredith, standing off to the side, felt her face growing hot. Lattimore and Ryland were up to their old tricks. So genial, so easy to get along with. A touch superior to everyone else. Well, it was a hell of a lot easier for them to put up with Raf: they weren't playing opposite him. They didn't have to moon at him and pretend to be in love with the macho bastard.

She had a moment of wishing she could walk out of the show and let them worry about replacing *her*.

After rehearsal, Patrick linked his arm in Meredith's. "Why don't we walk home? It's such a nice day."

She shrugged and stalked silently beside him. In fact, it was a little too warm for her taste, and muggy. The rehearsal studio was in the West Forties, not her favorite part of town. Grimy, noisy, squalid.

Coming down Sixth Avenue didn't please her either. Their building was smack in the middle of the flower district, and they had to sidestep plants the size of trees. Water oozed along the sidewalks and splattered her shoes.

God, she was disgusted. With everything in general, and Raf in particular. He simply irritated the hell out of her. Even the way he stood, with his thumbs in his jeans pockets, fingers pointing to his crotch. As if she didn't know it was there.

Patrick, glancing at her sullen face, said, "I'm sorry you're having such a tough time, baby. I know it's not easy working with Raf—"

"I'll do it," Meredith snapped. "I just don't want to talk about it."

Only half an hour before, Jenny had spoken similarly to her about Raf. Meredith hated to be the object of pity, and she burned with resentment. Patrick and Jenny must have been talking about her. Just because she didn't grin and bear it the way they did. Tweedledum and Tweedledee. Smirking at each other, making private little jokes. Damn them, Patrick was *her* husband, not Jenny's.

Meredith had gone from being the star singer to the star brat. Everybody tiptoed around Raf Garcia as if he were the king of Broadway. Yet *she* was the one who had to carry the show. But nobody really cared what she thought. When push came to shove, Raf got his way every time, and she had to shut up about it.

Only at home did Meredith veer from her obsession, involving herself with her daughter, and hearing how Lissa had fared at day camp.

Later, in bed, when Patrick gently caressed her bare arm and shoulder, Meredith said, "I'd love to but I'm dead tired, darling. I can hardly keep my eyes open."

"Close them, then," he murmured, kissing each one. He hugged her and held her close. "Good night, baby. Sweet dreams."

Meredith awoke hours later, damp with perspiration, her heart palpitating. She had had a nightmare. Lissa had run away and she was trying to catch up to her. But because she could only move through the crowded streets in slow motion, her daughter disappeared. As Meredith shouted her name, an angry mob menaced her. It was the chorus from the show, magnified to four million, intoning that it was her fault, all her fault.

Trembling, Meredith got out of bed and went to make sure that Lissa was all right.

The child was sleeping, her fine hair spread on her pillow, her arms around her raggedy panda. Meredith bent and gently kissed her head, adjusting the covers.

She went back to bed but her anxiety didn't leave

her. It grew, in fact. As she thought about her dream, she didn't need to ponder the symbolism of the four million people who menaced her. Four-million-dollars-plus was at stake in the show, and her role was crucial to its success.

She suddenly panicked. If anything happened to her, then what?

Patrick stirred, and she looked at him, lying asleep on his back, his hair, like Lissa's, falling softly over his forehead.

Meredith sighed. He was a dear man, really. Almost always gentle with her, and understanding. Well, why shouldn't he be? She loved him, she believed in him. Hell, she had turned down richer men to marry him.

She sighed again. Was she really cut out to be a star? Had she been fooling herself all these years? Sure, she had the voice, the looks, the presence. But inside she felt like tissue paper, thin, fragile, afraid she would tear under pressure. If the show flopped, millions would be lost. All her hopes and dreams. And Patrick's too.

No. She'd be fine, she told herself fiercely. She'd sing her lungs out. Identify with Helen, an enigmatic creature, by turns sad and funny, seductive and fiery. Everyone would love her. The show would be brilliant. Patrick would be acclaimed.

But wouldn't women be after him? Younger, more beautiful? Success and power—what woman could resist that combination? Patrick was still so young and attractive. At thirty a man was just becoming interesting, whereas a woman was on her way down, and maybe out.

The thought of losing Patrick made her panicky again. Meredith moved over to him and kissed his forehead, his cheeks, his lips, so warm and soft in sleep. She rubbed her breasts against his bare chest while she entwined her fingers in his hair.

"Darling, I want you," she whispered.

Slowly he awakened, put his arms around her, caressed her.

"Oh, Patrick, Patrick," she moaned, moving her hands down to his belly, his thighs.

He responded warmly and made love to her beautifully. She cried loudly in his ear, raking his back with her nails at the moment of climax.

His climax. Well, she was pleased, even if the earth didn't move, or whatever it was supposed to do.

"I love you, darling," she murmured. "That was so wonderful."

Meredith was finally able to get back to sleep, lying with her head in the crook of his arm.

Rehearsals began to go a little more smoothly.

"Okay," Milo called one morning, "Let's have 'Do I Love Him?/Do I Love Her!' "

Meredith took her place next to Raf.

When Lattimore and Ryland had sung the number at the backers' audition the key hadn't been set. It never was until rehearsals, so that it could meet the needs of the performers.

Patrick now set it at G for Meredith and Raf.

The melody was complex, with a wide range of highs and lows, and as she sang, Meredith felt a strain at the highest note.

Gary Stroh, the musical director, who would also conduct the orchestra, was sensitive to the expression on her face. "Is that key okay for you, Meredith?"

She hesitated. "It's a little high, I think—"

"Oh, shit, here we go again," Raf said angrily. "Are we going to quibble over every goddamn note? As soon as something's right for me, it's wrong for her."

"Milo looked imploringly between the two singers. "Meredith?"

"Well, if you could take it down a tone—"

"It'll be too goddamn low! My voice'll be in my shoes."

"Try it in F, Raf, just to see," Milo pleaded.

They did. Meredith preferred it but Raf made such a hash of his low notes that he got a laugh from the cast.

Meredith, furious, felt all eyes upon her and sensed that everyone sided with Raf. "Okay. Leave it in G."

Patrick called out from the piano, "Are you sure? I could narrow the range—"

"Or I could play around with the words, so the high note would be easier for you," Jennifer added.

Meredith fixed a smile on her face. "No, no, it's fine," she insisted, pretending they were arguing over something totally inconsequential.

Damn them, damn them, damn them. Instead of disapproving of Raf, they were patronizing *her,* making it seem as if it were her problem alone.

"Meredith, are you sure?" Patrick asked again.

She nodded, still smiling. "I'm absolutely sure."

She was sick of being treated like the heavy. Let that bastard have it in G. She hoped he choked on it.

11

One afternoon, as rehearsals were winding down, Jennifer and Patrick got into a dispute with Milo about the placement of a comic song. The argument went on and on, with everyone against Lattimore and Ryland, for once.

"I need a drink," Patrick said angrily. He grabbed Jennifer's hand and pulled her along with him before she could object.

They went to Joe Allen's and sat at the bar.

"Gin and tonic, lots of ice," Jennifer ordered.

"Same for me." Patrick sighed. "Maybe it's this heat. Everyone's on edge."

"I know. And nervous about the tryouts. Even so, it's maddening that nobody can see our point."

"Yeah. Wait until Boston. When that song fizzles, they'll see we were right."

"Thanks for the invitation," Meredith said angrily behind them. "What the hell are you two, anyway, a closed corporation? I'm supposed to be the star of this goddamn show."

"I'm so sorry," Jennifer said, immediately moving to the next stool so that Meredith could sit next to Patrick. "It wasn't your scene, so I didn't think—"

"That's right, you didn't think," Meredith snapped. "Everything in this show concerns me, *everything*."

"Please lower your voice," Patrick said tensely. "What would you like to drink?"

"A double vodka and tonic," she ordered loudly. "And I still think you're both dead wrong about that song." She reiterated the opposition point of view while she gulped her drink.

Jennifer was silent, and Patrick tried to calm his wife, unsuccessfully. Meredith was furious. "You two know best, don't you? The rest of us are morons, right? Nobody in the whole fucking company has a sense of humor except Lattimore and Ryland—"

"Meredith, stop it, please," Patrick begged in a low voice. "This isn't the place to have this conversation—"

"Where then? In our bedroom? With Jenny?" Meredith jumped off her stool and stomped out.

Patrick covered his face with his hand.

"Shouldn't you go after her?" Jennifer asked gently.

"No. I'm too goddamned angry. And I'm sorry you had to hear all that. When a couple work together, artistic disagreements can be sticky, I guess." He moved onto the stool Meredith had vacated.

Jennifer, not replying, stirred her ice with her swizzle stick, understanding Meredith's anger at being slighted.

"We shouldn't have left without her," Jennifer said at last.

"Maybe not, but she was being as obtuse as everyone else. I was just so annoyed." He sighed and glanced at Jennifer reflectively. "You're lucky your husband's in another business."

"Maybe. But that can have its problems too."

"For instance?"

"Well, if he's interrupted when he's working, he

can go right back. But if I'm interrupted, the lyric that popped into my head can pop out again unless I've jotted it down. Other people don't always understand."

Patrick nodded. "I know. If I stare into space while I'm at the piano, it doesn't mean I'm daydreaming, but that an idea is taking shape."

"Exactly. 'Did I interrupt you, dear?' is enough to interrupt me."

They looked at each other and smiled, the look of recognition, of shared understanding, causing a strong wave of sympathy to reverberate between them.

Patrick suddenly kissed Jennifer lightly on the lips.

It was only a peck, but her lips tingled, and she felt a fluttering in the pit of her stomach. Although she didn't dare look at him, she felt his eyes on her. In a low voice he said, "Let's get out of here."

"Uh, yes. I have to go home," she murmured, not entirely truthfully. "It's after four and—"

"It is? Oh, hell. I have an appointment. Late as usual. I'll have to run."

Jennifer got into a taxi, mercifully air-conditioned, gave her address, and then sat back, feeling anxiety creep over her. The one place she didn't want to be was between Meredith and Patrick. That would spell disaster for the show—and maybe for the collaboration.

She shut her eyes, tried to relax. It was impossible.

Patrick was sending her signals; she could no longer deny it. The way he looked at her . . . And his lips had felt so hot, even during that momentary contact.

In the apartment, the emptiness hit Jennifer with particular force. Tony was in L.A. for two days, and she felt his absence keenly, needed to be with him to reassure herself of her own feelings.

The ringing of the phone shattered the silence.

"Jenny? Meredith. Sorry I had a fit this afternoon. Nerves, I guess. And the heat doesn't help. What are you doing right now? Patrick won't be home for dinner—an appointment he forgot about. I have lots of food, and maybe if you haven't cooked yet—"

"I'd love to come. Tony's in L.A."

"Okay. It'll just be us girls."

Jennifer hung up, feeling vastly relieved. She badly wanted to strengthen her friendship with Meredith. Among other reasons, she believed it would help her avoid forbidden thoughts about Patrick.

On her way to Meredith's she picked up a bouquet of red and white carnations and a bottle of wine.

Lissa was standing by the open door when she got off the elevator. "Hi," the child said shyly, smiling.

"Hi, Lissa. How nice to see you." Jennifer hugged her and kissed her cheek, then handed her the flowers.

"They're pretty. What kind are they?"

"Carnations."

"Oh. They don't smell very much." Lissa sniffed at them in disappointment.

"No. Next time I'll bring roses."

"Pink roses, please. Oh, I love pink roses." Lissa danced ahead on her toes, her shiny hair bobbing down her back.

Meredith, wearing an apron over her shorts and a sleeveless shirt, was flushed and a little breathless. "Impossible to air-condition this place effectively. So I didn't fuss too much. Just some broiled chicken and a salad."

"That's perfect. Need any help?"

"No, thanks. Lissa will set the table, won't you, honey?"

"Yup. Company dishes or everyday dishes?"

"Oh, please, use everyday," Jennifer said, smiling at her. "Let's be casual."

"Okay, let's be casual," Lissa agreed, reaching for three plain white plates. "What does 'casual' mean?"

"No fuss, no muss."

The child laughed with delight. "My daddy always says that."

"Well, lots of people say it. It's a common expression," Meredith said, annoyed.

Over dinner, Jennifer focused on Lissa. She felt very much drawn to the child. Also, Meredith seemed extremely edgy and was trying to hide it from her daughter.

Had Meredith made up her fight with Patrick? Had he, in fact, been the one to suggest that she invite Jennifer tonight?

After they had eaten and washed the dishes, Lissa wanted to play cards. "Do you know Hearts, Jenny?"

"I used to. Refresh my memory."

The three played, and Meredith won several games handily.

"You always win, Mommy," Lissa complained.

"I've taught you how to win. Just pay attention. One more game and then bed."

Meredith held back this time. Jennifer should have been the winner, but she deliberately played carelessly so that Lissa could beat her.

"I won, I won," the child cried happily.

Meredith and Jennifer exchanged a smile she didn't see.

"I want Jenny to read me a story, too."

Meredith seemed a little calmer and better disposed toward her, Jennifer felt. Maybe because it was obvious that she was so fond of her daughter.

More than fond. Not only was Lissa a lovely child, but in an eerie way Jennifer felt comforted by her. Lissa encompassed little-girlness for Jennifer and brought the memory of Melissa closer.

"I wish Jenny were my aunt," Lissa said sleepily after the stories had been read.

"Well, honey, you can pretend she is," Meredith said.

"Oh, goody. Because I don't have a real aunt. Everyone in my family is an only child," she added a little petulantly.

"I'm an only child too," Jennifer said. "Only children are special, and we grow up to do special things. You will too. And I'd love to be your aunt," Jennifer said, kissing her.

Lissa smiled. "And I'll be your niece."

"Okay, no more talking," Meredith said, tucking her in and kissing her good night.

Jennifer kissed her again, resisting the impulse to hold her tightly.

The women went back to the living room and had another glass of wine.

"It's hard on Lissa, having no relatives to speak of. Patrick's parents and cousins live in Michigan and she rarely gets to see them. My mother's in Florida, in a home. Bad arthritis." Meredith sighed. "I wish I could take Lissa to Boston with us, but that wouldn't work out. She'd have nothing to do all day, and then she'd miss the beginning of school. Yet leaving her in New York with nobody but Bridget . . . She's reliable, but still. Lissa isn't her own child. You probably think I'm silly to worry so much."

Jennifer's face darkened, and she swallowed some

wine. "No, I don't," she murmured. "I think you're right to be concerned. It's so easy for something to go wrong."

As it had for her, five years ago, in San Francisco. . . .

12

"Tony, we've got to put everything out of Melissa's reach," Jennifer told her husband as he came into the kitchen.

She was kneeling on the floor next to the cabinets under the sink. Melissa had worked the doors open, pulled out soap powder, and spilled it all over the floor. "If she ate this stuff . . ." Jennifer shuddered. "I never thought she'd be able to get these doors open."

"Maybe we should have locks put on." Tony strode to the stove and burned his finger on the coffeepot. Cursing under his breath, he drew his hand away and looked for a potholder. "Where's Harriet this morning? I'm very late, *cara*."

"It's her day off. I'll pour the coffee in a sec." Jennifer lifted her two-year-old daughter and put her back in her chair. She handed the child her cereal spoon, smiling at her encouragingly. Then she poured coffee and buttered a roll for Tony.

He was preoccupied. "I just hope the new line of handbags will go over. They love them in L.A. but here it's a different ballgame."

Jennifer smiled at Tony's use of the American idiom.

Melissa was making a mess of her cereal, and

when Jennifer looked disapproving, the child laughed
with delight.

Jennifer knew all parents thought their children
beautiful, but Melissa really was, with her dark
curly hair, round eyes as black and shiny as buttons,
and a rosebud of a mouth. Strangers would stop
them in the street to admire the child, while Jennifer, terribly proud, confirmed that Melissa looked
like her father.

Jennifer answered the phone. "You can't? Oh.
That complicates things. Do you know anyone else
who could sit? No, never mind, it's all right. Thanks
for letting me know.

"The sitter can't come, Tony, and I have to be at
the club by six for a dress rehearsal. We're putting on
a new show."

"Do they really need you?"

"Well, there are always last-minute changes, and
everyone's so nervous. I don't know who else to call.
I'd ask Harriet to switch tonight, but she's out of
town. Damn."

"Damn," Melissa repeated loudly, grinning at her
parents and spitting a mouthful of food down her
chin.

They laughed.

"Oh, dear, I'll have to watch what I say. Little
monkey repeats everything," Jennifer said, wiping
her daughter's face.

Tony drained his cup. "I can get home early tonight, if you wish it, *cara*."

"Oh, can you really? That would be wonderful.
I'd have her supper ready. You'd just have to see she
eats it, then put her to bed."

"Fine. I'll be back about five-thirty. That should
give you enough time, if you have a taxi waiting."

Tony kissed her good-bye, and then hugged his daughter, laughing at the way she had smeared her mouth with cereal again. "There's no place to kiss you, *ragazza mia*," he said, finally pecking her on top of her silky head.

Jennifer cleaned up the kitchen, humming a song from the new show. She hoped it would be well received. Nice skits, gentle parody, nothing too difficult or inaccessible for the audience. And the songs and dances were charming. It was light, easy entertainment.

She suddenly missed New York and the big time, but the moment passed. Sometimes one had to make sacrifices. She had a successful, loving husband and a wonderful daughter. What kind of mother would she be with a full-time career? She didn't relish having someone else caring for her child, at least not when she was so young.

Tony's business was booming, and money was rolling in, which made it easier to keep up the house with his housekeeper Harriet's help and a cleaning woman three times a week.

Once in a while Jennifer felt they should sell the too-large Victorian mansion, though she really loved it. High on Vallejo Street, it commanded a view of the Golden Gate Bridge and the Marin headlands in the distance. It had belonged to her grandfather, and she cherished his memory. Also, Tony kept pointing out that they would have more children and then would welcome the space.

As Jennifer stacked the dishes in the dishwasher, she had an idea for a skit. Grabbing Melissa's hand, she hurried into the den and scribbled quickly on a piece of paper.

Once the morning fog lifted, it was a lovely day,

sunny and breezy. Putting Melissa in her stroller after lunch, Jennifer called the dog, Toto, a golden retriever, and they walked over to the Presidio. She let Melissa out of the stroller and made a game of letting her run away, then chasing after her, Toto outrunning everyone.

Later, Melissa, her thumb in her mouth, fell asleep in her mother's arms. Cradling her daughter gently, Jennifer had an ineffable feeling of love. Motherhood was so satisfying. In fact, she and Tony had begun trying for another child. A three-year difference between children would be ideal, Jennifer felt. Tony wanted several children. Well, they would see. One at a time, anyway. She wondered if each child would seem the miracle Melissa did.

When they got home Jennifer defrosted a quiche and prepared a salad for Tony's dinner.

To save time, she took Melissa into the shower with her, and they had wonderful fun splashing each other.

While Jennifer was dressing, Melissa opened the bedroom door and disappeared.

"Melissa? Melissa, where are you?"

Jennifer found her daughter trying to get down the stairs. "Come on, sweetie, let's get your supper ready."

At five-thirty the taxi arrived. Jennifer had him wait. Five-forty-five, five-fifty, six o'clock came and went, and still Tony hadn't returned.

Melissa was already eating, and Jennifer kept impatiently looking at the clock. She now regretted not having hired a sitter.

Tony arrived at six-fifteen, full of apologies.

Jennifer hadn't heard his car.

"I left it downtown and took a taxi to the corner.

Traffic was terrible. Wanted to save time. Okay, go now, *cara*. I really am sorry. Something unavoidable came up. Tell you later."

"Melissa's halfway through her meal," Jennifer told him, pulling on her jacket. "There's applesauce for her dessert, and pour her a glass of milk afterward."

Giving her daughter a quick hug and a kiss, Jennifer grabbed her purse. "She can climb out of her crib, as you know, and open the bedroom door. Today I found her halfway down the stairs. So look at her every fifteen minutes or so until you're sure she's fast asleep. I'll get back as soon as I can."

The players were running through their numbers for a second time. Although it was going well, Jennifer felt strangely anxious. She was finding it difficult to concentrate.

One of the actresses noticed her nervousness. "What's the matter?"

"Nothing, really. I guess I'm a little concerned about my daughter. I don't think Tony's ever taken care of her before, without my housekeeper there. I'll just phone him and make sure everything's all right."

She let the phone ring fifteen times but got no answer. Impossible. He had to be there. Had she dialed the wrong number? She tried again. Finally she got the operator to ring. Same result. No answer.

Something was wrong.

Just as Jennifer was about to leave the club, the bartender told her there was a call for her.

"Tony? Where are you? What's happened?"

"Jennifer, oh God!" His voice broke. He was at the hospital. There had been an accident.

* * *

No matter how many times Jennifer went over it in her head, it made no sense.

Tony had explained what happened, briefly, through his sobs, and she hadn't been able to grasp it.

He had put Melissa to bed after her supper. Pulled up the sides of the crib and left the door open at her request.

But she started to cry. Just then an urgent call came from Florence.

"I remembered what you said about keeping an eye on her, so I took the call in our room. But I needed some papers from the den downstairs. So I locked her door. But she wouldn't stop crying."

Tony had taken out the playpen and set it up in the living room, so he could go into the den and finish the call.

He got caught up in his conversation. There was a strike at his family's company. No leather was being tanned, and orders couldn't be filled. It was serious. The halt in production would mean a loss of customers.

Tony had been totally absorbed until the dog bounded into the room barking.

Then Tony ran downstairs to find that Melissa had climbed out of her playpen and was choking on something. He tried to dislodge it, turned her upside down, breathed into her mouth. Nothing helped, and she was turning blue. He phoned for an ambulance, but by the time they arrived it was too late. They worked on the child in the ambulance and at the hospital, without success.

Melissa had opened a candy dish on the coffee table and swallowed a handful of nuts.

In her shock and misery, Jennifer lashed out at her husband. "The playpen? Are you crazy? Where did you find the playpen? I put it away a year ago. She's much too big for the playpen! Of course she could climb out!"

"I didn't realize. She was playing, and Toto was with her. She seemed happy. . . ." He shook his head miserably.

"What do you mean you ran *down* the stairs?" Jennifer shouted at him. "I thought you were downstairs in the den."

"Well, I was, at first. But I'd left something upstairs—an important paper—so I finished the call up there. Oh, God, I didn't know what she would do. I'm a businessman, not a nursemaid."

"I told you this morning that she was getting into everything. You saw for yourself. and you offered to take care of her, it was your idea—"

"All right, I offered! I wanted to help you out. Every night she goes to sleep. I didn't know tonight she wouldn't. And I couldn't predict my family's factory would go on strike—"

"One time I left her in your charge. One time only, and you could let a thing like this happen—"

"It was so quick. Before I knew it, before I could turn around . . ." He began to cry.

Jennifer collapsed in tears beside him. "If only I hadn't gone to that damn rehearsal! I wish I'd never heard of the North Beach Players. Melissa . . . oh, God, Melissa! I just want my baby!"

Tony took her in his arms, his tears mingling with hers.

Later, in a calmer moment, she stopped blaming Tony. He was really no more at fault than she. It was true that he knew very little about taking care of children. He had adored his daughter, loved to play with her, fondle her, but he wasn't alert to all the possible dangers with a toddler.

Tony did blame himself, and Jennifer blamed herself.

They had plenty of time, in the painful, empty hours ahead, to deal with the if-onlys.

If only she had skipped that rehearsal.

If only he had told his brother in Florence he would call back.

If only she had encouraged Tony to take care of Melissa all along, taught him to bathe her, feed her, and run after her, see for himself what mischief she could get into.

If only he hadn't found the playpen.

If only she had given it away.

If only he had taken a course in first aid.

If only she had taught him the Heimlich maneuver to deal with a choking victim.

Jennifer, sleepless at five that morning, rose and went down to the living room. There stood the playpen in the dim light, mocking her.

She took a hammer from the toolbox and, using all her strength, smashed it into splinters, screaming with misery.

Tony found her asleep in the ruins, clutching Melissa's favorite toy, a stuffed bear.

"How terrible," Meredith said, shuddering. That Jennifer's child had also been named Melissa gave her goose pimples.

Meredith hugged Jennifer, who was now silent but tearful. "How terrible it must have been," Meredith repeated, "and I guess still is."

"Yes," Jennifer admitted, wiping her eyes. "We

could both hardly sleep for more than a year afterward. And Tony had terrible nightmares. I think he blamed himself, even though I kept saying we shared the blame equally."

They had sold the house as soon as they could find a buyer. And when Tony traveled abroad, Jennifer went with him. There was nothing to keep her at home. She never went back to the North Beach Players.

For the longest time, the reality of her child's death didn't register.

It had taken nine months for Melissa to be formed. Two years for her to develop, recognize objects, people. Learn to smile, sit up, talk, crawl, walk.

And less than ten minutes to snuff out her life.

"Did you and Tony think of having another child?" Meredith asked softly.

"Yes. After a year or so. Nobody could ever take Melissa's place, of course, but we both love children and we hoped . . . Well, anyway, we still hope." Jennifer smiled sadly. "I'd like to adopt, but Tony keeps wanting to try for our own."

Meredith was able to sympathize. What were Jenny's riches compared with the loss of her only child? What did it matter that Jenny made jokes with Patrick, when underneath was a sadness that would linger as long as she lived?

"Well," Meredith sighed, "how about some more wine?"

"No, thanks. I better go."

At the door she hugged Meredith warmly. "I'm so glad we're friends again. I find as I get older I really value people who knew me when. Sort of as a witness. There's a continuity to friendship I find very satisfying."

"Yes, I know what you mean."

Jennifer smiled. "I wanted to talk to you about the show but we got a little sidetracked, I guess. Maybe we can do this again."

"Sure we can. And I'm sorry about what happened today. I was being too touchy. I guess if you and Patrick didn't agree the way you do, you wouldn't be such good collaborators. So let's just forget it, okay?"

"Okay."

The cast began to run through the last New York rehearsal. After a week's vacation, the company would leave for Boston.

The show had been shaping up well, and that day, as they finished the second scene, Milo was reasonably satisfied.

During the third scene, Meredith and Raf started to sing their duet, "Do I Love Him?/Do I Love Her!"

"It sounds terrific," Jennifer whispered to Patrick.

"It really does. And they look good together, too. Of course, it's all pretense. They still can't stand each other."

" 'Do I Loathe Her?/ Do I Loathe Him!' " Jennifer murmured.

Patrick smiled at her in appreciation, his eyes taking on a silvery intensity.

Jennifer quickly turned back to the performers.

The singers were continuing to soar, until Meredith hit the high note that had once troubled her. Suddenly her voice cracked.

Milo waved to the piano player. "Stop! Stop a minute. Meredith, are you all right?"

Meredith tried to reply, but she couldn't utter a sound.

13

It turned out that Meredith had strained her vocal cords and would not be able to use her voice for at least a month. Gayle, her understudy, would take over for the week's rehearsal in Boston and a week of previews.

The first rehearsal in Boston was a disaster. Songs that had sounded fine in the small hall in New York got lost in the much larger space of the Shubert Theater with its seventeen hundred seats. All the singers were having difficulty, and Gayle was in such a state of hysteria that she could hardly project her voice at all.

Milo quarreled with everyone and he kept threatening to walk out.

And Patrick's good humor deserted him. Whether it was worry over Meredith or all the other pressures, he joined the snarling majority. Even Jennifer found herself embroiled in some of the disagreements.

During the problem duet, Gayle was able to hit the high note. However, her voice sounded thin and weak throughout, and was almost inaudible at the lower register.

"This is impossible," Milo shouted, losing his patience with her. "You're supposed to be the most beautiful woman in the world, not a teenage virgin."

Gayle burst into tears, and everyone began to talk at once.

Milo strode back and forth on the stage, waving his arms. "I can't go on with this, it's simply beyond me. Either we replace Meredith or I quit."

"I'm with you," Gary said. "This show is Helen. In other words, Meredith. Maybe it can be someone else, but it can't be Gayle. Sorry, it's nothing personal. You're a terrific Cassandra but simply not believable as Helen."

"My two co-producers are ready to pull out," Sharon told them, coming down the aisle. "And I can't blame them. Carla Andrews' show is being postponed. If we offer her a contract, she'll come running. And that's what we're going to do."

Patrick's face was ashen. "Please, we can't. Meredith will be all right. The doctor assures us it's a minor strain. How will you feel signing Carla when, say, two weeks from now, Meredith's ready to sing again?"

Jennifer backed Patrick up, adding, "I've seen Carla. She's a pro, but not right for this show, in my opinion."

Raf began to shout that he wouldn't work with Carla no matter what. To everyone's surprise, he actually said Meredith was the only one he wanted playing Helen.

"And what if Meredith doesn't recover?" Milo wanted to know.

Raf waved his hands. "Then we'll get someone—anyone but Carla."

While Milo and Raf shouted at each other, Patrick moved to Jennifer's side. "Thanks for your support." He sighed. "I'd like to tear up every note of music, I'm so disgusted."

"Take heart," she said lightly, trying to cheer him up. "The plot offstage is developing comic overtones. Imagine Raf, of all people, defending Meredith."

"That hypocrite. He ought to be drawn and quartered," Patrick muttered.

"He is, in the third act." Jennifer finally drew a small smile from her collaborator.

"Jennifer, Jennifer, what would I do without you."

Immediately she looked away and suggested that they narrow the vocal range of the duet.

"If we do, the words will probably be off in the refrain."

"Then we'll fix the words."

They found a corner of the theater and began to work. Within an hour they had made the song easier to sing without destroying it.

Gayle performed much better, Milo and Gary calmed down, and Sharon was persuaded to hold off on Carla Andrews.

"We need a really strong love number before the finale," Gary declared that Friday morning at rehearsal.

"Oh, no, not at this late date," Raf cried.

Gayle added her objections at having to learn yet another song. Previews were starting on Monday.

But Gary insisted, and after he elaborated, Milo came around to his opinion.

"How about it, Lattimore and Ryland?" Milo asked.

They looked dismayed but conceded that the directors had a point.

"Okay, you two, get to work on the duet. No, not here. Give me a moment. I think I can arrange a studio," Milo said.

Patrick was scowling as he and Jennifer walked out of the theater into the glaring sunlight. The streets were steaming in the late-August heat.

"Just what we needed. Another number. Oh, shit, how about a quick drink?"

"Okay," Jennifer agreed.

The cocktail lounge they found nearby on a side street was dimly lit and grimy-looking, but at least it was cool.

"Any ideas, Lattimore?" she asked.

"Negative." He sat next to her on the banquette, and she found his closeness disturbing.

Halfway through their drink, after kicking around some ideas and coming up with nothing, she asked how Meredith was doing.

"No change, and frankly, I'm worried sick," Patrick burst out. "This whole thing has me baffled. I've heard of strained vocal cords, throat infections, laryngitis, for a few days, but she's still not able to make a single sound and it scares me. Just between us, the doctor said that the cause could be psychological. Suggested that Meredith see a psychiatrist, but she refused. I don't know what to think. And I don't know what to do. I keep hoping that tomorrow she'll be back to normal. But tomorrows become yesterdays . . ." He trailed off unhappily.

"I'm sorry, Patrick. I wish I could help."

"I do too. Did she confide much in you, the night you two had dinner alone?"

"No, not really. I'm afraid I did most of the talking—about my daughter."

He looked at her with compassion. "Yes, that's right. She told me. I didn't realize both our daughters had the same name. After Durrell's Melissa, wasn't it? I had the same idea. Remember, *Jennifer*, when we read the *Alexandrian Quartet* together?"

She nodded, not able to look at him, feeling him watching her.

"I should have realized then what you meant to me," he murmured, putting his arm around her shoulder.

DANGER.

But she was paralyzed.

When he moved his hand to her head, turned it, and tried to kiss her lips, she suddenly jerked away, overturning her drink.

They grabbed their napkins and began to mop up the liquid.

"Sorry," she murmured, getting up.

"It's my fault," he said in a low voice.

He got up as well and stood facing her, looking at her with luminous eyes.

She wanted to throw her arms around him, kiss him, be with him. . . .

"Don't," she said, stepping back.

He bit his lip and called for the check.

Jennifer waited for him outside. She could feel the alcohol streaking through her bloodstream, and her head was buzzing. When she tried taking a few deep breaths, the steamy air only made her feel worse.

It had been madness to think she could work with Patrick. She had been fooling herself, and now things were getting out of hand.

Thank God today was Friday, and Tony was coming up for the weekend. She would move out of the small hotel where the cast and crew were staying and into the Ritz-Carlton. She needed Tony to be here, needed to be with him.

Suddenly Patrick was at her elbow. "Do you know where this street is?" he asked in his normal voice.

She glanced at the piece of paper Milo had given him. "Not really."

"Let's get a taxi. Damn this heat," Patrick muttered irritably.

The studio was large, posh, and the piano it held was a concert grand. Patrick sat down, looking distrustfully at it, and played a series of chords. "Even 'Three Blind Mice' would sound good on this thing."

"We could stuff the back with newspapers," she suggested facetiously.

He didn't respond, but glared at the keys.

Jennifer couldn't bear to look at him. She took a turn around the room, the nicest studio she had ever been in. Yet, she felt empty of inspiration.

"Well, shall we begin?" Patrick called out wearily.

"Okay with me." Leaning on the piano, she tried her best to come up with something, and so did he, but it was slow going, and they made several false starts. Hours went by without their being aware of it. Lunch never even crossed their minds.

Gradually their words and melodic line were turning more romantic. Jennifer felt herself being caught up in the spell but she didn't dare stop it. It was impossible for her to write romantic words unless she was feeling romantic.

By four they had their duet, and a reckless feeling of euphoria gripped them.

"You know, Ryland, I think we're the best that ever was," Patrick said.

"I think you're right."

She leaned on the piano, printing her words over

his music, while on another piece of paper he transposed his musical notations over her words.

"Okay," Patrick announced, "once more, with feeling."

She began to sing.

"Look at me," Patrick instructed. "We have to pretend it's for real, to see if the song really works."

A wave of heat flooded through her but she steeled herself.

" 'No one but you/ Will do,' " she began again, looking at him.

"Wait." He played a chord, then altered it, looking at her questioningly.

She nodded. "Better. Very good, in fact."

"Again."

She sang, and then he sang, while he caressed her with his eyes.

They went on singing to one another. But she began to quake, and her voice did as well. The papers were rattling in her fingers, and she had to put them on top of the piano and hold them down with her fist.

The song ended with the "No one but you" refrain, sung together.

Patrick's eyes burned. Suddenly he stopped playing and said huskily, "No one but you, Jennifer. I love you."

"No! Don't say that, please!"

"I have to. Because it's true and getting worse every day. I know it's madness. There's nothing you can tell me that I haven't already told myself—"

"Please," she broke in weakly. "It's . . . it's just the situation. Having to write a convincing love song—"

"No, Jennifer. No matter what you say, it's there

between us. I don't want it to be, but it is. I love you."

"No!" She put her hands over her ears. "I won't listen."

He bit his lip and forced himself to play their song.

When she saw his eyes on the keys once more, she uncovered her ears, feeling childish.

While she leaned on the piano, her fingers clutching at the shiny wood, they sang the duet from start to finish.

Patrick's face was thrilling to her, his eyes glowing, his mouth vulnerable and so sensual. How she wanted him to kiss her!

After the last note, she abruptly turned away, trying to catch her breath. "Patrick, you must stop tormenting us," she said in a voice that wasn't as forceful as she wanted it to be.

Abruptly he got up from the piano and walked in front of her, looking at her with restrained passion. He was so close that she could feel his breath on her face. Her pages fluttered to the floor.

"Tony's coming tonight," she babbled, her skin on fire. "So if we're finished—"

Patrick tensely stepped back. "Yes. Of course. Oh, Jesus!"

He grabbed his things and rushed out of the studio, leaving her standing there, her emotions as scattered as her papers.

Patrick walked aimlessly, not knowing where he was going, not caring. How had he come to this point, after vowing repeatedly that he would not?

His longing for Jennifer was cumulative. Seeing her morning, noon, and evening, working with her, eating with her, confiding in her.

He had tried hard, but his feelings were so strong. Every day he loved her more. In spite of everything: worrying about the show, worrying about Meredith. His wife was ill, maybe having a breakdown, and he wasn't helping.

Jennifer loved her husband. She would be in Tony's arms all weekend.

The thought drove Patrick mad. Yet he knew that he had no right to such feelings, no right at all.

What sort of insane perversity had taken hold of him? He could understand why, in olden days, people believed they were victims of the devil. That evil spirits had invaded their bodies, tormenting them with impossible passions.

Tormenting. The very word Jennifer had used when she begged him to stop. If she was in torment, did she have some feeling for him too?

He must simply stop thinking about it. He would never get through the weekend otherwise.

When he got back to the hotel he called New York. Bridget told him that there had been no change in Meredith's condition.

Panic rose in his mouth like bile. He had to force himself to talk to his daughter calmly. She was fine, having a wonderful time at day camp. She had made a new friend and learned to float on her back.

"That's wonderful, sweetheart."

"I wish you were home, Daddy."

"I do too. I'll see you very soon."

When he hung up, his temples were throbbing.

The room was too tiny, claustrophobic. He couldn't stay there. Nor did he want to have dinner with the company, having to pretend everything was normal. The absence of Jennifer. The coarse jokes about her husband.

Patrick changed into shorts and shirt and put on his running shoes.

He jogged around the Common, his breathing controlled, his pacing steady.

Although he tried to make his mind a blank, images kept creeping in. Images of Jennifer.

Old incidents surfaced from the morgue of his memory.

Jennifer, sleeping in the bedroom of their Village apartment, night after night, while he tossed on his lumpy sofa and dreamed of Meredith.

Jennifer, sympathetic listener, unselfish and caring, and always there.

Hadn't she helped him to choose a present for Meredith? He relived the incident, sweat pouring out of him.

He had asked Jennifer to help him buy a gift for another woman! After she had given herself to him only a short while before! How could he have been so stupid, so callow?

Jennifer hadn't been in the least promiscuous, he recalled. In fact, he couldn't remember that she had dated at all during the time they lived in New York.

So if she had slept with him . . . Jesus, had she been in love with him? And if so, was there a vestige of feeling still there? Was that why she had used the word "tormenting"?

He simply must leave her alone. It wasn't fair. He was bound to Meredith. She was in a bad way, and it was all his fault.

Patrick ran until his clothes stuck to him and he couldn't draw another breath.

14

"I'm sorry, *cara*, I won't be able to come up tonight after all." Tony's voice sounded strained and very far away.

"Oh, no! Why not?" Jennifer cried, clutching the phone. "You promised."

"I can't help it. Several things have come up—"

"What things?"

"Well, first, the workmen who were supposed to lay the carpet this morning couldn't make it until this afternoon. They're here now, and the place is such a mess—"

"Can't they finish on Monday?"

"Too late. The furniture is being delivered, and the stock. I must have the men's department open before I come to Boston for your opening. Has something happened to upset you? You don't sound like yourself."

How could she answer that question? She didn't want to answer it. She just wanted him with her.

"Tony, even if you have to catch a late plane or get the limo and drive up at midnight, please—"

"No, I can't. Impossible. My other problem is in Palm Beach. There's been a theft in the shop."

While he talked, Jennifer's panic grew. She took a deep breath. "Tony, just this once, please let some-

one else handle everything and come to Boston.
Please humor me. Just this once."

"Jennifer, what is all this? Are you ill?"

"I feel terrible. I need you here."

"But, *cara*, what's wrong?"

"I . . . I feel I'm cracking up. The strain. Changes.
Pressures. Having to write a new song in one day
. . . I need you, someone from the normal outside
world." She babbled on, repeating herself, not caring how emotional she sounded.

There was a pause. "It's just a case of nerves.
You'll be all right."

"But I need you, Tony!"

"Be reasonable, *cara*. You can't expect me to drop
everything and come and hold your hand. If you
could give me a valid reason . . ."

She said nothing.

"I can tell you *my* reason," Tony was saying. "The
thief was caught in the act and arrested, so it's been
in the paper and on TV. Whenever anyone sneezes in
Palm Beach, all the world knows about it. Such publicity is harmful to the De Palma image. I must be
there to counteract it. Surely you can understand. I
promise faithfully to be with you next weekend."

Faithfully.

She was silent, wondering if she should fly to Palm
Beach. No, she didn't dare. If Milo didn't like the
new duet, she and Patrick would have to do more
work on it. Oh, God! She was on the point of
screaming out the truth to Tony. Would he come
then? Or would he dismiss it as nonsense?

"Jennifer?"

"I'm here," she said woodenly. Here she was, here
she would stay. Without Tony. She said good-bye
and hung up. In a daze she packed a few things. She

had to stay at the Ritz-Carlton as planned. The company mustn't know—*Patrick mustn't know*—that she wasn't spending the weekend with her husband.

Tony shut his carry-on bag and looked around his bedroom while he sipped the last of his Campari and soda. God, he was tired. What a day.

American workmen exasperated him. Those carpet people, with their coffee breaks, their personal phone calls, in the meantime earning overtime pay. Not that he was a slave driver. He simply thought men should take pride in their work, do it as quickly and efficiently as possible. As he had always done his job, even when it had been menial.

They had messed about until eight-thirty without finishing, damn them. Left rolls of carpet all over. His assistant would have to supervise the work on Saturday.

Constant problems. The more boutiques he had, the more things that could go wrong. Naturally. Yet, it gave him such pleasure to think of the De Palma name earning prestige in the world of fashion. And it was he, the youngest brother, the one for whom there had been no room in the tanning business, who was making the family world-famous.

While his driver maneuvered the Bentley along the Long Island Expressway to La Guardia, Tony frowned, thinking of his wife. He had never known her to be so difficult—not since their child's death.

He put her nervous state down to the theatrical temperaments all around her. Much as he enjoyed being a spectator at a good show, he deplored the overdramatic way those people behaved offstage.

Meredith, for example, losing her voice. Simple hysteria. It could be nothing else.

He thanked God he hadn't invested in the musical after all. Show business was too unpredictable. It wasn't the money so much as the lack of control. With his shops, he knew where he was. Leather and fabric were tangible. Sure, things could go wrong, but not the way they did in the theater. The star of a show with no voice. And more than four million dollars down the tubes. No, thank you, not for him.

The night flight to West Palm Beach was irritatingly noisy, filled with the sorts of money-saving passengers he usually avoided by flying by day and first-class.

Well, this was an emergency.

Tony was met at the airport by a private limo and whisked to the Breakers. He had a cooling shower, dinner, and a brandy. Wavering over whether or not to order a cigar, he decided against. Many years ago he had stopped smoking to please Jennifer. During one period he had slipped back into the habit, giving it up again after his daughter died.

Tony rose after a restless night's sleep, broken by bad dreams of Melissa. Well, dreams were only dreams, he told himself, not entirely believing it.

After breakfast he went to see the thief in jail. The young man who had pilfered several thousand dollars was a twenty-two-year-old Cuban, very handsome and contrite.

Why had he done it? Because most of his family, in Miami, was out of work. His sister-in-law was pregnant with her fourth child, and his brother was unable to find a job. And so forth.

The young man had no record in Miami, and the manager of the De Palma shop said he was a good salesman and had been honest and hardworking for two years.

As long as the story had already appeared in the press, Tony agreed to an interview on television. A little good publicity couldn't hurt.

Tony had his hair trimmed, washed, and blow-dried, and his nails manicured. He dressed in a crisp white suit with pastel shirt and tie.

During the taping, Tony smiled a lot, totally at ease, and expressed sympathy for his employee's plight. No, he wouldn't press charges. In fact, he had worked out a program for restitution of the money and intended to keep the young man in his employ.

By seven Tony was back at the hotel. He wondered briefly if he ought to fly to Boston after all. Jennifer would be pleased. And it would be nice to hold his wife in his arms, make love to her.

But did he feel like getting on a plane now? Was he in the mood to listen to all the problems of the production? The squabbles, the irrational outbursts?

The answer was no. He decided to stay put.

"Put the news on, will you, Debbie?" Charlene called out to her sister.

Debra Dillon, reclining on an old couch and smoking, didn't move immediately. As she lethargically turned the pages of the Palm Beach *Daily News*, her bones felt heavy, moisture-laden. She had forgotten how hot and humid Florida was in August.

Of course, she hadn't intended to be here so long, but the days had somehow slipped by, one after another. Slowly all her money was draining away. Charlene lived so poorly. She was working now as a hairdresser in a Palm Beach salon, but she didn't earn much. And in the summer, the salon closed.

"Debbie, please. My hands are soapy," Charlene called again.

Debra moved lazily to the new color TV she had bought for Charlene. To go with a couple of bedroom air conditioners and a washer-dryer. Gadgets that were sturdier than the aging frame house and only showed up the shabbiness of the furniture.

After switching on the set, she fell back on the couch exhausted.

Charlene came into the living room, wiping her hands on her apron. Debra thought her sister looked more like fifty than thirty-five. Lord, time was running out. Pretty Debra might be, but it was a fast-aging family. In a few years she would have lost her chances for an advantageous marriage.

If only she could get herself moving again. She had to go back to New York, return to circulation so she could line up new prospects.

A familiar face on the TV screen snapped Debra to attention.

Photos didn't do Tony De Palma justice. He looked even more handsome than she remembered, with some strands of gray in his hair.

Tony De Palma, the love of her life. She watched, riveted, listening to his mellifluous voice, his exotic accent.

What a fantasy she had woven about Tony De Palma. Rich and handsome and so romantic. Unlike the grubby manufacturers and other businessmen she had known. Or the androgynous photographers who tended to find her too voluptuous for their tastes.

In his most charming manner, Tony was telling the interviewer that he was not going to press charges against his thieving employee.

"Sure," Charlene said through lips holding a cigarette. "When you're rich, what's a few thousand bucks more or less?"

Debra, her face flushed, puffed her cigarette tensely. She had never told her sister about Tony. By the time there was something to tell, it was over, and she had been too ashamed.

But now that she thought about Tony, she wondered. She had been awfully dumb back then.

Tony De Palma was rich, all right, richer than before. A new shop in Vienna. A shop in New York—and it was being expanded.

Debra smiled wryly at the free publicity Tony was giving himself, probably worth more than the sum stolen from the boutique.

He had been crazy about Debra once. And she had been awestruck, taken in by his smoothness, his charm. A charm that still made her feel funny inside even after all this time.

After she had learned he was married, she had done some scheming of her own, but circumstances had been against her. She had let him go easily—too easily, she thought now. He owed her a lot more than a good-bye kiss.

While Debra studied him now, a new plan began to take shape. A plan that would solve her problem once and for all.

15

Jennifer walked around the suite Tony had reserved at the Ritz-Carlton. The suite overlooked the Public Garden, and would have been spacious for two; for one it was ludicrous. The only purpose it served was to allow her to pace back and forth, thinking.

The thing she had dreaded from the very beginning had happened. Patrick wanted her. And she wanted him. Even though she was happily married to Tony. She was, wasn't she? Then why didn't it help?

She remebered Patrick's words: *No matter what you say, it's there between us. I don't want it to be, but it is.*

Well, thoughts didn't count, actions did. As long as they didn't give in to their impulses . . .

Tony's absence wasn't making her dilemma easier. Maybe she should have been more clever, devious, inventing another reason to get him here. But she hated to lie outright. Yet if she had told him the truth, it would have hurt him deeply.

No one but you/ Will do. The words of the song ran through her head like a litany. And the face that flashed before her was Patrick's.

It was crazy. Impossible. She would avoid spending any more time alone with him. They had written the song. Milo had better like it, because he was stuck with it.

On an impulse, Jennifer phoned the Lattimore loft and spoke to Lissa.

The child sounded happily surprised, and chatted for a few moments, being her delightful self.

Before hanging up, Jennifer said, "Tell your mother we really miss her and want her back in the show as soon as possible."

Jennifer felt a little better, but only for a moment. Wishing Meredith well didn't help. Nothing helped.

No one but you, Patrick.

Oh, God, what was she going to do?

She was going to *do* nothing—except stay out of Patrick's way. What she was going to feel was really the question.

Rehearsal was called for nine Saturday morning.

Jennifer, dressed and carefully made-up, practiced looking radiant in the mirror, looking the way a woman would after a happy night with her husband.

As soon as Milo spotted her at the theater, he said, "The duet's good, very good, tops. But Helen's second verse is a little tricky to understand. You'll see what's wrong when Gayle sings it."

Patrick was there, looking pale and drawn, with dark circles under his eyes. He barely nodded at Jennifer as he went to the piano. "Let's get this over with," he said in a flat voice.

Jennifer's heart was beating thunderously against her ribs but she was thankful for small mercies. It was only the last four lines of one verse Milo wanted fixed, and she could work on it right there.

When Gayle and Raf sang the duet, Jennifer understood what Milo meant about the verse. Unfortunately, her mind was blank. Being so near Patrick was torture. Instead of words for the verse, the words that came to her were "Do I Love Him?"

No, I don't love him, I won't love him, she told herself fiercely. Then she stole a look at Patrick, in profile, observing his silky, sandy hair falling softly forward, his long lashes brushing his cheek as he looked at the keys, his pale blue shirt with the mandarin neck and neatly rolled sleeves, his white summer pants, his De Palma loafers.

Jennifer felt the blood draining from her head. "I . . . I have to sit down for a moment," she said to Gary, who was standing near the piano.

He got her a chair and recommended that she put her head between her knees, while he sent the production secretary for a glass of water.

"Too much husband last night." Raf snickered, while Gayle glared at him and told him that wasn't funny.

Patrick sat stonily, playing, not looking at anyone.

Jennifer drank the water, trying to get a grip on herself. She had never fainted, and this was not the time to do so. After a few moments she felt better.

Noticing Patrick's lack of involvement, Gary looked between him and Jennifer. "You two quarrel or something?"

Jennifer shook her head at the same time that Patrick said moodily, "No quarrel. Just pressure. We worked on the duet all day yesterday—"

"I know, I know," Gary soothed. "Listen, I think you're both terrific, I really do. This is a dynamite song. If you can just fix four lines."

Jennifer tried her best, and Patrick did his part by sticking to the music and not looking at her.

He's trying, he really is, she thought. But it didn't help. She was aching for him, and she didn't know how to stop.

Rehearsal had to continue, and Jennifer finally told Patrick she would try to come up with something on her own. She took herself to the last row of the theater with a pad and pen, trying to work out the new lines. But she simply couldn't. All she could think of was Patrick, Patrick, Patrick.

This was hopeless. She needed a walk.

Having been to Boston several times, Jennifer knew it pretty well. She took the subway to the North End, an Italian district that reminded her of Tony. Oh, how she wanted to think of Tony!

The day was hot, muggy, and it was threatening rain.

She walked slowly down Salem Street, glancing at the shops with their displays of sausages, barrels of olives, wheels of cheeses hanging from ceiling hooks. She stopped for an espresso in a little café, while she grew more discouraged by the minute at her failure to come up with a corrected verse.

When she resumed her walk, the darkening sky mocked her mood. A crack of lightning was followed by an ominous rumble. Within moments rain poured down with the force of a garden hose. Unmindful of how soaked she was getting, Jennifer continued to walk through the deserted streets. When her shoes became sodden, she took them off and walked through the puddles barefoot.

She arrived at the Ritz-Carlton looking like a shipwreck victim. Although some guests in the lobby eyed her curiously, the man at the desk barely glanced at her as he handed her the key.

When you could afford a suite for four hundred dollars a day, eccentricity was acceptable.

She showered, and after ordering up an early dinner, watched a little television, read the paper. She was hoping that if she took her mind off herself the words would come.

But they didn't, and she couldn't stop thinking of Patrick. It was as if all her old feelings for him had returned, fiercer than ever.

I could have him for my lover. All I have to do is say yes.

But she couldn't say yes. It would mean betrayal. Of Tony, and of Meredith.

Maybe if she phoned her husband in Palm Beach . . .

He sounded sleepy.

"Did I wake you up?"

"No. I was just resting. It's been quite a day." He gave her a brief report but sounded impatient to get off the phone. "Was there anything special, *cara?* I haven't had dinner yet."

Tony had solved his Palm Beach problem by the afternoon. He could have come to Boston if he had wanted, but he had chosen not to. It hurt her, but she swallowed her disappointment.

She had to escape from the hotel.

Afraid she might be seen by someone from the company if she walked around Boston, she took the subway to Cambridge. It comforted her to be in a college town. Reminded her of her coed days, when her life had been simpler.

A local movie theater was showing a revival of *Casablanca*, with Bergman and Bogart. She had seen it once, many years ago, and she went in, though the film had been on for more than ten minutes. What she wanted was to be with a crowd in a dark place, to lose herself in someone else's story.

As it turned out, the plot reminded her of her own. Married woman in love with another man although she also cares for her husband, who cherishes her.

Jennifer found the ending so moving she almost sobbed aloud. The film reinforced loyalty to one's mate, at the sacrifice of love.

Jennifer went up the aisle and into the crowded lobby.

Suddenly she was face to face with Patrick. They both stopped—oblivious of others having to sidestep them—and stared wide-eyed, as if at a mirage.

Patrick glanced behind her and then into her eyes. "Tony?"

He's in the men's room. He's at the hotel. He's waiting outside.

Jennifer merely lowered her eyes and tried to get past Patrick, to escape. . . .

He grabbed her arm. "Wait. We have to talk."

"I can't. There's nothing to say."

"There's a great deal to say. Too much has been left unsaid. Please, Jennifer. Are you meeting Tony now?"

She shook her head.

"Then let's get some coffee." He put his hand on her elbow and steered her firmly out of the theater.

She bowed to the wisdom of his suggestion. She had known they must clear the air, somehow, but had been too cowardly to suggest it herself.

They found a place nearby, frequented by students but not very crowded in summer. Their table was in a quiet corner.

"Patrick—"

"Jennifer—"

They spoke at the same time, and stopped, looking at each other and smiling nerviously.

"You first," she said.

"Are you and Tony all right? Nothing's happened?"

"Nothing's happened. He couldn't make it up here. Business."

Patrick looked relieved.

She forced herself to talk, in spite of her ragged breathing. "Patrick, we can't have an affair." As she made that announcement, she felt silly, prissy.

"Don't you think I know that?" he answered in a low voice. "I'm not trying to have an affair. I'm trying my best not to."

She exhaled sharply.

"I think we both feel the same way, Jennifer. Committed to our mates, upset at what's happening between us. Yes?"

"Yes."

There was a long silence. Then Jennifer frowned. "I'm so upset I can't make any headway on that damned duet. I've been trying to rewrite those four lines all day."

"I'm sorry." He sighed and stirred sugar into his espresso. "And all day I've been thinking of us, in the past. Trying to get it straight in my mind. I want to know if . . . if when we spent that night together in the Village . . . if you were in love with me."

She was silent.

"Jennifer, it did happen, didn't it? I haven't dreamed it?"

"It happened," she murmured, "but it was only half the night. You sent me back to my room—"

"I was an idiot," he broke in huskily, studying her face. "You haven't answered my question."

"I guess I was a little in love with you. Does it matter now?"

"Of course it matters. Are you . . . are you still?"

Again she was silent, wanting to conceal her feelings but not able to do so. Finally she whispered, "I don't know. I'm so confused."

"I am too. If it were only lust, I'd suggest we have a fling and get it out of our system. But it's much more, for me. Ever since you came back into my life, I've felt so drawn to you. In every way. I keep thinking that we belong together. We're so right for each other. Our work. Our thinking. Even both of us seeing the same film tonight. I just wanted to escape, take my mind off you. Instead, I thought of nothing but you. And suddenly, there you were."

Jennifer looked at him, and felt a sharp pain in her chest. As if her heart had become detached and was bouncing back and forth like a rubber ball.

I love him. I really do love him.

How could that be? She loved Tony. Was it possible to love two men at the same time?

"I was so dumb in the old days," Patrick said softly. "I had very odd ideas. It didn't occur to me that a woman I thought of as a good friend could also capture my romantic imagination."

"Patrick, if you could undo the last ten years, would you?"

His adoring eyes glazed as they turned inward. Finally he sighed. "I have to be honest and say no. I've had some wonderful times with Meredith. I did love her, and still do, in a certain way. Besides, there's Lissa. Doing away with those years would mean denying her existence. I love my daughter too much for that."

The truth of Patrick's words brought tears to Jennifer's eyes. She felt the same way about Tony and Melissa. "I had my daughter for two precious years," she said softly, "years I could never wish away. Oh, Patrick, I don't understand any of this. I have a good marriage. And I think you do too."

He compressed his lips thoughtfully, then nodded. "Yes. In some ways. But I'm not entirely satisfied. When I saw you again, when we began to work together, laugh together, appreciate each other—"

"Please don't. I don't think I can bear to listen to any more," she interrupted tensely. "I feel so disloyal to Meredith—"

"So do I, believe me, so do I," he said miserably. "She trusts me. I feel like such a bastard. Especially since my song caused her voice to give out. That's why I wanted to talk to you. Don't you see, I'm trying to explain it all away, all the feelings and fantasies I keep having about you. Demystify the attraction."

Unfortunately, his words were stimulating her imagination instead of dulling it. She was crazy to sit here, facing him, drinking coffee, and listening to things he shouldn't be saying. Yet she couldn't tear herself away.

A group of young people came into the coffeehouse, laughing and clowning.

Patrick and Jennifer exchanged a look. "Us, a few years ago," he said, smiling wryly. "When I married Meredith and became a father, I grew up in a hurry. If I'd been mature before then, I'd have known that you're the woman for me, Jennifer—"

"No," she whispered. "You can't really know for sure if we . . . we'd be so good as a couple."

"I know it for sure." His eyes burned through her, and she began to tremble.

She noticed that each of them kept looking up as new patrons walked in. This is the way it would be if they were to have an affair. Sneaking around. She hated it. Conspiracy wasn't her thing.

"I'm feeling the incredible frustration of realizing what I could have had," Patrick murmured. "I love you."

Hot and cold shivers assailed her backbone in contrapuntal waves.

"But I won't try to kiss you again, Jennifer, or do anything to tempt you. That's a promise."

As she looked at his sensitive face, the eyes so wanting, the mouth so sensual, she found herself asking the dangerous question: "And what if I should tempt you?"

"I won't be able to resist," he answered huskily, "so don't tempt me unless you can accept the consequences."

She lifted her cup and lowered her eyes to hide a surge of love for him.

It was insane for her to be feeling this way toward a man who had once rejected her. Probably it was *because* he had rejected her.

It was fantasy, pure fantasy, on both their parts. If they went to bed together once more, they might see that fantasy was all it was.

But what if it turned out to be something more?

They ordered more coffee. At the same time that they were convincing themselves to let this tantalizing situation die a sensible death, they didn't want to part just yet.

She felt so close to Patrick. Closer than she had ever felt to Tony in spite of his many wonderful qualities. Tony had a special kind of reserve she recognized as European. While she respected it, at times she longed to be more open with him. Open and equal.

Tony didn't treat her like an equal. He was often paternal. Paradoxically, at other times—after Melissa's death, for instance—he had almost wanted her to mother him, to keep him from his nightmares.

But she and Tony had been together for almost nine years. Together they had had Melissa. Together they had lost her. It was a strong bond between them.

"Let's go, Patrick," Jennifer said firmly.

They stood in the street side by side.

"Would you like to walk back across the bridge?" Patrick asked.

She nodded. The coffee had made her wide-awake, jumpy, in fact.

During the walk they spoke very little. When they reached the Boston side of the river, Jennifer said, "I'm going to the Ritz-Carlton."

Patrick nodded, and they walked on, a little uncertainly. The streets were dark in places and, unsure of their bearings, they asked directions several times.

At one point, just as they stepped off the curb, a motorcycle zoomed around a corner and almost hit them.

"You crazy ape!" Patrick shouted after the rider. "Jennifer, are you all right?"

"Yes." Trembling, she leaned against a car for support. He stood next to her, clenching his hands at his sides, peering at her in the dim light.

"I'm a little cold," she murmured, trying to stop her tremors.

"Let's get a taxi." He stepped into the middle of the street and waited until one came along.

Gratefully she got in.

Within moments they were at her hotel. And she didn't want to leave him.

"Good night," she said quickly, her hand on the door. It wouldn't open.

He leaned across to help her, and as she felt his arm brush her knees, she gasped involuntarily. "Patrick. Oh, God, Patrick!"

In the next moment she was in his arms, and he was kissing her feverishly.

She shut her eyes and pressed against him, her fingers digging into his shoulders.

"Are you folks staying or going?" the driver asked in a tactfully neutral voice.

Patrick reached for his wallet.

Jennifer, still tasting his lips, gave a long, quivering sigh of surrender.

Just this once. She had to be with him, just this once.

She couldn't remember how she got to the suite, but when they were inside the door, she felt helplessly in the grip of her passion.

They fell onto the sofa in the front room, grabbing each other, and losing themselves in long, breathless kisses.

Jennifer felt on fire. His caresses were so exciting that she thought she was going to explode.

"Jennifer, Jennifer, my darling love," he whispered, nipping at her ear, while his hands gently undressed her. "How I have loved you, wanted you, all these months."

Impatiently he pulled off his clothes.

The two became nothing but flesh, hair, fingers, lips, their bodies snaking over one another, exploring, embracing.

"Just this once," she kept whispering, as if to explain the greedy way she was devouring him.

Her head had cleared of thought and filled with passion, longing, and such love.

No one but you, Patrick.

He forced them to go more slowly, gently kissing her, nuzzling her with his soft lips, making her cry out.

She experienced the full ecstasy of each moment. This was how she had once imagined it would be.

They were attuned to one another, their rhythms complementary, their timing exact. Their cresting was simultaneous and explosive, yet it left them hungering for more.

They showered together, the most sensual shower of Jennifer's life. Soaping one another, then standing with their arms around each other, kissing deeply, while water cascaded over them.

They were too aroused to wait. Patrick sat down in the tub and pulled Jennifer on top of him.

Had she thought reality might puncture her fantasy? Wrong, wrong, wrong. No dream she had ever had could approach the pleasure of making love with Patrick.

Later they reclined on the bed, she in a robe, and sipped wine, and looked at each other.

"Let me see you, please, Jennifer."

She observed him, so unselfconscious in his nakedness, and shyly removed her robe.

His eyes burned and he became aroused. "You're even more beautiful without clothes," he murmured, reaching for her. "Let me have you, darling. God, I must have you."

"Just this once," she whispered, not knowing how she would ever again resist him.

All night long they made love—wonderful, inventive, magnificent love. Understanding that if this was to be their only night together, they had to make it last a lifetime.

As Patrick brought her from one level of ecstasy to another, Jennifer knew that she loved him as she had never loved before.

Toward morning they finally dozed in each other's arms.

They awakened at the same time and looked into each other's eyes.

Jennifer smiled. " 'No one but you/ Will do,' " she sang softly. " 'My lord, my king/ To you I sing/ To you I bring/ True, everlasting love.' "

She had found the ending to Helen's verse at last.

16

Jennifer and Patrick faced each other over breakfast in the suite.

She was feeling wonderful. Wildly in love, and so glad to be here with him that she couldn't even muster any guilt. The one imperfect thing was this elaborate suite, which she thought of as Tony's.

"I have to move out of here, Patrick."

"Yes. Let's take a room in Cambridge, darling, for tonight." Giving her a beautiful smile, he continued softly, "We're already damned. Will one night more make a difference?"

It would, oh, it would. She would love him that much more than she already did. God. She wanted to be with him so much it took her breath away. Although she lowered her gaze and studied the remainder of her omelet with pretended concentration, he wasn't in the least bit fooled.

"Tonight. Cambridge."

"Tonight. Cambridge," she affirmed, finally locking eyes with him.

Electrical charges of passion reverberated between them.

Within moments they were back in bed, making love with renewed urgency.

Jennifer was awed by her incredible sexual responsiveness. It had never been this way with Tony, not even at the beginning.

Patrick was so totally on her sensual wavelength that her slightest movement elicited from him the touch she most wanted, and where she wanted it.

He was an exquisite, fantastic lover. Her passion reached such a pitch that she cried out during her climax, and even sobbed for a few moments, from sheer joy.

They dozed briefly. When they awakened, he kissed her, murmuring, "Jennifer, Jennifer, I want you so much, it's unbelievable."

"I want you too," she replied, suddenly feeling a pain of guilt. "But we're not being fair to . . . to them. It's not as if we have a reason—"

"The heart has its reasons," he interrupted softly. "We're soulmates who discovered it too late. I mean, I discovered it too late."

"Yeah, not a very quick study." She kissed the tip of his nose.

"Shut up," he said, playfully smacking her bare bottom.

When it was checkout time, Patrick offered to go on ahead and get them a place in Cambridge.

Her conscience told her it was wrong, but her heart couldn't resist. She simply wouldn't be able to get through this Sunday without him.

An hour later, her heart going like a jackhammer, Jennifer opened the door to a room in a Cambridge hotel overlooking the river. The room was lovely, with one wall of brick, one of walnut paneling. Cozy, exactly right.

She expected Patrick to be waiting for her in bed, but he wasn't even there.

Automatically she walked to the window. It was

then she saw him, standing next to a canoe. He waved and blew her a kiss.

Delighted, she changed into shorts and a shirt, grabbed a floppy straw hat, and went to meet him.

"Room okay?" he asked.

"Perfect. Reminds me of another room with a river view. In a hotel in Manhattan, where I stayed a couple of days before going to New Haven."

She got into the canoe gingerly.

At first it went in circles because Patrick was a much stronger paddler, and Jennifer laughed helplessly as her view kept changing from Boston to Cambridge.

Her mirth changed to reflection. Being on the river between two cities seemed a metaphor for their situation—between their mates and each other.

But the thought passed because of her joy at being with Patrick.

She suddenly smiled at a memory.

"Tell me," he demanded.

"The first time I was in a boat, I fell overboard. Let's see, it was the Fourth of July. My parents and I were sailing under the Golden Gate Bridge. I was about five, I guess. I was looking up at the bridge, and the next thing I knew, I was in the water. Mother couldn't swim, and she was hysterical until Daddy dived in and got me. Funny. I wasn't scared a bit. As I remember it, I paddled like a puppy."

"I wish I'd known you then," Patrick said, looking at her with love. "You must have been adorable. Still are."

"What were you doing on July Fourth when you were five?"

He shrugged. "Probably something forbidden, like playing with firecrackers."

"You haven't changed much."

He grinned and made a face at her.

As she looked at him, she knew that she hadn't been mistaken when she had first loved him all those years ago.

She didn't realize she had stopped paddling until the canoe swung around. The next moment she felt the paddle slip from her fingers. In a swift motion she leaned over to retrieve it.

"Hey, don't do that," Patrick called. Too late.

The canoe, unbalanced, turned over, spilling both of them into the water.

"You haven't changed either," Patrick shouted. "You're still falling overboard."

"Only for you," she shouted back, drawing an appreciative hoot from him.

Laughing and spluttering, they managed to turn the canoe right-side-up. She held on while he retrieved the paddles. Then he heaved himself into the boat and held out his hand.

"Oh, wait. My hat." Jennifer swam toward it, while Patrick followed her in the canoe.

When she finally joined him, they were weak with laughter, looking at each other, dripping. For a few moments they couldn't paddle at all.

"Come on, enough of this," she said finally. "We've got to get out of these wet clothes—"

"—and into a dry bed," he finished, in a renewed burst of laughter.

A while later they left their sopping clothing on the bathroom floor, but before she could fully dry herself, Patrick was kneeling at her feet, embracing her legs, and bestowing feathery kisses on her calves and up to her thighs.

They made love with a quickness and intensity

that astonished her anew. Then she lay in his arms, overcome with happiness as he held her tenderly and kept kissing her hair, her forehead.

"God, I've never felt anything like this for anyone," he whispered. "My darling Jennifer. Infinitely more wonderful than I remembered."

Infinitely more wonderful than I remembered, Patrick.

But she didn't say so. She couldn't. If he knew how much she loved him . . .

Instead, she got up and went to the window. "I love to face the water. I guess I got used to it." She described the view from her grandfather's house. And as she spoke, she realized that Tony had always chosen where they would live, consulting her only at the last minute, presuming she would agree.

She suddenly felt Patrick's exquisitely sensitive hands on her bare shoulders, and she shuddered.

He nuzzled her neck gently. "Shower. Walk. Lunch."

She turned and found herself in his arms, tightly pressed against his naked body, which began to respond to hers.

"Bed," he amended.

"Uh-uh." Gently she squirmed out of his embrace. "Shower. Walk. Lunch."

A while later they joined the throng of people strolling on Boston's Lewis Wharf, with its cobblestone paths and flower garden, alongside a former warehouse turned into an arcade of shops.

"What if someone sees us?" Jennifer asked nervously.

"We'll say we're working on the duet. Our duet, to be precise. Anyway, nobody will see us. Don't you know you never get caught when you take risks?"

While he went in search of something to drink, she bought them a picnic lunch at one of the gourmet shops. Then they sat on the terraced steps facing the harbor, grateful for the breeze blowing gently off the water.

Patrick reached into a shopping bag and with a flourish produced a bottle of chilled white wine, uncorked, and two wineglasses.

"How the devil did you get someone to sell you that on Sunday in this town?" Jennifer asked, impressed.

"Well, lassie, it's like this," he explained in a credible Irish accent. "I threw meself on the mercy of the bartender. 'Sir,' I says, 'Paddy Lattimore is me name. I wouldn't dream of incurring the wrath of the Almighty on the Sabbath, but the honest-to-God truth is that I'm about to pop the question.' As you see, it did the trick."

"It did, huh?" Jennifer smiled skeptically. "You mean that blarney plus a twenty did the trick."

Patrick regarded her with a mock-hurt expression. "Lassie, you underestimate the romanticism of Boston bartenders." He paused and picked up the bottle. "It was only a tenner."

Laughing merrily, she held out the glasses while he poured.

He raised his glass to hers and said huskily, "No one but you, Jennifer."

"No one but you, Patrick," she replied, feeling her blood turn to lava.

Quickly lowering her eyes, she took a sip. "Hm. A modest little wine, don't you think?"

He savored his. "I don't know. I'd call it just a tad presumptuous."

While they drank, they nibbled on chicken legs,

cucumbers and tomatoes, and several kinds of cheese, finishing with fruit.

Playfully Patrick dropped a cherry into Jennifer's wine.

She drank it slowly, chewed the cherry, and leaning over to kiss him, pushed the pit into his mouth.

Smiling, he carefully retrieved it and polished it with his napkin. Then he dropped it down the front of her blouse, just as a middle-aged couple, formally dressed, with Back Bay written all over them, walked past. They frowned in disapproval.

"Never mind," Patrick called out loudly after them, winking lasciviously at Jennifer. "I'll dig it out later, Sis."

She doubled over with laughter.

Afterward they strolled to Quincy Market, browsing at the stalls. He bought her a little basket of potpourri "for your unmentionables"; she bought him a fragrant bar of soap on a string "for yours."

They drank espresso at the counter of a café, threw all their change into the hat of a street musician, and wound up in the Public Garden exhausted from their walk.

Patrick was ready to sink down on a bench, but Jennifer propelled him to the swan boats, preferring a floating bench, and promising to remain aboard.

Several children were playing a noisy game all around them, and Jennifer, unable to hear Patrick over the din, grabbed the arms of a boy and girl. "Lindsay! Tracy! Behave yourselves."

"Otherwise no TV tonight," Patrick added sternly.

The children, looking at them as if they'd gone crazy, moved to the other end of the boat.

Patrick and Jennifer exchanged a thumbs-up signal, laughing and looking delightedly into one another's eyes.

As evening fell they wandered around the Common, arms entwined, enjoying the jugglers and mimes and listening to the rousing music of a brass band.

Every once in a while Jennifer glanced at Patrick, marveling that she was here with him, yet feeling it was the most natural thing in the world.

She loved him. Had always loved him. And was going to make the most of every precious moment they could be together this weekend.

"I'm hungry," Patrick announced. "You?"

"I could nibble something."

"Chinese?"

"Terrific."

They took a taxi to Chinatown and chose a casual place loaded with Chinese patrons eating at large tables, family-style.

As Jennifer and Patrick were seated, he smiled at her. "Ah. The Greasy Chopstick, Boston branch."

Jennifer smiled back, her heart thumping. He remembered!

Only this time . . .

Only this time the food was secondary to the talk for both of them. This time as they ate they looked deeply into each other's eyes. And kept starting sentences with, "Do you remember when . . . ?"

This time, as soon as they got into the taxi, Patrick pulled Jennifer into his arms, saying gruffly, "God, what a fool I was back then. I'm going to make it up to you."

There was no way she could have stopped him. She was caught in the vortex of her love for him, her passion, and the intoxicating knowledge that this time he returned her feeling.

In the room, their mutual adoration gave them the impetus to make love again.

"Jennifer, Jennifer," he cried hoarsely, "if only we could run away from everything and be together always."

"If only," she echoed, clinging to him as if she would never—could never—let him go.

Patrick couldn't sleep, and he got out of bed quietly, not wanting to disturb Jennifer. He went to the window and looked out at Boston across the shimmering river.

He was more in love with her than he had imagined possible. And he wanted to be with her openly.

God, what a mess. Two marriages. And one child.

Patrick's parents had always been devoted to one another, and he realized how much that had meant to him. Children of divorced couples had so many additional problems. He couldn't put his own daughter in such a position now. No matter how much he loved Jennifer.

For more than an hour he sat on the bed and watched his beloved sleeping, etching in his mind the way her golden-brown hair lay softly on her neck. The curve of her cheeks, the rosiness of her lips, the slender, shapely arm thrown across his pillow, the swell of her buttocks under the thin sheet.

The thought that another man would again be the beneficiary of Jennifer's passion, would have the legal right to embrace her, to renew himself day after day in her beautiful presence, made Patrick very unhappy.

Finally he crept into the bed, wrapping himself

around his love, his face buried in her fragrant hair, pain and pleasure colliding and causing an aching in his chest that nothing could alleviate.

Jennifer awoke early, feeling such a sense of doom that she could hardly bear it.

Patrick was lying on his back, asleep, breathing softly, looking so endearing. She was filled with tenderness for him, and deep, enduring love.

She forced herself to get out of bed, to shower and dress.

Looking at her face in the bathroom mirror was a revelation. She appeared wickedly exhilarated. Surely anyone seeing her would know she had just spent two days with the love of her life.

And nobody must ever suspect that that love was not her husband.

Guilt flooded her. She had no right to be so self-indulgent. Remembering the film both had seen, Jennifer smiled wryly at her sated face in the mirror. Sacrifice was mostly for the movies, a myth. In real life people got divorced and remarried every day of the week, no matter who was hurt. Not she and Patrick, though.

Still, they had sneaked a weekend together, with no one the wiser. No one but them.

Patrick was awake, sitting up, his arms around his bare legs. He looked sad as his eyes grazed over her.

"So this is it, eh, Ryland?"

"This is it, Lattimore."

The feeble attempt at humor fell flat.

Patrick unwound his arms and got off the bed, standing straight, looking incredibly desirable in his proud manliness. "Are you sorry?" he asked quietly. "Are you sorry we had this weekend?"

She shook her head slowly, unable to tear her gaze from him.

"Neither am I. It was the most wonderful weekend of my life. If only it didn't have to end. If only there were a way, somehow—"

"No!" All her reserve, and her resolve, evaporated. She burst into tears, turning her back, weeping into her hands.

In seconds he was beside her, holding her to him, kissing her wet face, stroking her hair. "Don't, darling, please don't."

"I can't help it," she sobbed. "Patrick, I love you so much! I can't bear to leave, but it's impossible for us to go on . . . like this. . . ."

While she gasped for breath, he held her tightly, shutting his eyes for a moment. "It's the first time you said you love me."

She couldn't speak for sobbing.

He released her gently and put on his robe. Then he found some tissues for her.

"Don't cry, please, Jennifer. Forget what I said. I don't want you to be hurt. I'll do anything to prevent that. I'll let you go, hard as it is. I just want you to know that I love you as much as it's possible for me to love any woman. I'll always cherish what we had."

"I will too," she murmured, wiping her eyes and feeling a little better. "It's the right decision."

He sighed. "I guess so."

Jennifer quickly turned and left the room.

17

On Wednesday afternoon Tony sat in the spacious office of his boutique on Fifth Avenue, going over bills. Adding the men's department was costing a fortune. He had decided to use Florentine colors—the pastels of the natural stone found in his native city—for the walls, carpeting, and furniture, and he thought the effect was different, and stunning.

The sales personnel would wear uniforms: beige suits, pale yellow shirts, and striped pastel ties for the men; stylish short-jacketed pale blue suits and pink blouses for the women.

The men's department was opening in two days. And in half an hour there would be an orientation meeting for the new salespeople, followed by drinks and canapés.

Engrossed in his paperwork, Tony found himself a little behind schedule. He didn't get to the meeting until it was already under way. In addition to the new people hired, the existing staff was present, to mingle and impress the others with their contentment at working for De Palma.

The sales manager finished his pep talk and introduced Tony. He came to the front and began his speech of welcome, one he had made many times, but always with enough variation not to bore the people who had heard it before.

He had an intimate way of speaking, looking from one face to another, as if his words were directed to that person alone.

It was in the course of scanning the faces that his eyes riveted on a familiar one. Debra Dillon.

He was so stunned that he faltered for a moment, almost losing his train of thought. Quickly he forced his attention to move on to the next person, and he recovered himself, but the rest of his words were spoken automatically.

What was Debra Dillon doing here? How had she managed to get herself employed at his store? And more important, why? She was a model, not a salesperson.

And why was his pulse fluttering, his heartbeat irregular?

She had come and gone in his life, and he hadn't thought of her in years. The last person he wanted working in the Fifth Avenue boutique was Debra Dillon.

After his speech, and the start of the cocktail party, he moved easily from one person to the next, smiling, shaking hands, saying a few words to each in turn.

He kept the smile on his face as he shook Debra's hand. "Miss Dillon, how nice to see you again," he said smoothly. She was standing with several others, and he carefully recalled their past meeting.

"You were modeling in San Francisco, I believe."

"Yes," she acknowledged, taking her cue from him. "Footwear. I worked for the Fishman Modeling Agency in L.A. and was sent to San Francisco for your new line of shoes."

As the others gradually drifted away, Tony and

Debra glanced at each other with a quick nod of recognition. "Debra, what are you doing here?"

"I needed a job, Mr. De Palma," she said softly, looking appealingly at him. "I'm still modeling, but it's not enough to . . . to keep me occupied. I've been through hell."

"We can't talk now." He arranged to meet her afterward.

Moving away, Tony went on greeting people, but his brain was actively working, trying to deal with Debra's unexpected appearance. He was careful not to look at her when she could observe him; still, his eyes followed her around the room for the next half-hour.

Even in that attractive crowd, Debra Dillon stood out. She was tall, with a model's proud, graceful way of carrying herself. The uniform only emphasized her broad shoulders, full bosom, narrow waist, and curving hips. He had been startled by the way the blue suit brought out the color of her eyes to a special vividness.

Tony felt distinctly uneasy. If she needed money, he would give it to her. If it was a job she wanted, he would get her one—somewhere else.

An hour later, he had his driver stop at the corner of Fifty-third and Fifth, where Debra was waiting for him.

Tony caught a glimpse of a long, beautiful leg as she slipped into the backseat beside him.

While the driver cruised, Debra described her engagement to Arnold Brody, and her shattered hopes when he committed suicide.

"I remember reading about it," Tony murmured, glancing at Debra with increased respect, laced with a touch of jealousy. Brody had been a multimillion-

aire, but Tony didn't doubt that Debra had capti-
vated him.

She was the most exquisite woman he had ever
known—a rare combination of innocence and dar-
ing. A child-woman. Irresistible.

Her story about Brody touched him. "I'm so sorry.
It was a bad break. If you're short of money, Debra . . ."

"No, please, Mr. De Palma. I don't want anything
except my job."

He was disarmed by her respectful way of ad-
dressing him, without presumption, without refer-
ring to their former intimacy. He felt suddenly
protective of her. "I don't understand why you want
to work as a saleswoman, when modeling pays so
much more."

"To take my mind off my troubles. Modeling is sort
of automatic. Stand here. Put your foot there. I do it
without really thinking. But when I'm talking to a cus-
tomer it's a one-on-one. So I forget about Arnold and
how happy I was going to be—"

She broke off, sobbing into her tissue.

Tony absolutely couldn't bear to see a woman cry.
Especially not this woman—this child, really—for
whom he felt a great deal of responsibility.

"It's all right, Debra, it's all right," he said soothingly, permitting himself to pat her shoulder.

By now his eyes had adjusted to the dark interior
of the car, and he could see her clearly. She was
wearing a black-and-white vertical-striped shift,
which all the same revealed her magnificent bosom
and the flare of her hips.

"You stay on the job as long as you need it,"
he said, before letting her out at the Barbizon Hotel.

He sat back in his seat, rationalizing his change of mind. She was going through a bad time, poor kid, and it would be unfair of him to ask her to quit her job just because he found her attractive.

She hadn't asked for anything. If she had wanted to, she could have put him in a very awkward position. Very awkward indeed.

He sighed and had his driver take him home.

If the girl became a problem, he could always get rid of her later.

Debra entered her room, triumphant. Her plan was going to work.

Tony had tried to conceal his interest but she had seen the sly glances he kept casting at her, the way his eyes had been riveted to her bosom.

In fact, with his wife in Boston, the situation couldn't have been more perfect. Debra had made it her business to find out that particular piece of information, by calling the De Palma housekeeper, pretending to be a theatrical agent.

Tony was more vulnerable than ever before. Older now, married to an independent career woman who didn't have Debra's beauty or youth.

Debra felt no qualms about her scheming, either. Not at this point. Tony had taken her highly prized virginity under somewhat dishonest circumstances. And she had been truly hooked on him. She was still.

Last time he had been able to finesse her out of what she wanted. This time she was going to get it.

18

Patrick, speaking to Bridget on the phone, learned that Lissa had had an accident. She had been running in the loft and tripped on a rug, knocking over a large vase. She fell on the broken glass.

Meredith had found her covered in blood. Fortunately, it wasn't as bad as it looked. At the hospital, the doctor cleaned her up, and discovered only some deep cuts on her legs that required a few stitches.

"Bridget, unplug the phone and bring it to Lissa's bed. I want to talk to her."

Patrick wiped the sweat off his forehead, suddenly furious with Meredith because she couldn't speak to him.

"Lissa, how are you feeling, sweetheart?"

"Okay, but it hurts, Daddy. My legs are all bandaged up."

He reassured her, terribly frustrated at being so far away, with no chance to get home before the opening in a couple of days. He had to be on call every minute.

When Bridget came back on the phone, Patrick told her Meredith was to bring Lissa to Boston for the opening. Then he hung up and went down to the bar for a stiff drink, aware of feeling slightly guilty.

Lissa's accident had reminded him that his family was his first responsibility.

* * *

"Ah, *cara*, I'm so glad to be here at last," Tony said, kissing Jennifer's cheeks and looking around the luxurious room at the Ritz-Carlton.

"I'm glad you could come," she said, kissing him back. "I rented a room rather than a suite," she added quickly. "A suite seemed so big, so extravagant, somehow."

"This will do nicely, *cara.*"

She busied herself helping him unpack, chattering about the problems the show was having, and asking about the opening of the men's department.

In truth, she found it confining to be in the room, and suggested an early dinner.

They were shown to a table near the window of the hotel's dining room. There, under subdued lighting from crystal chandeliers, and with unobtrusive piano music in the background, Jennifer was able to relax somewhat.

Their waiter was attentive, the French food very good, and the wine Tony chose excellent.

Normal living. Husband and wife, appropriately dressed, dining in their usual style.

Everything as usual. But not really. Although it was only two weeks since they had seen each other, Tony appeared to be a stranger. How could he have changed that much?

Had he changed at all, in fact? He smiled at her, listened to her attentively, spoke to her of the opening of the men's shop, which had gone very well.

Did she imagine that he was more reserved than usual?

Or was she merely comparing their polite conversation with the intimacy she had shared with Patrick?

Jennifer felt as if her spirit had split from her body and she was hovering invisibly, watching her corporeal self go through the motions of Mrs. Tony De Palma.

The spiritual Jennifer was aching and couldn't help thinking of another man's face, and voice, and words.

Several times during the meal Tony kissed her hand across the table, looking at her seductively. Said he had missed her terribly. Hadn't been sleeping properly.

"I've missed you too," she said, her face growing warm. Would she be struck dead for insincerity? Yes, she had missed Tony, in a way. But not as much as she missed Patrick.

She must stop it, she must. She was counting on Tony to help her put Patrick out of her mind and heart, as he had done once before in San Francisco.

It was different now, though. This time Patrick loved her back. Even though he had behaved correctly to her all this week, she could feel his caring, sense it, quietly there.

"*Cara*, you hardly eat a thing," Tony noted, watching her pick her way through a veal dish and a salad.

"I'm not very hungry," she apologized. "Too much to think about."

"I understand. But you must try, my sweet. Or you will fade away into nothing."

She noticed that he quietly checked out every attractive woman who passed their table—especially the ones very well endowed.

Patrick thinks I'm beautiful, why don't you? She immediately felt ashamed of her thoughts. She was inventing reasons to be annoyed at her husband.

Meredith had arrived this evening with Lissa. Jennifer had a moment of wondering if Patrick, spending time with his wife, was thinking of Jennifer as much as she was of him.

That was precisely what was wrong with divided love. It tended to spoil something that had, up until then, seemed perfectly adequate.

In bed that night, Jennifer willed herself not to compare Tony with Patrick. Yet, comparisons made themselves. The room dark, husband and wife under the covers most of the time. Always a certain propriety. Tony didn't let himself go horizontally any more than he did vertically.

Afterward she felt anxious rather than exhilarated.

Patrick had been so free, so open, so frankly sensual, so admiring of her, unable to stop looking at Her, kissing her, touching her. . . .

Tony lay on his back, his hands behind his head. "I need you, *cara.* I'll be so glad when you come home." He kissed her before rolling over and going to sleep.

Dear Tony. So agreeable and civilized. Jennifer told herself that they had a fine marriage. Tested and proven. Whereas she and Patrick might be a flash in the pan, a quick, intense passion that would soon burn out. Maybe, in fact, it was only the forbidden quality that lent their love such excitement. Any two people got used to one another in time. Even if she and Patrick could bear to destroy other lives in order to be together, they might wind up as complacent as the De Palmas were. Or, probably, the Lattimores.

She fell asleep fairly quickly but awakened in a panic from a dream about Patrick. They had been

walking arm in arm through the Public Garden,
stopping every few moments to look into each other's
eyes, to kiss. And they had been joking, laughing,
having a wonderful time.

Jennifer's heart pounded so noisily in her rib cage
she was sure Tony would hear it.

Her dream had reinforced a truth she was reluctant to face: she loved Patrick. Wholly. Uniquely. As
she always had. They had been meant for each
other. Only now it was too late.

Helen, Helen! opened to lukewarm reviews—and
in the opinion of the producers and most of the
others, lukewarm was better than they deserved.
They knew how bad Gayle's performance was compared with Meredith's.

The critics praised the libretto for telling a story
for a change. They had grown tired of a series of musically staged moments. Generally they agreed that
there were some lovely songs, excellent lighting, sets,
costumes, and choreography. They were mixed in
their assessment of the actors, but when it came to
the star role, all agreed: Gayle was unbelievable as
Helen. One critic doubted that Paris would have kidnapped her in the first place. A second felt the Tro-
jans would gladly have sent her home. And a third
wrote scathingly of "the face that launched a thousand yawns."

Sharon cut the show's run from three weeks to two
because they simply weren't selling enough tickets.

Meredith, locked into her silence, had never felt so
awful in her life. It was her fault.

When she had watched the opening she had been
appalled at the way Gayle was butchering the songs.

Her understudy was only an ingenue, pure and simple.

Patrick, sitting next to Meredith, had his head in his hands during much of the performance. Maybe he was hoping that when she saw how lousy Gayle was she would rally, and her voice would miraculously return. Like in an old Hollywood film. Suddenly she would jump up, in full costume, and rush to the stage to deliver the songs as they ought to be sung.

Fat chance. That could be her up there, bombing out.

And later, after she saw the roasting the critics had given Gayle, she mentally substituted her own name for her understudy's.

Why had she lost her voice? Was it only straining at that high note? Or was it, as the doctor had obliquely hinted, some psychosomatic nonsense, her head and her throat ganging up on her?

Well, maybe there had been a good reason. What if she had been in Boston rehearsing when Lissa had fallen on that vase? Her daughter might have bled to death. Bridget was fine, as good as money could buy, but she wasn't Lissa's mother.

Still, the situation was intolerable. Meredith hated the way everyone mouthed words at her very loudly, as if she had lost her hearing as well as her voice.

Meredith O'Neill, musical-comedy star, reduced to the pathetic status of a deaf mute. It was humiliating.

Oh, God, how she wanted to sing Helen. All her life she had been waiting for a chance like this. How could she not take it? And yet, if she did . . .

The secret truth eating away at her was that her

voice had returned more than a week before. But she was holding back because she didn't trust it any longer. She was absolutely terrified that it would conk out again right in the middle of a performance.

19

The week that Tony spent alone in New York, after Boston, crept by slowly, and he was vaguely dissatisfied. His usual procedure was to go home after work, eat the dinner his housekeeper had prepared, and then retreat to his den and work some more. Afterward he might watch television until he could fall asleep.

He rarely phoned Jennifer. When he did, either she wasn't yet at her hotel, or if she was, he felt she listened with only half her attention.

Damn that show that was taking his wife from him. His mistake. He had been the one to urge her to do this collaboration, thinking she might conceive a child if her mind was on other things. But now he hardly saw her, so she was even less likely to get pregnant.

That Thursday Tony left his office feeling downcast. He could have arranged to meet someone for dinner, but most of his business acquaintances were out of town. September was turning out to be almost as hot as August, and his European contacts, who hated the heat, were postponing their trips.

As Tony rounded the corner of Fifth Avenue and Fifty-sixth Street, he ran into Debra Dillon.

"Oh, hello, Mr. De Palma," she said, smiling at him. The smile warmed him.

"How are you, Debra?"

"Much better, thanks to you. I'm so grateful to have my job. I really enjoy it, and it takes my mind off my loss."

As she spoke, her full red lips trembled, and she turned her head away.

Tony was suddenly moved. The poor child, she really was in a bad way. "Have a drink with me," he suggested.

"Well, all right."

They had martinis at the King Cole Bar in the St. Regis Hotel, a place he never went and was unlikely to be recognized.

He couldn't take his eyes off Debra's dress, the same color blue as her eyes. And the silk-jersey material clung revealingly to her bosom.

As she continued to address him as Mr. De Palma, he said, "In private you can call me Tony." A moment later he felt his face growing warm. He had spoken as if they were going to be alone in the future.

"Are you still living at the Barbizon Hotel?" he asked, to change the subject.

She nodded. "I don't know where to look for something affordable."

Tony found himself promising to help her find an apartment. "In fact, why don't you come up to my place right now and I'll make a couple of phone calls."

He ushered her past the doorman and concierge boldly. After all, she was only another model invited to his home, as others had been previously. Of course, this time his wife wasn't there. Well, he hardly cared for the opinion of the building personnel, whom he always tipped generously.

He left Debra in the living room with a martini

while he went to his den to phone his real-estate contacts.

When he returned to tell her he had set up an appointment for her to look at apartments, she thanked him profusely, but he was hardly listening. He sat down across from her, noticing that her clinging dress was hiked up slightly to reveal her exquisite legs enticingly crossed.

He tried to turn his attention back to what she was saying as she talked animatedly about furnishing a new apartment, but he was distracted because as she leaned forward, the jersey of her dress pulled tightly across her breasts.

She was one gorgeous woman, and he wanted her.

At that moment she rose and said she had to use the bathroom.

He watched her walk out of the room, swiveling her hips in a way she surely hadn't learned at modeling school.

Tony was in a state of desperate arousal. He realized that he had been even more lonely than he had thought. Lonely, and horny.

When Debra returned, Tony invited her to have dinner with him.

"Thanks, but . . . but I couldn't. You're married, and . . . and . . ." She reached into her purse for a tissue. "I was only going to marry Arnold because I couldn't have you," she burst out, sobbing. "He was good to me, but . . . but you were my first love, Tony. And I've never gotten over you. I don't think I ever will."

Tony jumped up and moved to her side, gathering her into his arms. The moment he touched her his arousal reached a new peak, but she resisted, saying she couldn't, it would be the same as last time, she wouldn't be able to stand it.

"No, no, it will be different, *amore*, I promise you. That apartment, I'll pay for it, it will be ours, ours alone . . . ."

Although she demurred, he kept talking softly into her ear while he fondled her magnificent breasts. "I want you, *Dio mio*, I want you more than I've ever wanted any woman in my life."

"I . . . I can't," she murmured, trying to back away. "I've got to go . . ."

He couldn't let her go. There was something about this woman that aroused deep primitive urges in him as nobody else had ever done. He would say anything, do anything, to have her right now.

"You must stay, *amore*," he whispered, pushing her against the wall and kissing her passionately.

She began to sob anew, and in a frenzy he kissed her and coaxed her until he had maneuvered her into his bedroom.

He was much too aroused to bother with romantic lighting or taped music. Removing her underclothes, he kissed her all over and then took her, groaning with ecstasy.

Shortly afterward he took her again, like a man possessed, sinking his teeth into her flesh, losing himself in her, his face muffled in her gorgeous breasts.

A while later, while she dozed, he lay beside her smoking a cigarette. Now that his brain was working again, he felt torn between a vow he had made some years ago and Debra's irresistible charms.

He puffed thoughtfully. His vow hadn't gotten him what he wanted anyway. What the hell. It was time to add a little variety to his life.

* * *

That Saturday morning Meredith stood in front of the mirror of their hotel room applying makeup. She could see Patrick fidgeting in his chair, turning the pages of the newspaper.

He seemed so restless.

Sunday was the last Boston performance, and the company would be leaving for New York Monday morning.

Meredith looked at herself with dismay. Each morning she had awakened fairly cheerful, sure that today was the day she would tell Patrick she was well again and ready to work.

But then her courage would fail her, and she would be certain that when she tried to speak, no sound would be forthcoming.

Suddenly she couldn't face watching the matinee.

"Going to Filene's," she wrote on her pad.

Patrick nodded, looking at her with compassion.

She left the hotel, feeling cowardly and hating herself.

Patrick remained, reading the paper, until Milo phoned, wanting to move a number.

"What, again? We've moved it twice already. . . . Okay, okay, I'll tell Jennifer."

About to phone her, he decided to knock at her door on the way out.

Jennifer, wearing her bathrobe, looked very sleepy. "Sorry. I'm not quite awake yet. What's the problem?"

"Achilles' song," Patrick replied glumly. "It's not going over. Milo wants it moved. One more time."

"Oh, no," she said wearily, letting Patrick into her room. "We've tried that number everywhere. I think the problem is Achilles. He's putting his foot in his mouth, heel and all."

Patrick began to laugh, and she laughed with him, their eyes suddenly locking.

Quickly Jennifer turned her back. As she moved past Patrick to get her papers, her robe lightly brushed the back of his hand.

She leaned on her dresser. "Where does Milo want it now?"

Hearing no answer, she turned, then gasped. Patrick had come up behind her unexpectedly.

He grabbed her and pressed her to him, kissing her ravenously.

She felt her bones dissolving, her flesh liquefying. Helpless to resist, she shut her eyes and wound her arms around his neck.

"I love you, I love you, Jennifer. I can't bear not being with you."

"I love you, too, Patrick."

What good was the promise they had made to each other? Words were meaningless when pitted against such deep feelings as they had for each other.

In moments they were undressed and rocking on her bed, so intensely fired that they couldn't wait. They devoured each other as if it were a matter of life and death, two people desperately in love, aching to be together.

She climaxed twice before him, stifling her moans against his shoulder, and then a third time with him.

Breathless, they lay entwined, their bodies covered with a thin film of perspiration.

"God, I needed that," Patrick murmured, kissing her damp forehead. "I love you so much."

"And I love you. At least as much."

"I'm glad. I've been trying like hell not to feel jealous of Tony."

"Well, there's no need. I'm not the same with him."

Patrick shut his eyes for a moment and said gently, "Thank you for that. I have no right to it, but it helps, a little."

She couldn't resist asking, "And Meredith?"

"I'm not the same with her, either."

When the phone rang, they looked at each other with dismay.

Jennifer rolled over on her stomach to answer it. "Yes, Milo. Yes, Patrick told me on his way out," she said smoothly. "I've been thinking about where to put it," she continued, moving her hand over the mouthpiece when Patrick hooted.

As she offered Milo a couple of suggestions for the placement of Achilles' song, she felt Patrick's hands and lips on the backs of her legs, thighs, and then her buttocks.

Hanging up, she squirmed and moaned under his embraces. "Love has made a liar out of me."

"It's made a sex maniac out of me," he said huskily, gathering her into his arms.

This time they went more slowly, savoring one another rather than satisfying a ravenous hunger.

While they showered, they agreed to play hooky for a couple of hours, convincing themselves that nobody would miss them.

It was a lovely day, much cooler than it had been during the past hectic week. Arm in arm they walked up the quaint narrow streets of Beacon Hill. Sidewalks paved with brick. Gaslight lamps. Wonderful landmark brownstones. Edwin Booth had lived here. Louisa May Alcott had lived there.

Jennifer admired a four-storied red brick with

black shutters and window boxes colorful with pansies and marigolds. "That's the one I'd choose."

"Me too. And someday they'd put up a plaque saying that Lattimore and Ryland slept there, among other things."

She smiled and kissed his cheek, wishing it were possible for them to walk into the front door and shut it behind them.

Patrick looked at his watch. "It's feeding time at the hotel."

Both of them shook their heads and drawled, "Noooo."

"We can always say we were working on our duet," Jennifer rationalized.

Holding hands, they ran gaily down the hill like a couple of kids.

Refusing to settle for any place less than ideal, they walked on until they found it: a charming outdoor café with fresh flowers on the tables. Sitting across from one another, their sunglasses resting on top of their heads, they munched on quiche and salad and sipped wine spritzers. As they ate they studied every nuance of each other's expression, storing the memory as a camel stores water for the journey across the desert.

When the curtain came up at the theater for the matinee performance, Lattimore and Ryland were in their usual places at the back of the orchestra.

On Monday when Jennifer let herself into the apartment at the Trump Tower, it felt so huge, so empty. But it wasn't only Melissa she was thinking of now. It was Patrick. She was wishing that "home" was his absurdly tiny studio on Houston Street.

She had lived a lifetime in the past month, and she

had a sudden fear that she wouldn't be able to go back to her role as Tony's wife.

What if the show closed after opening night? What would she do then? Could she stand collaborating with Patrick? And yet, to end such a wonderful working relationship would be a double loss to both of them.

Tony phoned the apartment, and his calm, welcoming voice allayed the worst of her fears. He would be tied up all day but wanted to have dinner out. He hoped she didn't mind that there would be another couple, a buyer and his wife.

That evening Jennifer realized how she could get through the next period of time: by seeing to it that she wasn't alone with Tony more than was necessary, so that their lack of true intimacy wouldn't contrast so painfully with what she had with Patrick.

Making love with her husband that night was difficult, however.

Tony never questioned the extent of her enjoyment. If he asked her anything at all, it was if she was pleased. Certainly his lovemaking was pleasing, and before she had known what it was like to feel such uninhibited passion, she hadn't realized quite what she was missing. But now . . .

"I'm glad you're home, *cara*," Tony said, caressing Jennifer's cheek. "I do so want us to have a child."

Jennifer's stomach fluttered fearfully.

For the first time she didn't want that to happen. It seemed wrong to have a child with one man when she was passionately in love with another.

* * *

Although dozens of women had auditioned for
Helen, nobody had been found by the first day of re-
rehearsals.

Was it masochism, Meredith wondered, that
drove her to be there? She didn't know. She simply
couldn't stay away.

Her presence did nothing to ease the tension. Milo
was at his absolute worst, rushing around, shouting
that everything that could be wrong with the production was wrong. Ten times he talked of walking
out. Let someone else put his name on this shambles
of a show.

In the next minute he would think of a way to
make it better. Maybe.

But the moment Gayle opened her mouth to sing,
Milo began to shout at her so viciously that she fled,
crying.

"You see how it is?" Milo shouted at Meredith. "I
can't take it anymore. I don't know what the hell
you're doing here except making everyone crazy. So
just go, will you?"

"Wait a minute," Raf said, coming forward.

"And you, shut your face," Milo screamed at him.
"Carla Andrews is free, ready to audition. Sharon's
with her right now. She's our only hope. You'll either
sing with her, Raf, or you can get the hell out too."

20

Tony got into his limousine and had the driver take him to the East Thirties, where he had set Debra up in an apartment. He had left his office early so that he could see his mistress before returning home for dinner.

His anticipation was mixed with uneasiness. He hadn't really dreamed, when he gave himself Debra as a special treat, that she would become a daily habit.

She had enchanted him when she was seventeen; at twenty-two her ripe body obsessed him.

All his life Tony had felt at the mercy of women. Starting with his mother and grandmother, who had doted on him and ruled over him long after his older brothers were at school and away from their influence.

In his youth Tony had gone from affair to affair, pleased that women of all types and ages adored him. And yet, he saw his promiscuity as a weakness. In those early days he had found it impossible to turn down a sexual episode unless the woman was actually repulsive.

Marriage, he had thought, would change him. And he had chosen Jennifer carefully. A modest woman, intelligent and companionable. When Jennifer had become pregnant so quickly, he had been pleased. And for several months he had been scrupulously faithful to her.

It was necessary for him to travel, of course, and she was reluctant to go with him during the later stages of her pregnancy. He understood entirely. However, wherever he went, women put themselves in his way. Mostly models, the kind he could easily resist. More like boys than women, not his type.

Then, during a trip to Paris, his sales manager's widowed sister, a handsome, buxom woman, flirted shamelessly with him. Later that night, she knocked on the door of his room, and he was unable to ask her to leave.

After Melissa was born, Jennifer begged off traveling with Tony because it was so difficult with an infant. It was during those trips that he had the occasional liaison, short, sweet, discreet. Those little treats left him happy and allowed him to give even more to his wife.

When two years passed without another pregnancy, Tony's affairs increased in frequency. Not producing more children made him feel anxious and somehow not as manly as his brothers, all of whom had several offspring.

In addition, as his fame grew he found himself besieged by women—buyers, sales personnel, secretaries, the wives of business associates, designers. But at one point, when he realized that he could have just about anyone he wanted, the novelty wore off and his affairs came to a halt. He had been an exemplary husband—until Debra Dillon arrived in San Francisco to model shoes in his shop.

He sighed as his car pulled up at her apartment house.

From the day his daughter died, he had kept his

vow to himself and had not touched any woman other than his wife. But now Debra had come back into his life, and she was getting to him.

Debra opened the door, wearing a black silk jumpsuit open to the navel. No bra. She was smiling and holding out a drink to him.

Before he had drunk half of it he was fondling her. For the next two hours he thought of nothing but Debra's body, and reacted with the fierce passion he had not experienced since he was twenty.

Meredith awoke, prepared to jump out of bed and go to rehearsal, when she remembered that not only was she no longer in the cast, she was actually persona non grata. And today Carla Andrews was going to audition for her role.

Meredith lay in bed alone—Patrick was already up—feeling disconnected, in limbo.

She could hear voices coming from the kitchen area.

Fighting off her depression, she dragged herself up, put on a negligee, and went to the kitchen.

Patrick was sitting at the counter while Lissa poured dry cereal for them. He was making a game of it.

They didn't see Meredith immediately, and she had a moment of jealousy, looking at father and daughter. Lissa had a special relationship with her father. Looked more like him all the time, too. Somehow mother and daughter, although they got along well enough, didn't have as much fun together. Maybe because Meredith worried too much. And she sensed a kind of rivalry between herself and her daughter. It was silly, of course, but it was there all the same.

The two looked up and saw her. Meredith kissed them good morning and sat down at the counter with them. She had no appetite, and only drank coffee.

"Bridget will be late this morning," Lissa informed her mother, "so Daddy's taking me to school on his way to the theater."

Meredith had a sinking feeling in her stomach. What was she going to do all day?

Patrick leaned over Lissa to kiss Meredith's cheek, looking at her with sympathy. She forced herself to brighten up, to smile when she saw the expression in his eyes. Dammit, she wasn't quite dead yet, even if she wasn't singing in that goddamn show.

"I'll go shopping," she wrote on her pad. "Lissa needs some things for fall."

After Patrick and Lissa left, Meredith felt as if someone had turned her upside down and shaken everything out of her, leaving just a shell.

When she finally dressed and got to the shops, her mood improved. Next to show business, shopping had always been her passion.

The one good thing depression did for her was take away her interest in food. She had lost eight pounds and come down a complete size, to her satisfaction. And when the salesgirl at Bendel's recognized her from *Me, Tarzan*, it made Meredith's whole morning. Flashing a note with the word "laryngitis" on it, she bought several new outfits, lapping up the compliments paid her like a starving cat swimming in a dish of cream.

In the children's department she picked up some adorable things for her daughter. Although Meredith felt a little guilty at spending so much money, she refused to worry about it. In fact, she became defiant. If the show bombed, she would have plenty of time to do without.

She economized by taking the bus home, then regretted it because it crawled in the lunchtime traffic.

As she entered her building, she was thinking of her new purchases. Suddenly she felt a hard arm around her neck, a knife at her ribs, and a man's erection boring into her spine.

"You do what I say, lady, or I'm going to cut you bad," a voice hissed at her ear.

She wasn't aware of doing anything at all, but when he released her and lunged out the front door, she realized that the high, piercing shriek she heard was coming from her own throat.

She kept screaming, absolutely terrified at the thought of being not only robbed but also raped.

The next moments went by in a great deal of confusion. She ran out the door, still screaming, and pointing to her would-be assailant. Unnerved by the unexpected noise, he was trying to get past a group of tree-sized plants blocking the sidewalk.

Several husky men who worked in the area and had often ogled Meredith as she walked by, grabbed the fleeing man and wrestled him to the ground.

Bridget appeared out of nowhere and put her arms around Meredith, crooning, "There, there, Mrs. Lattimore, it's all right now. Thanks be to heaven you've found your voice again."

The police arrived, and Meredith, accompanied by Bridget, was taken to the local station to file a complaint. While Meredith was relating her experience to the sergeant on duty, Bridget gave everyone in the police station a brief biography of her em-

ployer, describing how her voice had miraculously
come back because of the fright.

A reporter from the New York *Post* was waiting
for Meredith when she emerged from the station.
Flushed from the attention, and still not over the
shock, she said a few words to him but had no answer to his question of whether she would now be
appearing in her husband's new show.

Bridget had had the presence of mine to phone
Patrick at the theater.

He took a taxi to the police station and ran up the
front steps. Pulling Meredith to him, he held her
against his rapidly beating heart. "Are you all right?
He didn't hurt you?"

"No," she said. "No. But I was so frightened. I
don't remember it very clearly."

"Don't think of it," he soothed. "Think only of the
good part. Your voice is back, and judging from
what Bridget said, you could be heard for a mile in
every direction. I'm so glad, baby. Oh, I'm so glad."
He hugged her tightly.

When he stood back and studied her, he saw that
she looked more bewildered than delighted. "Let's
get you to the doctor. No arguing. You've had a
shock, and I want you examined right away."

The doctor nodded as Patrick told him the story
Meredith was tired of telling. Then the doctor asked
her to scream for him, and she did, so convincingly
that he put his hands over his ears, laughing. "That
mugger will be lucky if he's not hearing-impaired, to
go with his other troubles."

"Is there any chance of my wife's being able to sing
within the next couple of weeks or so?" Patrick asked
the doctor tensely.

The doctor shrugged. "She sounds great to me, and I can't find anything wrong. But then, I never really could. It might have been a strain, with maybe some psychological overtones."

"I don't know what to do," Meredith admitted, looking from her husband to the doctor.

"Do what's comfortable, Mrs. Lattimore. Your vocal cords have had a rest. Any physical strain should be over. But the psychological factor . . . well, I'm not the one to deal with that."

When they left, Patrick, holding Meredith's arm, said, "I don't want you to feel pressured. Of course I'd like you to sing, but it's your decision. The contract with Carla is being drawn up tomorrow. She's not you, but she can manage. Maybe you should talk to a psychiatrist—"

"No. I don't need that," Meredith said firmly.

He sighed, "Okay. Just do what makes you happy, what you feel you can handle."

She looked at him. "You'll be so disappointed in me if I don't sing. You've been disappointed ever since it happened."

"No, I've been terribly concerned. And now, after today's shock . . . Maybe you need time to get over it. There'll be other shows. Your health and well-being come first, always."

With his arm around her, he kissed her cheek tenderly.

A stab of guilt went through her. Well, she couldn't decide this minute. And she had until tomorrow, when Carla would sign the contract.

On their way home they collected Lissa from school so that Bridget could stay at the loft and cook dinner.

"Hello, sweetie," Meredith said, smiling at her daughter.

Lissa looked questiongly at her mother.

"Mom's got her voice back. Isn't that wonderful?" Patrick asked, beaming.

"Oh, yes." Lissa kissed her.

It was a lovely, cool afternoon, and they decided to walk. Lissa, holding each parent by the hand, was looking from one to the other happily.

"Tell us about your day," Patrick requested.

"It was nice. I like my teacher much better than last year." She told them everything she had done, liking to be the focus of their attention.

As they were nearing home, Meredith cleared her throat.

The child looked up at her, frowning. "Mom, will your voice go away again? Remember, the last time it came back and then went away?"

Patrick shot Meredith a look of astonishment.

She looked uncomfortable.

"Don't you remember, Mom? When I fell and was all bloody and everything. You kept saying, 'Oh, God,' and you called the hospital and asked them to send an ambulance. But then you stopped talking again."

"I'll be all right now," Meredith assured her daughter.

Patrick waited until Lissa was asleep before confronting his wife. They were sitting in the living room having their coffee. "What was Lissa talking about?"

Meredith sighed. "When she hurt herself I suddenly seemed to talk. But I was so upset I wasn't thinking. I knew I had to call an ambulance. I didn't realize that Lissa had heard me."

She hesitated. "I thought I'd wait a little while to make sure my voice really was back for good . . ."

"Are you serious? You didn't say a word to me, didn't see the doctor, have been faking all this time . . ."

"I was meaning to tell you, but—"

"Goddammit, Meredith, you don't tell me anything! You keep it all locked away inside. Don't you think I have a right to know? I'm your husband, aside from being the composer for the show, a show I thought meant so much to both of us—"

"That's the trouble," she burst out. "It meant too much." Tears began to flow.

"But you were doing so well," he said, subdued by her outburst. "We all told you how well you were doing. Sure, there were problems. In any production there are bound to be clashes, you know that."

"Yes, but this was different. Everyone was so anxious to please Raf they'd do anything."

"No, not anything. I asked you at the time if you really wanted the duet taken down a tone. I would have insisted, fought Raf and Gary and Milo and Sharon and anyone else. If you had admitted that it really was a strain."

"I didn't realize it was that bad until it was too late."

"Meredith, if only you'd told me about your fears. Letting us agonize all this time, performance after lousy performance—"

"I know. I'm sorry. I was only waiting a little longer to see if my voice lasted. Because . . . because what if I had said, 'Hey, I'm fine, no problem.' And then I'm back in the show, right? I'm on the stage, and I open my mouth and nothing comes out. I saw that happening in my dreams almost every night.

The silence. Then a few giggles, people nervous, wondering if it's part of the show or what. Then the pity. Poor thing. Some star she is. A bust, a total bust. That's why I quit. I just couldn't stand it anymore." Meredith lowered her head and cried.

"Baby, baby, come here." Patrick put his arms around her, soothing her the way he soothed his daughter when she fell and hurt herself.

"I've been too afraid to tell you or anyone," Meredith sobbed into his shoulder. "I wanted the show to succeed so much. But I was afraid of that, too. Afraid that if it did, you wouldn't want me anymore."

She spilled out all her fears about younger women going after him, as they undoubtedly would, because of his fame, his money. "Alan Jay Lerner's been married, what, seven times," she sniffled.

Patrick, one hand on her back, pushed his other hand through his hair, his face stony.

Her confession shook him. Especially the part about her fear of losing him. She sensed his conflicts, even if she had the reason wrong.

She finally lifted her face and looked mournfully at him. "I want to sing Helen, Patrick, I really do. Only I'm so afraid."

"I'll help you, baby. I promise. I'll do everything I possibly can—"

"I need you, Patrick," she cried, flinging herself into his arms. "I need you with me at the theater, every minute. Otherwise I'll never make it. I'm so afraid you're going to leave me. Tell me," she begged, her eyes fearful, "tell me you'll never leave me."

White-faced, he held her close and promised he would stay with her always.

21

Debra turned off her alarm, hating the moment she would have to leave her warm, comfortable bed and get up to go to work.

Much as she hated selling, however, she had to pretend to Tony that it was wonderful. Too many previous plans had gone awry. This one must succeed.

Tony might not be as rich as Arnold, but he was infinitely more appealing. So attractive, such a passionate lover. How she enjoyed teasing him, working up little scenarios designed to drive him out of his mind with desire for her.

Tony continued to be very generous with money, and she used much of it to buy exotic, sexy, but tasteful clothes.

She was providing Tony with everything she sensed his wife did not: undivided attention, appreciation, youth, and novelty. How fortunate that Mrs. De Palma should be spending so much time at the theater. Tony had gone from just drinks with Debra to dinner. But he hadn't spent the whole night—yet.

She was trying to work quickly. Once the wife's show opened, she might have more time to spend with her husband. Debra wanted to be sure that Tony was good and hooked by then.

At work she put on the De Palma uniform and took up her duties in the men's department. Mostly she waited on lone male shoppers, the type who needed a beautiful woman to help them in their purchases. Men shopping with their wives were usually taken care of by salesmen, who addressed themselves to the women.

Debra came home tired but alert. She had a complete Italian dinner sent up from an excellent caterer.

Her table was set with good china, silver, and candles waiting to be lit.

After showering, she put on lacy white panties and a camisole, then a white cotton dress with puffed sleeves, tightly fitted on top, belted at the waist, and flaring to a full, very short skirt that revealed a wide expanse of thigh. On her feet she wore flat white sandals.

She applied very little makeup, and gathered her blond hair into a demure braid down her back.

Regarding herself critically in the full-length bedroom mirror, she was satisfied with her nymphet appearance.

When she greeted Tony at the door, the look of surprise and pleasure he gave her was gratifying.

She was careful to sit on a straight-backed chair in the living room across from him, to cross and recross her perfect legs, to smile archly at him.

She watched him sipping his Campari and soda, his dark eyes velvety with desire.

When she refilled his drink, she leaned over him so he could sniff the fresh light perfume she wore, as a young girl would.

He put his hand on her calf and moved it up slowly

until it reached her thigh, then the edges of her lacy panties.

She acted coy, then gasped as his fingers insinuated themselves into intimate places.

"Amore, amore," he moaned. Sliding to the floor, he buried his face between her thighs.

Debra rejoiced at her power to make him lose all reason, so intent on possessing her that he did, then and there, on the living-room rug, with both of them half-dressed.

Afterward, during dinner, she wore a white silk lounging robe, open enough for her breasts to be partly revealed, her hair now hanging loose. By candlelight she looked at him with knowing eyes. The child-woman devirginized.

After dessert he pulled her into the bedroom and made love to her once more before he had to leave.

Debra had a long, hot bubble bath, a brandy at her side, a smug smile on her face.

She dialed her sister in West Palm Beach, and for the first time told Charlene about Tony De Palma, swearing her to secrecy.

The company press agent did a terrific job for *Helen, Helen!* planting stories in the media to take advantage of the fairy-tale situation: star loses voice, understudy takes over and can't carry the show, which does poorly out of town. Star recovers and is ready to resume her role. It was the sort of thing the public loved.

Meredith appeared on the Merv Griffin show and *Live at Five*. With Patrick's encouragement, her confidence was being bolstered. Everyone was in her corner, and she was coming out fighting.

Newspaper stories were written about Lattimore

and Ryland and their history, and the result of all the ballyhoo was the soaring of ticket sales. All fifteen hundred seats were sold for opening night, and advance sales were good enough to ensure that the show would run for two months even if the reviews turned out to be less than enthusiastic.

Opening night was a glittering affair, with all the media coverage anyone could wish.

The De Palmas were photographed entering the theater. Jennifer wore a sleeveless Valentino gold lamé dress, with a cowl neck and intricate gathers in the front, topped with a fox jacket, both a present from Tony for the occasion.

The atmosphere in the theater was one of heightened excitement. But all the buzzing stopped at the first notes of the overture.

And the moment Meredith appeared on the stage, she received a two-minute ovation. Nobody would have guessed that she had been sick to her stomach an hour earlier.

She gave the performance of her life, carrying the rest of the cast with her. Raf was at his absolute best, and Gayle's Cassandra number was superb and greeted with applause.

To avoid being recognized, Lattimore and Ryland watched the show from the wings. They had the exquisite pleasure of seeing the work they had agonized over playing the way it should. Not that they didn't find things wrong; but the audience didn't seem to notice.

Meredith and Raf had to do an encore of "Do I Love Him?/ Do I Love Her!" That song, at least, was going to be a hit.

After the intermission, Tony came backstage with

two of the backers in from Paris. "It is brilliant, *cara*," he said, beaming proudly at Jennifer.

Sharon was at his heels with her co-producers, simply ecstatic, everyone kissing and hugging. "The critics love it," she declared. "I can tell by their faces. They just love it. And I love all of you."

The minute the final curtain went down, the audience jumped up, yelling bravos, cheering, whistling.

The cast got curtain call after curtain call, especially Meredith, whose appearance was greeted by a roar of approval. Bouquets of flowers covered the stage. Then a shout went up for "Author," and Lattimore and Ryland took a bow.

It was a dream come true, for everyone.

The cast party, held at Sardi's, was a gala affair. Champagne corks were popping all over the place, as everyone forgot the weeks of bickering because it had been worth every bitter moment to have a triumph like this.

Jennifer drank a lot of champagne, feeling wonderful about the show. However, every time she caught a glimpse of Patrick, who never left Meredith's side she had a pang of sadness.

Had she believed that she would be able to admire him from afar? False. The alcohol pushed aside the veil she had been keeping over her emotions, revealing what she really felt. She loved Patrick here and now, and wanted to be with him tonight. Oh, how she wanted that!

She forced herself to mingle with the crowd, talk, smile, praise, and acknowledge the praise heaped on her. Several of the backers wanted to know if she and Patrick were hatching another idea. She said no at the same time that he said they would see. They quickly looked at each other, and just as quickly looked away.

He apparently was intending to go on with the collaboration. She didn't know how she could.

They all sat down to supper, and there was no flagging of the euphoric mood of the celebration. Especially when they learned that the reviews in the *Times* and the *News* were terrific.

Finally, as guests began to trickle out, Meredith was surrounded by people, the heroine not only of the show but also of the evening. But Patrick wasn't with her.

He was standing next to Jennifer. "We did it, Ryland. We really did it."

"Yes, Lattimore, we did," she said tensely. Hardly trusting her voice, she was unable to look directly at him. Instead, she kept her gaze on Meredith. "This is her night, maybe even more than ours."

"True. And it thrills me to see it, after what we've been through. We almost didn't make it."

"I know. When I think it took a threat to her life before her voice came back . . ."

"Well, not exactly." Patrick hesitated, then quickly told Jennifer the story. "She was afraid if the show did well she'd lose me. No, she doesn't know about us, but I guess she senses a change."

Eyes down, Jennifer murmured, "It seems to me that you and she are close again. And that's as it should be."

"Jennifer, look at me."

She lifted her eyes to his, tremulously, knowing all her love was beaming out at him. And that he saw it. "It's all right, really," she babbled. "This is the way it has to be . . ."

"Yes, this is the way it has to be," he echoed huskily, "even though I love you as much as I did in Boston. I'll always love you. But I can never leave Meredith."

22

"Patrick, I can't stand to live in this loft for another day," Meredith said after their boiler broke down in January and they were without heat for four very cold days. "I want a real apartment, and we can afford to buy one now."

Patrick looked at her, somewhat dismayed. "Yes, I suppose so."

"You sound doubtful. For God's sake, Sharon told me only yesterday that the backers will soon be completely repaid. In record time, too."

Patrick knew all that. It was as hard to get a ticket to *Helen* as it had been to *Cats* the year it opened. In the three months since it had been running, several road companies had already been formed, the record album was doing fabulously, and the movie rights had been sold for a half-million dollars.

For Patrick it wasn't a matter of the money but a reluctance to make a change. As if he had a long-term investment in the marriage. He sighed. Of course that was exactly what he did have.

Anyway, since Meredith's incident with the mugger he had been worried about his wife and child in that neighborhood.

As it turned out, Ed Zinn, one of the co-producers, was moving to California and wanted to sell his three-bedroom co-op on East Seventy-second Street.

He offered it to the Lattimores for a reasonable price.

"Why are we moving, Daddy?" Lissa asked one Saturday as they were having lunch at home.

"Because your mother wants an apartment with walls and doors for all the rooms."

"Well, I don't," she pouted.

"No, sweets? Why not?" He refilled her glass with apple juice.

"I don't like walls. I like to hear what's going on."

Patrick laughed. "You do, do you, little nosy bird."

She made a face at him, and he made one back at her.

Patrick, feeling a little selfish, was very much enjoying his time alone with his daughter. They had breakfast and lunch together on weekends, and breakfast on weekdays, when she ate lunch at school. Most nights they met Meredith at a restaurant near the theater. While father and daughter ate dinner, Meredith nibbled cottage cheese and drank orange juice. Except for Mondays, it was virtually the only chance she got to see Lissa, because the child was asleep by the time she came home at night, and had gone to school before she awoke.

"I don't want to go to another school," Lissa said. "I like my school and my friends."

"You won't have to change schools. It will just take a little longer to get there."

"Will Bridget still take me?"

"Yup. In fact, there's more room in the new apartment and we're thinking of asking Bridget to live in. Would you like that?"

"I guess so." Lissa furrowed her brow. "If she lived with us, you'd pay her more, wouldn't you? That would be good, because she sends money home to Ireland."

Patrick leaned over and kissed his daughter's cheek. "That's a lovely thought, sweetie. You have a kind heart."

Lissa smiled, and then asked if she could give a party in their new apartment. "My friends would like to meet Mom. She's a celebrity," Lissa said proudly.

"Okay. We'll see what we can do. We may not be settled for a while, though."

"That doesn't matter. If we're a little messy, you won't care if my friends aren't so neat or anything."

While Lissa cleared the counter, Patrick got a call from Sharon, who was after Lattimore and Ryland to get cracking on another idea. "Now is the time to get backing for another property—when you're hot."

"I see your point, Sharon. But Jennifer's been out of town. Palm Beach, I believe, for a month."

With her husband, of course. A cold shiver hit Patrick.

"Well, phone her. Get her up here, or you go down there. Listen, at this point you two could write a shopping list to music and the angels would lap it up."

Sharon wouldn't let him go until he had promised to think really hard of another idea, and to get Jennifer thinking too.

Before Jennifer had left New York she had been lukewarm about collaborating on something new quite so soon. And Patrick had shared her reluctance, in a way.

It was very difficult for him to see her, now that the wonder of their lovemaking was becoming only a memory. Although they spoke on the phone, she avoided meeting him.

He had begun to miss working, though. He was writing two TV scores, but it wasn't the same. Musical comedy was what he liked best. And he couldn't imagine doing another show without Jennifer.

Jennifer finished a round of golf, not disturbed that she was way over par. She played mostly to please Tony and to be sociable, the same way she played bridge. She had always found it difficult to take games very seriously, whereas Tony played to win, using all his powers of concentration.

Although they had first taken a suite at the Breakers, they soon moved to a private mansion complete with servants.

Jennifer had a welcome rest. She swam, walked on the beach, dined out or at home, read, and relaxed.

Tony went to work, as usual, overseeing his boutique in town.

The De Palmas gave several dinner parties and were invited to others. They socialized with people named Pillsbury, Mellon, Firestone, Vanderbilt, and Singer.

Tony seemed tense, thinner, and he was secretly smoking. She could smell the tobacco on his breath. She wished he wouldn't hide his habit from her. She told him that if he had to smoke he should do so openly. He denied it utterly, however, claiming she was imagining it.

Although she kept trying to get closer to him, she wasn't succeeding. The smoking discussion was one example of his inability to talk openly with her.

And in spite of her resolve, she thought of Patrick often, and dreamed of him. She missed collaborating

with him, and toward the end of their stay in Palm
Beach, was chafing to get to work on another musical. Even if it meant dealing with her emotional turmoil.

"I hope you know what you're doin' with that guy,
Debbie," Charlene told her sister one evening while
they were having dinner at La Crêpe de Paimpol in
Palm Beach. Charlene greedily tucked into her dessert, crêpes Suzette, which she had heard of but
never tried. "Married men are tricky. Look, we're
way over here in his neck of the woods. What if he
walked in with his missus—"

"He won't." Debra had chosen the place carefully.
Tony didn't eat crêpes for dinner, and certainly not
at six. If the De Palmas went out to a restaurant,
they would probably dine three hours from now at
the Café L'Europe, all French and snooty, and
packed with the high and the mighty.

Eating her ice-cream crêpe, Debra glanced at her
sister with affection mingled with slight embarrassment. Although she loved Charlene dearly, her sister
was all wrong in her look, tastes, and manners. And
Debra's infrequent attempts to soften Charlene's
rough edges were greeted without enthusiasm. "You
tryin' to make me over or somethin'? Listen, I'm too
old to learn new tricks. Eatin' with fancy people,
havin' to hold my pinky in the air, just ain't my idea
of fun."

The one new thing Charlene had learned was how
to cut and style hair. Debra thought her sister did her
hair as well as anyone in New York. Anyway, Debra
resigned herself to keeping her in a separate com-
partment of her life. She would buy her a good house
in West Palm Beach and send the boys to college.

As far as Tony knew, Debra was an orphan. She would keep it that way.

Although she resented being tucked away in a motel, Tony at least gave her plenty of money for shopping. Now she could afford to buy from the sorts of places she had once admired: Jourdan, Ralph Lauren, Ungaro, Yves St. Laurent.

Charlene refused most gifts but liked to accompany her, and seemed not to care—if she even realized—that shop assistants took her to be Debra's maid.

"See, Debbie," Charlene would say as they left a store laden with purchases, "I knew someday you'd wind up wearing the best. But it's not enough. I want to see you settled with that guy, all legal and proper."

So did Debra. She didn't let on to her sister, but she hated being a back-street mistress. She wanted a room at the Breakers. Wanted to go everywhere with Tony De Palma.

With avid longing she read the Palm Beach *News*, scanning the names of the rich and famous. The De Palmas were reported dining on someone's luxurious yacht, or attending a match at the Palm Beach Polo and Country Club, or viewing a performance of a play at the Royal Poinciana Playhouse.

Yet, sooner or later Debra's phone would ring at the motel or at her sister's—she had told him it was the number of her hairdresser—and Tony would be breathless to see her. Whatever his wife had to give him, Debra had a lot more. More than even he knew, yet.

"Welcome home," Patrick told Jennifer on the phone. "How was Palm Beach?"

"Rich, relaxing, warm," she said, sounding nasal. "But I caught a bad cold the minute I got back."

Her heart was hammering away, although his tone was impersonally friendly. She thought he might be calling from home.

"How's the new apartment?" she asked.

"Rich, warm, not so relaxing. Quite a mess, in fact. We're still trying to get settled."

After several minutes of desultory conversation he said, "I've got a new idea. Restoration comedy. Sheridan's *The School for Scandal*. I've been playing around with a couple of numbers. Care to hear more?"

"I sure would."

"Are you housebound or can you come to the studio?"

"Not today. How about tomorrow?"

She went to bed feeling awful but she was much improved by morning, although she thought she still looked terrible. A red nose and swollen eyes to go with her lovely tan.

Patrick looked smashing, standing in the door at the top of the stairs, wearing battered brown corduroys, a black turtleneck, and a tan suede vest.

"Good to see you," he said, pecking her on the cheek.

"Careful, I'm lethal."

She didn't intend her words to have a double meaning but he took them that way, looking broodingly at her.

He had a little electric heater blowing gently, and she huddled near it, hoping she hadn't made a mistake going out in such cold weather.

After almost three months apart, they kept glancing at each other quickly and shyly.

Patrick played her a little of what he had done, and she loved it. She had reread Sheridan's play and come up with a few ideas of her own.

Without her noticing, the time sped. Then the ringing phone shattered her concentration.

"Yes. I'm on my way."

Patrick hung up, looking gloomy. "Meredith," he explained. "I've got to go. I'll keep working on the idea. Let's call each other when we have a little more to show. Sharon's antsy. Feels she can get backing for a new show as soon as she has a decent sample from us."

When they were in the street, he said, "Let me drop you home in a taxi."

"It's out of your way."

"A few blocks. No problem."

In fact, by the time a taxi stopped for them she was shivering with cold. She kept to her corner, trying not to breathe on him.

Patrick finally said, "For God's sake, stop worrying about a few germs. If you think a little thing like a cold could keep me from taking you in my arms this minute . . ." He halted and exhaled sharply. "Don't cringe. I'm not going to do it."

"I'm not cringing. Just shivering."

"Have something warming when you get home. I wish it could be me," he said, making a grim joke. "Have you missed me at all?" he suddenly asked.

"Yes, I have," she answered truthfully. "And I hate being noble, but I don't see any alternative to what we have now. You can't leave your wife and child, and I can't leave my husband. We can't hurt innocent people. If we did, we'd both feel so rotten I think it would sour our love."

He nodded and looked at her with luminous eyes.

"The love is there, anyway. Working together as well as we do is part of it. The part we can keep and cherish."

She couldn't argue with that.

When the taxi stopped in front of her building, Patrick gave her a quick hug. "Feel better."

She got out and waved at him, quickly turning as the taxi pulled away.

An elated Meredith took four curtain calls. To-night's audience had been superb. But then, most audiences were.

Everything she had ever wanted from Broadway had become hers. Fame and acclaim. There were newspaper interviews, television appearances. She loved the fact that crowds waited before and after the performance to catch a glimpse of her, and she didn't at all mind the requests for autographs.

At last she was somebody. Broadway was where she belonged, and acting was what she did best.

Her beautiful new apartment, with a view of the East River, was being redecorated to her specifications. When the renovation was complete, she would be proud of where she lived, for once.

What she did mind was not seeing more of Lissa. But she was pleased that her daughter had changed toward her. It wasn't only "Daddy" now, but also "Mom." Lissa was a big deal at school because of her mother's success.

And then there were Meredith's many admirers. They sent her flowers, phoned her, wrote her love letters, proposed to her. How wonderful to be so adored.

Patrick remained devoted to Meredith, and was at the theater every matinee and every evening just before the performance, to hold her hand and cheer her on. Usually he brought Lissa with him.

In fact, Meredith no longer required Patrick's presence at the theater. Hadn't for a couple of months, but she had no intention of letting him know. She didn't want her fame to overshadow his, and perhaps make him resentful.

Besides, if he was with her at dinnertime, and picked her up after the performance, he was less likely to fall prey to some scheming young thing who would consider it a great triumph to take him away from Meredith O'Neill.

23

Patrick phoned Jennifer on a Saturday morning at home. "How would you like to catch today's matinee of *Noises Off?* You know, the English farce. Everyone who's seen it says it's excruciatingly funny. Say yes, Jennifer."

"Uh, wait, let me think a minute," she replied, flustered. "What about Meredith?"

"She's working. Anyway she doesn't care for the theater unless she's the star. Say yes, Jennifer."

Patrick's voice sounded light, buoyant. She suddenly saw herself sitting next to him at the theater, laughing with him, sharing the enjoyment. Tony had already left for his boutique. There was no real reason not to go, was there?

"Don't you spend Saturdays with Lissa?"

"She's been invited to a birthday party today. I'm dropping her off first. Say yes, Jennifer."

"Okay, okay. Yes," she said happily.

They arranged to meet in front of the theater.

Patrick was there before her. As she stopped across the street, observing him in his soft belted coat and rakish broad-brimmed hat, she experienced a quiet moment of pure love.

He saw her, smiled, and tipped his hat, making her grin.

"I'm so glad you could make it," he said, kissing

...er cheek. "I've been wanting to see this play since it opened."

"Me too. I sure could use a laugh. January, I think, is crueler than April."

"Much. But the dreariness vanishes the moment I see you," he said softly, putting his arm around her shoulder and giving her a hug.

She hugged him back, feeling so happy to be with him.

Their seats were in the first row of the mezzanine.

"I hope you don't mind not being in the orchestra," Patrick said.

"Not at all. In fact, this is my favorite spot. I like having an overview of the stage."

"Close enough to see the actors, not so close as to destroy the illusion," he added.

"Exactly." They smiled at one another, and sighed simultaneously.

"Oh, Christ, this is stupid," he murmured. "We're so good together—"

She put her finger against his lips. "We agreed."

"You agreed. But there's no reason not to be affectionate, is there?" He stroked her hair for a moment and kissed her forehead.

No, there wasn't. She kissed him back, feelings of affection welling up in her. God, how she loved him!

The play was a spoof of a typical British sex comedy, in which the women wind up scantily clad and the men with their trousers around their ankles. The plot involved a troupe of third-rate actors going from town to town presenting a dreadful farce, while backstage their own lives were equally farcical. In the second act the playwright presented the stage from behind, showing the backstage turmoil that resulted in pratfalls onstage: props removed, spiteful actions by the players because of jealousies, causing endless accidents and desperate improvisation.

Both onstage and offstage problems had a special meaning for Jennifer and Patrick, and they laughed until they were breathless.

"Exit laughing," Patrick said as they left the theater. "That's the funniest thing I ever saw."

Jennifer had the hiccups.

"Stop a minute," Patrick advised. "Take a deep breath."

She tried but hiccuped in the middle.

Suddenly he grabbed her, kissed her, and swung her around right in the middle of Forty-seventh Street.

When he released her she was gasping for breath and her heart was pounding. "Patrick, for God's sake!"

He feigned innocence. "Just trying to help, ma'am. How are the hiccups?"

"Gone." Jennifer smiled sheepishly.

They went to the West Bank Café for a bite, and discussed how the play reminded them of all the things that had gone wrong with their own productions.

For instance, the day in Boston that the scenery had suddenly collapsed during Raf's romantic number.

"And remember, in *Make Love*, when Betsy was doing her big number and she danced right off the stage into the orchestra pit?" Patrick reminisced.

"Oh, God, yes. And she went right through the drum," Jennifer said, laughing. "Let's stop, please. I don't want more hiccups."

"I don't know why not, after I've developed the perfect cure."

Their merriment subsided, and they gave each other a long passionate look.

Suddenly "No One But You," the hit from *Helen*, began to play on the jukebox.

Patrick smiled sadly. "You see? Fate."

Flustered, Jennifer looked at her watch. "It's after five. I have to be getting home." She called for the check. "My treat. You got the tickets."

In front of the restaurant they faced each other.

"It was a wonderful afternoon, Patrick. Thanks."

"My pleasure." He put his hands on her shoulders. "I miss you so much."

"I know. I miss you too."

"Jennifer, can't we—?"

"No, Patrick, we really can't."

He nodded and hailed a taxi for her, watching until it pulled away.

On Valentine's Day the Lattimores gave a party at their new apartment.

Tony had surprised Jennifer with a stunning outfit: an evening sweater composed of petals of sequined silk in various shades of gray, over a tight-fitting long black satin skirt. He even chose her shoes, sequined satin pumps.

There were easily two hundred guests in the big Lattimore apartment—Broadway luminaries mixed with prominent socialites and people in all the arts. Such celebrities as Mary Tyler Moore, Mikhail Baryshnikov, Beverly Sills, Betty Comden, Adolph Green, Oscar De La Renta, and Angela Lansbury.

Meredith, resplendent in a form-fitting black sequined dress with the thinnest of rhinestone shoulder straps, greeted her guests warmly, looking proud

nd beautiful amid the heart-shaped red decorations
anging everywhere.

She was quite friendly to Jennifer, who responded
s best she could while suffering from stabs of disloy-
lty. In spite of her affection for Meredith, she
ouldn't stop wanting Patrick.

When she spied him, looking achingly handsome
n evening dress, her heart flipped over. The two
voided one another but it was inevitable that guests
vanted to talk to Lattimore and Ryland, inquiring
bout any new properties. Then they drifted away,
eaving Patrick and Jennifer by themselves.

"Stay a moment," he said, his fingertips grazing
er arm. "If we never talk together, people will won-
ler why."

"I can't help it," she murmured, moving back.
I've had a couple of drinks and my inhibitions are
owered."

"Same here. But we're safe enough talking shop in
his crowd," he said, gazing at her.

"I can't talk shop when you look at me that way."

"Only for a moment," he whispered, his eyes
ourning through hers. "Especially on Valentine's
Day. Jennifer, I love you."

"I love you," she whispered, giving him one pas-
ionate look before walking rapidly away.

They did not speak again.

Later she saw Meredith leaning all over him, insis-
ently kissing him for so long that guests milling
earby began to clap.

Patrick looked embarrassed, Meredith radiant.

Jennifer wanted to flee to the ends of the earth.

She didn't appear at the studio during the follow-
ng two weeks, telling Patrick on the phone that she

had to work on the libretto at home before continu‐
ing to meet and go over the songs.

The libretto wasn't going well. She was too agi‐
tated to concentrate properly.

Tony had been meeting business associates for
drinks most weekday evenings, and she felt lonely.

One evening at the end of February she wandered
around the apartment restlessly, unable to rouse her‐
self from her black mood.

She was relieved when at eight she heard her hus‐
band's key in the door, and she went to greet him.

They kissed. "Have a good day, *cara*?"

"Yes, pretty good," she fibbed. No point telling
him how she really was feeling when she couldn't re‐
veal the cause.

They had begun drinking Perrier instead of cham‐
pagne, as Tony would already have had as much al‐
cohol as he wished before dinner.

After they had raised their glasses in their ritual re‐
membrance of Melissa, Tony said, "I've been speak‐
ing to someone whose wife had a problem getting
pregnant. Then she took a new fertility drug and
gave birth to twin sons. So maybe you should con‐
sider it."

"The last time I took fertility drugs, they made me
sick."

"Well, maybe this one won't. If you would just try
it. I'm assured that it's safe."

Did she really want a baby now? Tony's baby? She
remembered how happy she had been with Melissa.
The three of them had been fine. If she had another
child, it might change everything.

"Jennifer, you will try the drug?"

"Yes."

"Good. Then you must visit the doctor very soon."

Over dinner Tony told her about his day and the difficulties he was having with the Italian interior-design firm he had retained to add men's departments to his Rome and Milan shops. "Americans are so much more—what is the word?—easy for change than Europeans. How do you say it?"

"Flexible?" Jennifer suggested.

"Exactly. Flexible. My countrymen get in a rut. They've always done things a certain way, so why not continue." He sighed. "I'm going to have to go to Italy for three weeks or so. I'm happy you have a new show to keep you busy while I'm fighting with everyone over there."

Jennifer looked at him thoughtfully. "When are you planning to go?"

"In two weeks. While I'm abroad I'll stop off in Paris and London—"

"I'd like to come with you."

He frowned. "You would? But, *cara*, it will be all business. I won't have a moment free. And what about your work?"

"I'll be working. In fact, I really need to go to London to research the Restoration period." She talked on, trying to convince herself as well as him. She didn't think she could bear to be left alone here for three or more weeks, and think about Patrick, work with him . . .

"You don't mind that I want to come with you?"

"No, *cara*, of course not. It's just unexpected."

In spite of his denial, she had the distinct impression that he wasn't really pleased. Well, at least he didn't argue.

She had to get out of New York. It was easier to miss Patrick when she was away than to miss him when she was here.

* * *

Long after Jennifer was asleep, Tony sat on the couch sipping a brandy, chain-smoking, and berating himself soundly.

Why hadn't he waited until the last minute before mentioning his trip?

Because he had never dreamed that Jennifer would want to go with him, that was why. She hadn't done so for such a long time. And now, when she was working on a new libretto . . .

Women. Just when you thought you had them figured out, they did something totally unexpected.

Tony exhaled a puff of smoke slowly. He had been congratulating himself on how well he was dealing with his life. Being with Debra didn't take anything away from his marriage. On the contrary, he never desired his wife more than when he was happy with his mistress.

In fact, he had left work early this evening, gone to Debra's, and had sex with her twice—which hadn't prevent him from making love to his wife after dinner.

Jennifer was at her most fertile time, too. Maybe a miracle would occur. And in a couple of weeks, when she had missed her period . . .

Please, God, let it be so, he prayed. No matter what, he would have to think of a good reason to leave Jennifer behind.

He had already promised this European trip to Debra.

24

Meredith was not happy.

Ever since the Valentine's party, she had been furious with her husband.

"What do you mean, I shouldn't have kissed you like that?" she shouted at him after their guests had departed. "What's wrong with a wife showing some affection to her husband?"

"Please don't shout," Patrick requested, looking pained. "Even if it was spontaneous, I'm very uncomfortable with public displays. It could have waited—"

"You ungrateful bastard!" Meredith yelled. "Dozens, hundreds of men would give their eyeteeth for a smile from me, let alone a kiss."

Patrick looked at her apologetically. "I'm sorry, dear, forget it. I didn't mean to upset you—"

"Well, you certainly have upset me! I thought you'd be flattered that I was showing the whole world I still want my husband, even though I could have anyone else."

He sighed. "Okay, okay. I apologize. It's late, we're both tired, a little drunk."

She had a good mind to sleep in the guest room to teach him a lesson. But she decided against it. Damn him. She was afraid if she held out on him he'd get his satisfaction elsewhere.

But when they went to bed she was cool and slept as far away as she could get.

She slept restlessly and had a dream about her father, someone she scarcely remembered. Awaking, she felt shaky and turned to her sleeping husband and snuggled against him. She began to caress him until she had awakened him in every sense and he had made love to her.

However, in the days that followed, she continued to feel resentful, even though he had been very sweet to her ever since, making a special effort.

Something wasn't quite right, she felt, but she didn't know what it could be.

Patrick was not happy.

Ever since his quarrel with Meredith the night of their party, he had felt himself losing control. It had been so tactless of him to have forced the issue of the public kiss when he was feeling frustrated over Jennifer and had been drinking.

The situation seemed hopeless. It was true enough that Meredith was looking more beautiful than ever. True that she was a star, and men were panting after her.

If only she weren't so dependent on him. He had promised he would always be there. How could he tell her he had fallen in love with another woman? And not any woman. Jennifer.

Yet, how could he go on this way, not loving Meredith the way she ought to be loved, and could be by someone else?

And there was his daughter.

He wished he knew what to do. How he hated living this way, hated the guilt he felt.

He was ashamed that when he made love to Meredith he often involuntarily thought of Jennifer.

It was a fine mess. And there was a new show to work on. Jennifer had been stalling for a couple of weeks, since that damned party. Working at home on the libretto, she said.

His pulse raced when he conjured up her voice on the phone, low, a little depressed.

She was avoiding him, he felt, and was relieved, in a way. He feared that the next time he saw her climbing the stairs to his studio, her soft hair flowing around her face, her incredibly passionate eyes that showed just what she was feeling for him, he would scoop her up in his arms, lock the door, and never let her out of there.

"You're going to Europe for three weeks?" Patrick's voice sounded edgy on the phone. "What about the libretto?"

Jennifer paused, feeling her hand sweating as she held the receiver. "I'll work on it over there. Tony will be busy. And in London I'll do some research at the British Museum. I can get at original source material . . ."

Excuses.

"I see." Patrick sounded weary, unhappy. "Well, at the moment I'm completely stymied. I've written some stuff but I need you to hear it before you go."

She took a deep breath. She would have to hear it sooner or later. Now was as good a time as any, when she was only a few days from leaving.

"Okay. When?"

"As soon as you can get down here."

She hung up, telling herself it would be all right.

The day was nasty, raw, and she wore flannel pants and a heavy hand-knit sweater.

As she climbed the stairs, her heart began to beat faster, with something more than the effort to get to the top floor.

Patrick was waiting for her. He didn't even help her off with her coat, but went directly to the piano and began to play. She leaned on it and listened.

"Well?"

"Well," she repeated, and then hesitated. "It's not bad, but it needs a little more . . . bounce. Snap. 'Wit,' I guess, is the word I'm looking for. I'm sorry, Patrick, but I must be honest."

"Yes, of course." He rested his hands on the keys glumly. "I kind of liked that tune, but hearing it again, I guess you're right."

She showed him her libretto, as far as she had gone, and he tried to get inspiration from it, but nothing came to him.

After an hour he said, "I can't make it today. I'm off, that's for sure. Dammit, Jennifer, I hate the fact that you're going away."

"Please don't. Don't make everything worse."

He ran his fingers over his forehead. "I've got a headache. Need an aspirin."

While he was in the bathroom, Jennifer decided it was time to leave.

When he walked back into the room and saw her holding her coat, he looked at her glumly. "I guess we'd better call it a day. A wasted day."

"There'll be better ones," she mumbled, not believing it. It had come to her during this session that they were never really going to work well again with the terrible thing they called love standing between them.

As they were coming down the stairs, a door opened and a young woman in jeans and a man's sweater said, "Excuse me. You're from the top floor, right? My name's Penny, and I wonder if you'd do me a favor. I've got to get to the bank before it closes, and if you'd just watch my little boy for five minutes, I'd be so grateful. He's getting over a cold and I don't want to take him out."

Penny looked too young to be a mother. Single Unmarried Parent was written in her large, dark, rather frightened eyes. "If I don't cash my check, we'll have nothing for supper."

"Sure, go ahead," Patrick said. "Take half an hour and do your shopping, too."

"Thanks a lot. You're a doll. Just make yourselves at home."

As Penny flew down the stairs, Jennifer hesitated. "I might as well keep going—"

"Oh, come on, stay for a few minutes. You never know. Inspiration may strike."

She doubted it but had no strength to argue.

The apartment was a little shabby, with attempts at prettiness in two circus posters and a small colorful Indian rug hanging on the kitchen wall.

The boy, about nine months old, was lying on his stomach sleeping in his crib in one of the rooms off the kitchen.

Jennifer unbuttoned her coat and sat down on a kitchen chair, looking around her.

"Not much in the way of possessions," Patrick commented, "but she thinks the world of her son. I've seen her carrying him close to her in one of those baby harnesses."

Jennifer said nothing. From the corner of her eye she could see Patrick lolling on the only other chair, his legs extended. With his finger he was absent-mindedly tracing the pattern of the cotton place mat on the table.

Those beautiful fingers—she wanted them to caress her.

She began to tremble and jammed her hands in her coat pockets, trying to think of something to say. But her mind drew a blank on small talk.

The baby began to cry.

"Amazing," Patrick commented. "As if he knows his mother's gone out."

Patrick, closer to the boy's room, reached him first, and lifted the child, holding him against his shoulder. "It's okay, little fella, it's okay."

The baby stopped crying.

"There, that's better." Patrick cradled him in his arms. "You're pretty cute at that. Give us a smile. That's right. Uncle Patrick's going to put you back in your crib. Now, sleep." He gently stroked the baby's shoulder until the child dozed off.

Jennifer stood in the doorway watching Patrick patting him. She felt the tears rising as she saw the man she loved gently handling the child, and she was overwhelmed by sadness.

That could be her baby, hers and Patrick's.

"Come and look at him, Jennifer. He really is sweet. And he's gone right back to sleep."

She couldn't move.

As Patrick glanced up in surprise and came toward her, she turned and began to swipe furiously at her eyes, willing herself not to cry but unable to stop the flow of tears.

"Oh, God, Jennifer." Patrick wrapped his arms around her. "Darling, I would so love to have a child with you."

She burst into sobbing and clung to him while he
stroked her hair, held her, murmured that he loved
her very much.

She must stop, she must. She backed away, and he
let her go.

"I'm sorry," she sniffled, glancing at him.

It was then she saw the tears in his eyes, the tender
look of pain on his face. She loved him unbearably.

"Don't be hurt," he murmured. "That's the thing I
can stand least, hurting you."

She nodded, trying to compose herself. "I don't
want you to be hurt either. That's the trouble with
all this. Someone gets hurt, no matter what we do."

Penny came in then, and they were able to leave.

Jennifer steeled herself to go down the stairs, but
Patrick wouldn't let her. He looked devastated.
"Please, please, darling, come home with me."

Her lips parted with longing as she looked at him,
feeling white-hot with desire. "It's wrong."

"It's even more wrong not to be together when
we're so much in love."

Gently he drew her into his arms.

Just one kiss. And then she would go.

But the kiss was endless. Patrick stood above her,
his back to the staircase, mounting the steps back-
ward, one at a time, drawing her with him.

Her whole body was quivering. She felt a part of
him. How could she not move where he moved?

"Patrick, if you knew how much I miss you—"

"I do know, darling." He unlocked his door.

On the futon they made love fiercely, then tenderly, the joy of their mutual adoration banishing
everything else. Afterward they reclined on their elbows, face to face.

When he smiled at her, her heart turned over. "I

love to see you looking so happy, Patrick. When I first came up those stairs you looked so sad."

"I know. I could say the same of you." He gently traced the shape of her cheek with his finger. "Jennifer, loving you makes up for every pain or disappointment in my life. You make me so incredibly happy." His eyes suddenly lit up, and rising, he went into the other room. Jennifer heard him playing the piano. Whereas earlier the music had sounded uninspired, now it was joyous, intricate, wonderful.

"Patrick, you've got it!" she cried, scrambling up.

She got to the door of his room and stopped, mirth bubbling up as she watched him, naked, on the bench, plunking away, all smiles.

He looked up and laughed with her, making some notations. "Come here, Ryland, I've got something to show you."

"I'll bet," she drawled, her right eyebrow raised, her smile mischievous.

Feeling like a character in a French farce, she went to lean on the piano. Astonishingly, she came up with some decent lyrics for his new composition.

In half an hour they achieved more than in their previous hour of work.

As they dressed, each had the same thought. Patrick voiced it. "Imagine what we'd be able to produce if we lived together." He sighed, and then leaned over to kiss her.

Inevitably the moment came for them to part, a moment she dreaded because the pain was in such contrast to her earlier joy.

"Well, have fun in Europe," he said.

"I'll try."

He reached into his pocket, drew out a key, and held it out to her.

He didn't have to tell her it was a duplicate to the studio.

"I want you to have it, darling."

The key was shiny in the palm of his hand. She didn't see how she could ever bring herself to use it. But if it made him feel better . . .

As she took it, he closed his hand over hers and pulled her against him, holding her motionless.

Then they exchanged a last loving look.

No one but you, Patrick.

No one but you, Jennifer.

She kissed his cheek and left.

"Tony, you promised," Debra said accusingly. "How can you do such a thing to me? I was planning the trip, looking at guidebooks, everything."

Lighting a cigarette, Tony looked at her guiltily. "I'm sorry, *amore*. I never thought my wife would be so insistent. But it seems she has some research to do in London—"

"I don't care," Debra interrupted angrily. "You made a promise and now you're breaking it. You're just using me, taking advantage of me, and I won't stand for it," she shouted.

"Please, Debra, calm youself."

"No, I won't calm myself," she shrieked. "I'm too good to be treated like this. I've always done what you ask, but give up Europe, no, I won't."

When he tried to touch her, she veered away from him, continuing to yell and stamp her foot.

He looked at her in astonishment. He had never before seen her like this.

He had come to her apartment this evening prepared for her pouting disappointment, and he had even bought her a lovely bracelet at Tiffany's, which he didn't dare give her when she was in such a rage.

At the same time that he was appalled, he was excited by this unexpected side of her. Her eyes were flashing as she stomped around in her cerulean-blue satin jumpsuit that revealed every curve of her body.

Tony knew he didn't want to lose her.

Could he possibly put Debra up in another hotel in every city he was intending to visit? And manage to sandwich her in between his appointments?

When he suggested it, she grew even angrier.

"No! No! No! I don't want that. I'm sick of being hidden away like a leper or something. What do you think I am? Don't you think I have feelings?"

"Of course I do, *amore*, and I never wanted it to be this way, believe me. I was looking forward to the trip."

"If you don't take me, I won't ever see you again. I mean it. Especially now."

To his utter astonishment, she threw herself into his arms and clung to him, sobbing like a child.

"Debra, *amore*," he murmured, the feel of her voluptuous body against him involuntarily arousing. Insistently he tilted her face up and kissed her, forcing her lips open with his deeply thrusting tongue.

She stopped crying and let him kiss her and fondle her breasts while he murmured soothingly, "Don't be so upset. I'll cut the trip short, I'll come back sooner, and then—"

He had said the wrong thing.

Furiously she pushed him away. "No! I don't want you back sooner, I want to go with you. I *will* go with you. I must go with you or I'll do something desperate, something terrible." She stopped and tried to catch her breath.

"What do you mean, terrible? You aren't thinking of harming yourself?"

"No, not myself, my baby," she blurted out. "Oh, I wasn't going to tell you this way," she wailed, flinging herself on the sofa and rocking back and forth, her head in her hands.

Tony stood motionless, not able to believe what he had heard. Surely she was just saying that to throw him off balance.

Slowly he walked to the sofa and sat down beside her. "You told me you were on the pill."

"I was," she sobbed. "But a few months ago the doctor said I had to come off it. Bad side effects." She had been using another contraceptive device, but because she was unfamiliar with it, she hadn't done it properly, and she had been caught.

Making an effort, she dried her tears and looked up at him with an appeal in her eyes. "I . . . I don't mind, really, Tony. I love you and I want to have your baby. Say you're glad. Say you don't want me to . . . to do away with it."

He found his tongue. "No! No, don't do anything like that." He felt bewildered, and his head was spinning.

"Then you're glad?"

Her appeal touched him greatly. "Yes, I'm glad," he replied, half-meaning it. He had to think this through. And in no event must she be allowed to do anything without his permission.

"Dry your tears, *amore*, get dressed. We'll celebrate."

"At the Four Seasons?"

"All right." At this point he saw he had to make a concession to Debra and buy some time to think. She was more than two months gone. If only she had told him sooner.

While she changed, he mixed himself a stiff Scotch and drank it down, trying to take in this incredible development.

At the restaurant, where he was well known by the maître d'hôtel, Tony smiled and brazened it out. So he was dining with a woman not his wife, so what? Fortunately, it was still early, and he was unlikely to run into anyone he knew.

He ordered champagne, caviar, and châteaubriand.

Debra, delighted, had recovered from her tantrum remarkably quickly.

When he took a careful look at her, he saw that she was a little peaked, with unaccustomed circles under her eyes. She was pregnant, all right.

"Oh, Tony, it will be so wonderful to have a baby," Debra said. "I hope it's a boy and that it looks just like you."

She chattered on, smiling once again, apparently assuming he would now take her to Europe. She said nothing about their life together in the future. Not a word about his divorcing his wife and marrying her. But he could guess that this was what she had in mind. While he listened to her prattle, smiling encouragment at her, he was thinking.

Maybe getting pregnant was an accident, maybe not. It hardly mattered at this point. The pregnancy was real, and it thrilled him and made him uneasy at the same time.

The irony of it. It should have been Jennifer, not Debra. Yet, Debra was young, strong, at the peak of her childbearing years. She would no doubt have a healthy baby. Whereas Jennifer, almost thirty-two,

would probably not conceive wit.
Twins would be all right, but wh
were born? A litter, like puppies. It

Although he had never before consi
his wife for his mistress, he was forced to
possiblilty now. However, the more he h   ..o
Debra, the less enthusiastic he became. Her conversation was fatuous. Compared with his wife, Debra
was immature and shallow.

"I'd like an English pram for him," she was saying. "Anthony Jr., and we'll call him Tonino—little
Tony. Won't that be cute?"

"Very cute," Tony agreed, smiling faintly.

Sitting across from Debra, his attention straying
often from her conversation to her bosom, he wanted
nothing more than to take her home and spend himself on her magnificent body—a body as perfect as he
had ever imagined the feminine form to be. But marriage? Seeing her morning, noon, and night? Forced
to talk to her after he was sated? Her tantrums—a
good example of which he had seen this evening—
would quickly become tedious. He would greatly
miss Jennifer's reasonableness, her fine disposition,
good humor, intelligent conversation. He would
miss, too, the way she listened to him.

Debra really didn't listen to him at all.

The difficulty was that child. His child. In spite of
his attempts to reason the whole thing out, he kept
imagining a small version of Debra, blond, blue-
eyed, adorable. Or a sturdy boy, also blond. Probably very tall, long-legged, an athlete. No, Tony
wouldn't mind it a bit if his son looked like his
mother.

The champagne made Debra loquacious and also
seductive. Before they had reached the dessert

she was prodding her knee against his under
table, tantalizing him unbearably.

He had to have her.

While she was in the ladies' room he made a quick
call home, telling his wife he had been detained by a
client, was having dinner with him, wouldn't be
home until very late.

Tony took Debra to her apartment, beseeching her
to show a little decorum in front of his driver. Without being seen, she caressed Tony underneath his
coat, running her fingers along the insides of his
thighs.

By the time they were in her bedroom, he was insane with wanting her. Fired by the idea that he had
impregnated her, he took her again and again until
he was drained. It was three in the morning before
he got home.

25

Debra leaned weakly against the bathroom wall, wondering how it was possible for anyone to be as sick as she had been, morning after morning, for the past few days.

It had begun the day after her lovemaking bout with Tony. No doubt she had overeaten and overdrunk at the restaurant. And then he had churned her up like a milkshake for half the night.

Since then she had felt awful. But she had dragged herself to work each day, more heavily made-up than usual. Nobody at the De Palma shop must guess her secret. And she had to put up a stoic front for Tony. The brave little mother-to-be. She wanted him to admire and desire her, not pity her.

In fact, that night five days ago she had nearly blown the whole thing. Fortunately, the situation had righted itself. Tony had been intrigued by the idea of her having his child. Had behaved beautifully. Taken her to the Four Seasons, greeted the maître d' without flickering an eyelash. Spent a fortune on dinner. And the following day he had given her a bracelet from Tiffany's.

Wearily Debra brushed her teeth and stepped carefully into the shower. She hadn't seen Tony since. He had claimed to be busy, trying to settle all his affairs before his trip. Anyway, she hadn't felt up to early-evening frolics after a day of standing on her feet.

"I'm going with you, aren't I?" she had asked every day when they spoke on the phone after work.

"I'm trying, *amore,* believe me, I'm trying."

But he still hadn't told her definitely.

After she was dressed she sat in her kitchen trying not to be nauseated while she munched on some dry crackers. She felt worse today than at any time she could remember.

Listlessly she consulted her calendar. She was ten weeks pregnant. The idea was suddenly repellent to her. She felt bloated, her breasts hurt, and she was nervous because she had stopped smoking.

Not only her doctor but also Tony had scared her by saying a baby could be damaged by its mother smoking, could be born undersized. So smoking was out. So was drinking more than one glass of wine per day.

Somehow she got through her morning's work, feeling weak and depressed. Instead of going out for lunch, she ate a yogurt in the lunchroom and returned to the floor early, hoping to leave early.

Unexpectedly, she came face to face with Tony and several associates. He nodded and smiled briefly at her, just as if she were any anonymous employee, then moved up the carpeted aisle with his companions.

Debra's face flushed with humiliation. How could the same man who was incoherent with passion for her in private greet her so coolly in public? As if she meant nothing to him.

For an hour Debra waited on an expansive businessman from Baltimore who spent two thousand dollars on clothes, winking at Debra every time she smiled at him.

A dull ache of anger and uncertainty smoldered within her, and she decided to have it out with Tony. She left the floor early but instead of going home took the elevator to Tony's office and announced herself to his secretary.

After checking, the secretary told Debra to go in.

Tony shut the door behind her and said sternly, "This is not wise. I've told you never to come here like this—"

"I don't care," she hissed, her voice low. "You're stalling. Am I going to Europe or aren't I?"

"Sit down, Debra, you look pale—"

"Just answer me. Yes or no."

She knew the answer before he spoke, because he wasn't able to look her in the eye.

"It's just not possible. There was no way to discourage my wife from coming with me."

Debra felt a wave of dizziness as she lowered herself into a chair. "I'm not feeling good. I've been heaving my guts up every morning. If you think I'm going to stay at home being sick while you have a good time with your wife—"

"Please, *amore*, be reasonable," he broke in softly. "First of all, if you're sick, you won't enjoy the trip, and it could be dangerous."

"If you leave me here, I'll have an abortion, I swear I will."

She enjoyed the look of horror on his face. "I'm not bluffing, Tony. I'm not a cow to be stuck here pregnant while you go bopping off to Paris and Rome—"

"Wait just a minute," he broke in angrily. "It was not my intention to get you pregnant. As far as I knew, you were taking precautions. Suddenly you spring this piece of news on me. What am I supposed to do, dump my wife just like that? She'd find out why, create a scandal, get a spectacular divorce, take all my money. Is that what you want?"

"No. All I want is to go to Europe with you. I don't care what you tell your wife. I'm going or there isn't going to be any baby—"

"Stop it!" he commanded furiously. "You are talking about a crime against God, and if you do such a thing, I will shun you like the plague. What's more, I don't like ultimatums."

She was suddenly afraid she had gone too far and was weakening her position. "Oh, Tony, you know I love you and want the baby," she said plaintively, "but I can't stand being left behind, with nothing to do and nobody to talk to." She used her tearful blue eyes to their best advantage.

After a few moments his face softened. Taking a seat next to her, he said in a lower voice, "It's not easy, I know. I'm sorry you're so disappointed. I wanted to take you to Europe, believe me. You know how much I want you," he finished, looking at her significantly.

"I know," she admitted, tears clouding her eyes.

"*Amore*," he crooned, pulling her into his arms. He kissed her gently and petted her. "I'll cut my trip short and . . . Sh, sh, just listen. As soon as possible, in April, we'll go to Europe together as I promised you. You'll be over your morning sickness by then."

"And your wife? What if she wants to go with you?"

"No, she won't want to go again so soon. And she'll be busy on her new show."

Debra sniffled against Tony's shoulder, letting him soothe her. Maybe it would be more sensible to wait until she was feeling better. She'd hardly be showing in April, and if she had him with her night and day for several weeks, he might never go back to his wife.

"All right," she agreed sulkily.

He dried her tears, kissed her again, and promised to visit her before he left for Europe.

The moment Debra had gone, Tony stopped smiling and lit a cigarette, telling his secretary to hold all calls.

He puffed thoughtfully. His little kitten had turned into a sneaky cat. She had him in a bad spot, and he hated being so vulnerable. He saw clearly that she wouldn't be happy until he divorced Jennifer and married her.

And that was the last thing he wanted. He liked things the way they were, his reasonable wife at home, his unreasonable mistress in her own bed, where she did her best work.

The trouble was that he wanted that child.

For the next few days Debra stewed, mulling over the situation and regretting that she had given in to Tony.

It seemed so hard to go on waiting. She had never imagined pregnancy would be like this. Sick in the morning, tired by afternoon. And so shaky, uncertain, lonely.

Although Tony had promised to see her before he left, he hadn't managed it so far. It was already Sunday afternoon, and he was leaving Monday evening.

Every time she looked at her shiny new passport with her picture in it, she wanted to weep.

She tried watching television, but what she tuned in to was a program about new procedures designed to help women bear children. Fertilization in a dish, implantation of an embryo in a woman's uterus, and for women who couldn't carry to term, surrogate motherhood.

Debra suddenly had the fearful thought that Tony's wife might be undergoing some of these treatments. If Debra allowed him to keep stalling her . . .

When her phone rang, she lunged at it, hoping it was Tony.

It was Charlene. "Debbie, honey, how're you doin'?"

"Just fine," she fibbed.

Assuming Debra was going to Europe as planned, Charlene talked on excitedly, pressing her for details.

Her face flushed, Debra lied through her teeth. She couldn't bear to admit that Tony was turning out to be as slippery as Charlene had predicted.

Debra's conversation with her sister snapped her out of her doldrums.

She was being idiotic. After having laid her plans so carefully, lied like hell—she had used no contraception of any kind with Tony—and succeeded in becoming pregnant, she was sitting around here waiting for something that wouldn't happen unless she made it happen.

She was almost eleven weeks gone. By the time Tony came back from Europe, it would be too late for an abortion, and then she would be in his power instead of the other way around.

Jennifer had her clothes laid out on the bed near her carry-on case and an overnight bag. She tried to select carefully and take as little as possible, but she would need at least three evening outfits.

With chagrin she realized that she saw this trip as a negative, an escape from Patrick, unlike former days, when her interest in her husband's business had made all the socializing, with its attendant formality, fun.

She suddenly imagined herself in Paris with Patrick, strolling arm in arm over the Seine, admiring the architecture, observing people, being relaxed, working on their new show, being together at night. . . .

The last time she had seen Patrick had been so wrenching. Her love for him was growing, not lessening. And the key to his studio was burning a hole in her handbag. How many nights she spent tossing, imagining herself using it, and finding him there. . . .

As she was about to pack, the phone rang.

It was someone called Debra Dillon.

Patrick was trying to read the morning paper, but the words were just a jumble. Today Jennifer was going to Europe. With her husband.

Patrick hadn't wanted to ask her again not to go. He had no right. Yet, he hated the thought of her being away for three weeks, maybe longer. At least here they could have seen each other while they worked on the show. It was difficult to be with her and not want her, but even more difficult not to see her at all. He had gone from enjoying her company to needing it. Badly.

When he looked at his watch he saw that it was late. Meredith had asked him to awaken her by eleven. The stage manager was calling a rehearsal for one-thirty because two new performers had joined the cast.

In the bedroom Patrick stood looking at his sleeping wife, her lovely hair framing her face. A strong feeling of affection and love welled up in him. But it wasn't the same kind of love he felt for Jennifer. His feelings for Meredith had become almost paternal over the years. When he had married her, he had found her exciting, beautiful, sexy, with tremendous vitality—all those things that she was onstage. But at home she had shown herself to be emotionally shaky. Meredith and Lissa, his two little girls.

Leaning over his wife, Patrick kissed her. "Time to get up."

"Mm," she mumbled without opening her eyes.

"Sleep well, baby?"

"Mm, but not enough," she mumbled. She turned on her stomach and pushed her head beneath the pillow.

He sighed. Maybe if he brought her a cup of coffee it would help. He had another cup himself. Although he went to sleep late every night, he got up early in order to have breakfast with Lissa.

His head was throbbing and he felt frazzled. Tonight Jennifer and Tony would be in London, at the Hilton, together in a big double bed. It would be Tony kissing those warm, responsive lips, Tony holding that exquisite, vibrating body against him. . . .

Jesus. He had to stop this. In the first place, Jennifer had told him she wasn't the same with Tony. He must believe that, cling to that. And why shouldn't it be true? Patrick wasn't the same with Meredith. Every couple was different. He didn't laugh with Meredith as he did with Jennifer, or banter with her, or have such intense, overwhelming feelings of passion. . . .

Stop it, stop it.

He brought the cup of coffee to Meredith, but she was fast asleep again and refused to be roused.

When the phone rang he had an irrational surge of hope that it was Jennifer. She wasn't going to Europe, she was in his studio, waiting for him. . . .

It was Lissa's teacher, telling him they were closing the school early because the boiler had broken down and there was no heat.

Patrick sent Bridget to get his daughter, then went back to the bedroom to prod his wife awake. If she missed the rehearsal, she would blame him.

He took a couple of aspirin but his head continued to ache.

Finally he coaxed Meredith out of bed and cooked a cheese omelet for her.

Lissa came home ravenous, since no school lunch had been served. Bridget had dropped her at the door and nipped out again to do the shopping. So Patrick prepared a hamburger and a salad for his daughter.

"And a glass of milk, Daddy," she requested.

"There isn't any milk. You'll have to wait until Bridget comes back. . . No, there's no Coke either."

"Well, I'm thirsty. What can I drink?"

Something in him snapped. "Drink water," he shouted. "I'm not the housekeeper around here! Somebody else take a little responsibility, for a change!"

His wife and daughter stared at him as if he'd gone crazy.

Shutting his eyes for a moment, he pressed his fingers against his throbbing temples. Then he looked contritely at them. "I didn't mean to yell. I'm sorry."

He put his arms around his daughter and hugged her tightly, feeling an ache in his throat.

"What's the matter, Daddy?"

"I guess I'm just upset today. My deadline for the TV special is next week and I'm only halfway through the score. And right now I've got a rotten headache."

"I'll kiss it better," Lissa promised.

Overwhelmed with love for her, he hugged her again and kissed her. "Thank you, sweetie. It's better already."

"Try Excedrin," Meredith said, eating her omelet. "It really works."

She meant to be helpful, of course. But didn't she realize she was repeating her part in a commercial of a couple of years ago? No, there wasn't a touch of irony in her tone or her expression. If that had been Jennifer, she would have grinned at him with that teasing light in her eyes . . .

Stop it.

Patrick looked at his family apologetically. "I'm just not fit for human company at the moment. I'm going to the studio for a couple of days, okay? I really need to get that TV score written."

Liar. Coward. He flung on a jacket, kissed his wife and daughter, and fled from the apartment before Meredith could say a word.

A blustery March wind nearly tore his head off. Grimly he set his face against the wind, putting his hands in his pockets, and walked to the bus stop.

When he climbed the steps to the studio, his heart was beating a tattoo against his ribs.

Of course Jennifer wasn't there.

The place seemed so small, shabby, barren. But at least he could be alone and not inflict his misery on the innocent.

He sat down at the piano, played some chords, and was shocked by the loudness, the intrusiveness of the sound.

Jennifer, Jennifer, Jennifer. No one but you.

God, how he loved her.

He didn't know how long he sat motionless at the piano.

Finally he began to work on the TV series, and the music came, slowly.

Being able to work well was the only thing that could make him feel better.

When Debra let Tony's wife into her apartment, she suddenly realized the enormity of her action.

Tony had phoned Debra last night to say goodbye, promising his trip would be short. He would buy her something fabulous in Milan, would miss her, et cetera.

The realization that when it came to the crunch he was choosing his wife over her had been upsetting. Debra had slept fitfully, awakened feeling awful.

For the first time, she hadn't been sick this morning. Maybe it was over. All the more reason to go to Europe with Tony. She had to go—or at least make sure his wife didn't.

Husband and wife on a trip together, alone a lot, in hotel rooms . . . Debra had never dared to ask Tony how he felt about his wife, and he had never volunteered any information. Debra had assumed he liked the woman well enough but was bored with her in bed. And tired of being childless. But on this trip, what if his feelings for his wife were rekindled? What if his wife became pregnant too?

Debra couldn't let that happen, and so she had phoned the wife, telling her she had to see her. And to the question of who she was, Debra had brazenly replied, "Tony's mistress."

There had been silence. And then, "Give me your address."

Tony's wife had sounded calm. Well, it was probably the shock. Wait until it had sunk in.

Although Debra had rehearsed what she was going to say, every word went right out of her head when she was actually face to face with Jennifer De Palma. She was slender, elegant in a charcoal-gray suit, and was much more attractive than her photos.

Even though the woman looked a little pale, there was a certain dignity about her, a presence that Debra found quite unnerving.

Tony's wife ought to be hysterical. Still, when she had looked Debra over carefully, and an expression of discomfort flitted over her features, Debra's confidence returned. She was years younger than her rival, and fertile to boot.

"May we sit down, Miss Dillon?"

The well-bred voice broke into Debra's thoughts, and she led the way into the living room, proud of the apartment Tony had furnished, in Italian modern.

While Tony's wife looked around briefly, Debra noticed that she had very disturbing, catlike eyes. Especially when she fixed them on Debra and sat there silently waiting for her to begin.

Debra was suddenly nervous. She desperately

needed a cigarette. Taking one from a pack she had hidden in a drawer, she offered them to her visitor, who politely declined.

Debra was intimidated, and fear made her aggressive. "You act like you're humoring me," she began harshly. "Like I'm making it up or something."

"No. I believe you. How long has your affair been going on?"

"Well, we first met almost six years ago." To Debra's satisfaction, she saw Tony's wife open her eyes wide and lean forward tensely.

"Six years ago?" she echoed incredulously. "In San Francisco?"

"Yes," Debra said smugly.

"You've . . . you've been seeing Tony all this time?"

"No. But the point is that I'm seeing him now. For almost six months. I work in the store, in the men's department."

"I see."

Debra was getting more upset. This interview wasn't going at all the way she had planned. Why was the woman so damned calm?

"When do you see him?" she now asked.

"Every chance he gets. After work, about three times a week. He comes here, to this apartment. Our apartment. He pays the rent."

"Of course." The woman's tone was wry. But she was getting paler and maybe a little less sure of herself. Debra watched as Tony's wife rubbed the fingers of one hand in the other and sighed.

After a long silence she looked directly at Debra, her narrow green eyes hard and, Debra felt, insolent.

"I suppose you're telling me all this because he promised to take you to Europe."

"He's told you!" Debra cried.

"No, he hasn't told me a thing. It's simply obvious that you're spilling the beans now because you're disappointed not to be going with him after all."

Debra felt rattled, and she puffed on her cigarette, longing for a drink, even though it was hardly noon. To hell with it, one Scotch wouldn't hurt the baby.

Tony's wife declined a drink, and her look of superiority made Debra furious.

Gulping half of her drink, she said shrilly, "I'm pregnant by Tony."

There. That was better. Watching the woman swallow and blink her eyes, Debra thought she was going to cry. But she didn't. She only looked very sad.

"Tony knows?"

"He sure does. And he wants me to have the baby," Debra said defiantly.

"Do you love him?"

The question took Debra by surprise. "Of course. He was my first lover."

The alcohol, hitting her on an almost empty stomach, loosened her tongue. Oh, how she had been longing to parade her conquest in front of this woman. With no encouragement Debra told Tony's wife how she had met him.

"You had an affair with him even though he was married?"

"I didn't know that. He acted like he was single. Came after me for weeks. Took me out in the evenings. I never dreamed he wasn't free. Not until I finally gave in did he tell me. So I . . . I went back to L.A."

Thrilling Fiction from SIGNET

*Prices slightly higher in Canada

†Not available in Canada

**Buy them at your local
bookstore or use coupon
on next page for ordering.**

More Bestsellers from SIGNET

Debra sipped her drink, knowing she was improving upon the truth. She had set her sights on the rich, handsome Tony, had flirted with him shamelessly. After she learned he was married, she had withdrawn, then surrendered once more, hoping he would leave his wife. Only when that hadn't happened had she gone back to L.A.

Tony's wife looked at her mournfully. "I will have that drink now, please."

So she *was* nervous. She just knew how to hide it.

"How did you resume with Tony?"

Handing her the drink, Debra said smoothly, "We happened to meet on the street. I needed a job, and Tony offered me one."

Determined to ruffle the other woman's composure, Debra boasted of Tony's preoccupation with her, of his limitless passion. Over a second drink she started to describe their lovemaking in some detail. But after a few minutes, Tony's wife asked her to stop.

Jennifer felt weak, and her head was spinning as she listened to the young woman's incredible story. Incredible, and yet believable.

When Debra had first phoned and dropped her little bombshell, Jennifer had been somewhat skeptical. But she had risen to the bait and come here to see for herself.

And what she saw appeared within the realm of possibility. The girl was young, beautiful in a sullen sort of way. Moreover, she had exactly the kind of figure Tony most admired.

Sitting on the sofa in a skintight black jumpsuit, with her prominent breasts half-exposed, Debra was

defiantly spilling out her sordid tale. Even if she exaggerated, her story had the ring of truth.

One glance around the apartment had revealed Tony's decorative touch. And Debra was a smoker. Tony's return to tobacco coincided with the time Debra said they had resumed their affair.

Hardly able to think straight, Jennifer drank her Scotch, recalling bits of past conversations with her husband. He had denied ever being unfaithful. A lie? He had said models didn't interest him. A half-truth? Most models, maybe, but what about this leg model with the big bosom?

"How pregnant are you?" Jennifer asked.

"Three months."

Jennifer wondered if she was pregnant at all, let alone three months gone. Her story might be true, but what if she were making it up? What if she were having an elaborate fantasy about her boss?

At the very least, Jennifer had to give Tony a chance to tell his side of the story. There was no point in jumping to hasty conclusions.

Debra was looking at her expectantly. Lighting another cigarette, the young woman said pointedly, "I just thought you ought to know."

Jennifer rose. "Thank you for considering my feelings," she said dryly. "I'll talk the matter over with my husband."

"Don't you believe me?" Debra cried. "Your husband's been screwing my brains out, and now I'm pregnant. And he wants me to have the baby."

"Yes, so you said. Well, children are very important to Tony. After our little girl died . . ." She trailed off, swallowed, then continued. "He's been disappointed that I haven't had any more children."

Jennifer felt terrible. Looking at Debra mournfully, she prepared to leave.

"Wait a minute," Debra cried, jumping up and rushing ahead to block the door. "Are you still going to Europe with him?"

"I really don't know."

Debra panicked. She had taken a terrible risk telling Tony's wife what she had. The only point in having done so was for the woman to throw a fit. Start talking divorce. It's what Debra would have done in her place. Instead, Tony's wife was not only giving her husband the benefit of the doubt, she had practically apologized for not having more children! As if that were any excuse for Tony's behavior.

Debra became desperate to knock some sense into the woman. And there was only one way.

To tell her something so terrible it would turn her against her husband forever.

Debra spread-eagled herself against the door.

"You haven't heard the whole story."

Tony spent a pleasant morning giving last-minute instructions to his assistant as well as to his secretary. Yet, something was nagging at him, something he had left hanging.

By lunchtime he knew what it was. Debra. He had the uneasy feeling that she wasn't resigned to his trip to Europe without her.

When he had spoken to his mistress last evening she had been quiet, true, and that had been worrying in itself. He toyed with the idea of canceling his lunch date and seeing Debra instead. But the thought that she might make another scene and renew her demands put him off. It would be better to leave well enough alone.

They were due at the airport at seven. Well, there was plenty of time. He was already packed, and he waited until four-thirty before leaving the office.

When he opened the door to his apartment, he was surprised to find it dark and silent.

He hung up his coat, puzzled. Surely Jennifer must be at home. He was about to try the kitchen when he heard a sound from the living room. "Jennifer? Is that you *cara*? Why are you in the dark?"

As he walked toward her, she stood up. "I saw Debra Dillon this morning," she said in a voice of deadly calm.

Tony stopped short, feeling cold apprehension flood through him. He expelled a sharp breath, thinking furiously. Someone had seen him with Debra, perhaps. Told Jennifer. There were always gossips ready to make trouble.

He must take it slowly. Not admit anything he didn't have to admit.

"Where was that?" he asked much more calmly than he felt.

"At her place. She phoned me."

Tony felt his hands grow clammy. The stupid, stupid little fool! This was serious. He switched on the light.

Jennifer's eyes were swollen, her cheeks streaked from crying.

"Dio mio," he muttered under his breath. Had Debra told her *everything*?

Jennifer was digging her fingers into the palms of her hands and fixing him with blazing eyes. "How could you?" she hissed. "How could you have kept such a secret for so many years?"

He stood stock-still, his mouth trembling, incapable of uttering a word.

"Tell me, damn you! Tell me how Debra happened to be in our house, *in our bed*, the day Melissa died!"

26

Tony would never forget his first sight of Debra Dillon, her golden hair falling to her shoulders, the tight sweater she wore revealing her magnificent breasts, the short skirt, her exquisite legs. Tony appreciated female beauty, and this lovely young creature was a feast for the eyes. Then she had smiled at him, overwhelming him with her innocent blue eyes.

He had never experienced anyone like Debra before. There was something so compelling about her that he had longed to touch her, embrace her. It was the oddest feeling. As if her very flesh were magnetized and drawing him to her.

He wasn't thinking of her as a replacement for his wife, Jennifer, whom he loved. This was something else. An elemental lust unearthed from his deepest sexual being. Love didn't enter into it at all.

He was desperate to have this girl. But at the same time that she teased him with smiles, she turned him down flat. Of course she was only a child, seventeen, a virgin.

It was madness. He knew it but he couldn't stop himself. He was simply enchanted by her.

Although her assignment to model shoes in his shop was limited to three days, he persuaded her to stay on in town, paid for her room, gave her money. He couldn't let her go.

Gradually she let him hold her hand, then kiss her. They had a long necking session in the back of his car—she didn't allow him in her room—which made him frantic with lust. A Botticelli face with a Rubenesque figure. Her breasts, like melons, high and firm. Her narrow waist, flaring hips. The perfect embodiment of beauty.

He caressed her long, perfect legs with their strong, shapely calves and the beauteous expanse of thigh. Higher and higher he moved his hands, but she wouldn't let him touch her between her legs.

After a week of being unbearably tantalized, he found an excuse to go to her room, talked his way in, and then fell upon her, stifling her cries with kisses. He used everything he had ever learned about women to arouse her. She succumbed, and they had a wild liaison for several days. In the throes of passion he told her he adored her. What he didn't tell her was that he was married. It seemed pointless. He thought of Debra as a toothsome treat, something he craved as he might a pastry. She had nothing to do with his marriage.

But when she discovered that he had a wife, she refused to see him again. She remained in San Francisco, however, and began to model for an agency there. She moved from her room, and for a while he couldn't even find her.

A few weeks later he saw her downtown by chance, followed her home, and implored her to come back to him, but she refused.

"I love you, Tony, but you're married. And you have a kid. Please, please let me forget you." The flow of tears made her eyes even more beautiful.

Tony offered to get her an apartment, to support

her, but she refused. "If you weren't married, it would be different."

He sighed, knowing she was right. He had no intention of disrupting his marriage. But oh, how he missed her. A month went by and he agonized.

The day he had promised to be home early so that Jennifer could go to her rehearsal, he found Debra waiting for him near his car, looking pale and washed-out, miserable. "I can't stand it anymore, Tony. I'm going back to L.A."

"Please, *amore*, you must not. If you knew how much I've missed you, wanted you . . ." Persuading her to get into the car with him, he drove aimlessly, not knowing what to do. But he had to get home; his wife was relying on him. Yet, he feared to let Debra go now.

"Come home with me, *amore*. We will talk everything over." He was ready to promise anything, he was in such a state of arousal. Her sadness, her trembling red lips, her brave renunciation of him, alternating with passionate looks, completely deranged him.

He left Debra in his car near a phone booth, telling her to wait for twenty minutes and then call his house. When the coast was clear, she drove his car to his front door.

Tony put Debra in the front parlor with a drink while he finished feeding Melissa. His instinct told him not to involve his mistress with his daughter.

He carried Melissa up to her room, put her in her crib, and kissed her good night.

When he came downstairs, Debra was having second thoughts, as he had feared, being in his wife's home that way. He reassured the girl and began to

make love to her. Her ripe body drove everything else from his mind.

Faintly he heard Melissa crying. He excused himself and went upstairs. There was nothing wrong. She just wanted a little attention. He picked her up, held her a little while, cuddled her. "Now, go to sleep, *figlia mia*."

But the moment he left the room, she began to cry. Again he went back to soothe her, but this time he locked the door on his way out.

When he got back downstairs, Debra was reclining on the couch exactly as he had left her, her clothes in disarray, her eyes hooded with lust.

Tony flung himself beside her and resumed his embraces. But Melissa started to cry again, louder. And their dog was scratching at the back door.

Tony could see a look of doubt pass over Debra's face. "Just one moment, *amore*. I'll settle her down once and for all."

"She's probably not sleepy," Debra said sulkily. "Maybe you should put her in her playpen or something."

Tony found his daughter out of her crib and trying to open the locked door, screaming with anger. It was as if she knew that exciting things were happening in the house and didn't want to be left out. He wiped her face, kissed and cuddled her, at which point she became very playful. It was apparent she wasn't going to sleep now.

He rummaged in the closet until he found the playpen. It was too big for the baby's room, so he brought it downstairs to the living room.

Then he carried Melissa down and put her in the playpen with a big pile of toys. The dog followed him in, and Melissa began to play with him, delight-

ing in trying to pull his tail. She seemed fine, and the dog was watching her.

When Tony returned to the parlor, Debra wasn't there. But her shoes were on the floor and her handbag was on the couch, next to her blouse and skirt.

"Debra, where are you?" he called.

No answer. She was playing games, and he smiled, intrigued. A trail of her clothes led up the stairs. As he followed it, picking up the items and sniffing at them, besotted by her scent, she appeared at the top of the stairs. Slowly, seductively, she took off her bra and panties and tossed them to him.

He caught them, and then ran up the stairs and grabbed her. Embracing her, he inched her into the bedroom and pushed her onto the bed. In a frenzy, fueled by their long parting, he flung himself on her, blocking out everything but his passion and her moans of ecstasy.

As he was just winding down from one of the most exciting experiences of his life, he heard the dog barking outside the door.

Melissa! Tony quickly got up, slipped on his shorts, and hurried downstairs.

The sight that met his eyes was horrifying. The child was lying on the floor, her face blue, choking.

What happened next was unclear to him, a nightmare. After phoning for an ambulance, he put his fingers down his daughter's throat, then tried to breathe life into her.

Debra came down, hurriedly getting into her clothes, as horrified as he.

"Go home," he told her, the tears coming down his face.

He didn't even notice when she slipped away.

The rest was a blur. Riding in the ambulance

while the attendants worked on the child. Sobbing in the waiting room. Having to call Jennifer.

Unable to believe that his daughter was dead.

He didn't think of Debra for several days, not until he was given a message that she had called the shop.

He saw her for only a few minutes. "My wife needs me now. We need each other."

Debra was pale, a little guilty. "It was an accident, Tony."

He nodded. "Yes. But we can't think of ourselves now. Don't you understand? My daughter is dead." He sobbed unashamedly.

Meekly Debra kissed him good-bye and went back to Los Angeles.

Tony now looked at his wife, who was ashen-faced, tears streaming down her cheeks.

"Believe me, *cara*, it was the most terrible thing that ever happened in my life. I would have given anything to undo that whole horrible day. You do see that it was an accident."

"You lied," Jennifer cried, her voice breaking. "Made up one lie after another. A strike at the factory in Florence, phone calls . . . Oh, God! While out child was choking to death, you were in our bed with another woman! I can never forgive you for that, never!"

"No! No, don't say that, *cara*, please. I didn't lie. There *was* a strike. I *did* talk to my brother in Florence that day. And if Debra hadn't picked that particular time, I would probably have spent the evening on the phone. The accident could have happened even without Debra—"

"No!" Jennifer was shaking with rage. "You would have heard Melissa. She wouldn't have been out of

the way in that goddamn playpen downstairs while you were upstairs!"

"It could have been us making love, not hearing the little one—"

"Never!" Jennifer yelled. "I'm her mother! I always heard her, always, no matter if I was asleep, no matter what else I was doing!"

"I adored Melissa, you know that. She was my darling. I didn't know what could happen. I didn't realize. I would give anything, *anything* to have her back. That night, I made a vow to God. I would never, never again be with another woman but you. If only God would forgive me, if only he would give us another child—"

"Stop it, stop it! I can't listen to any more," Jennifer screamed. She ran out of the room, then halted, not knowing which way to turn.

Then she headed for the guest room, locked herself in, and flung herself on the bed. She cried until there wasn't another tear left.

Tony took several deep breaths.

Well, the terrible secret was out at last. Jennifer was upset, naturally. But if he had told her the truth at the time, it would have been worse. She might have left him. Now, with six more years shared, she would get over it. She was strong, resilient.

He walked to the bar and poured himself a Scotch. Then he looked at his watch. Moving to the phone, he called his chauffeur to say they would not be going to the airport that evening. Then he wired his contacts in London not to expect him.

He thought of phoning Debra and telling her he was through with her. The little bitch, she certainly had made a mess. But he contained himself. He

couldn't antagonize her further now. She was unstable, liable to do anything, as today proved. And if she did what she had threatened about the baby . . . He lit a cigarette.

He was in a pickle, that was certain. He had to try to repair the damage to his marriage and at the same time prevent his mistress from aborting his child.

27

Jennifer came out of her room early in the morning, exhausted after a mostly sleepless night.

Tony was in the kitchen drinking coffee, his ash-tray full of cigarette stubs. He eyed her guardedly. "I have packed for you, Jennifer. We can catch a ten-A.M. Concorde flight—"

"I'm not going." She poured herself a cup of coffee and sat down at the table across from him.

He was unshaven and looked as if he had slept as little as she. But when Jennifer thought of their daughter, she was unable to pity him.

What she found incredible was that at the time of the tragedy, in spite of his tears, his genuine anguish, he had been able to concoct such a lie and stick to it. She had never imagined he could be so deceitful, so coldblooded.

"I don't blame you for being upset. It's a relief, *cara*, to have told you at last. It was heavy on my conscience, believe me. I only ask that you forgive me. That you believe I have mourned my beautiful daughter with every drop of sadness in my body."

"I do believe it," she said, her voice flat. "But I'm still outraged that you would have brought another woman to our home, to the very bed you shared with me."

"I explained how it was. I was not myself. She had cast a spell over me."

"Really. And it lasted for six years. So that when you met her on Fifth Avenue you offered her a job—"

"I did no such thing." He explained what had really happened. "She's a liar. I'm beginning to think she planned it this way."

Jennifer eyed him coldly. "No matter what she planned, seeing her again, didn't you remember? Didn't you make the connection? Jesus, that woman was indirectly the cause of Melissa's death."

He lowered his gaze. "It was a terrible accident. I didn't blame anyone. And you were in Boston for a month. I was missing you."

"So you took up with her again."

He lit a cigarette nervously. "It wasn't that simple. For months that show kept you busy. You had no time for me."

"You encouraged me, insisted, almost, when I was doubtful at first—"

"Yes. But I didn't realize what it would mean. I was remembering the showcase. A few hours a week."

"And what were you doing during those few hours, I wonder."

"Nothing, Jennifer, believe me." He looked solemnly at her. "Since Melissa I have not looked at another woman. I told you it was my pact with God, to be faithful, if only we could have another child. But there wasn't another. When you were in Boston, Debra used all the wiles of the temptress. Believe me, I love you and you alone."

Jennifer looked steadily at him.

"It's true. I'm not in love with Debra. No matter

what she told you. She would say anything now. She
wants you to leave me. She wants my name, respect-
ability, money. Don't you see that?"

"Of course I see it. And as far as I'm concerned,
she's welcome to it all."

He blanched. "No! No, don't say that, *cara*,
please. Debra was an amusement. Nothing more."

"How nice for her," Jennifer snapped. "And what
about the child she's carrying?"

He sighed and rubbed his chin stubble with his fingers. "I don't know. An abortion is a crime against
God."

"Then what are you planning to do about her?"

"I don't know. I haven't thought it through. Maybe . . . maybe when she has the baby we can convince her to give it to us. For a price."

It was a cruel thought. Even if, as he claimed, he
didn't love Debra. Even if she was scheming. To
want to deprive a woman of her own child by offer-
ing her money . . . The idea made Jennifer shudder.

Wearily she sipped her coffee. She could have
forgiven him for having an affair, if it hadn't led to
Melissa's death. If he hadn't concealed the truth all
these years. Jennifer blamed herself, too, for having
known Tony so little.

"Jennifer, I love you. You must believe that."

"What you call love doesn't mean much to me.
You had an affair with another woman. Are still
having it. Don't I please you enough as a lover?"

"You're my wife. That is very different. A wife is
sacred."

"I see. So scared you had to find another lover—"

"That had nothing to do with you," Tony said impatiently. "I don't understand this country. If a husband has a minor affair, his wife goes berserk. In

aly's a man's meaningless affair doesn't threaten a
arriage."

"What does?"

"Nothing. Marriage is a trust."

Incredible as it was, she saw that he wasn't being
onic in his use of the word "trust." "Before we were
arried, we were lovers—"

"No. You were my intended wife, my fiancée. I
as serious about you from the start."

"Even so, you made love to me before the cere-
ony. You knew what you were getting. And appar-
ntly I was satisfactory then. Did you get bored? Is
ebra a better lover than I am?"

"I don't compare you with her. It's different."

"In what way? From the very beginning you've
een romantic. Fine. I like candlelight and soft mu-
c. And I accepted your modesty even though I won-
ered sometimes. But not with Debra, apparently.
Vhy? Why have you always stopped me whenever I
anted to look at you, touch you, kiss you in certain
vays?"

"I made love to you with respect, with reverence."

"But not with passion," Jennifer cried. "The pas-
ion was all for Debra. She told me some details,
ony. Very impressive," she added dryly.

He raised his eyes to the ceiling, mumbling in Ital-
an and growing red with embarrassment. "A man
oesn't treat his wife like a whore. A wife is for com-
anionship, for children. Passion doesn't last, any-
vay. Not for the same person. In my youth I had
. . I don't know how many women. I never
vanted to marry one of them. They weren't worthy
f my love. You, Jennifer, you were a lady, born and
red. Delicate, discriminating, inexperienced. I was

glad. I wouldn't want someone who might be dissat
isfied, have affairs, perhaps."

Jennifer couldn't believe what she was hearing. "*
wife can't have affairs, but a husband can?"

"It's not the same thing. If a wife plays around
how would her husband know that the children wer
his?"

"That's medieval," she exclaimed. "Surely you
don't believe that stuff." Yet, looking at his face, she
saw he meant every word. "If you do believe it, what
makes you so sure that Debra's child is yours?"

Tony blew out a puff of smoke. "I'm not sure."

Jennifer's head was reeling. How was it possible
that she had been married to this man for nine years
Had they never discussed this sort of thing? She
guessed not. She had apparently assumed that they
shared the same ideas about love and marriage. In
fact, had they talked in depth about anything at all?

Jennifer had another cup of coffee. "When you
first met me at the club, you didn't know anything
about me, presumably. What made you so certain I
wasn't promiscuous, maybe with several abortions
behind me?"

He didn't look at her. "Well, you didn't seem that
sort of woman—"

"I didn't *seem*? You, who think a wife is sacred,
went looking for a bride in a nightclub? Chose a
woman connected with show business, who came
from New York? Whose history you didn't know?"

"I didn't ask you to marry me for quite a while—"

"One month. I was the one who wanted to wait."

He was silent.

"Was our meeting accidental? You didn't know
who I was? Where I lived? Or who my grandfather
was? Look at me, Tony."

He lifted his compelling brown eyes and gazed
softly at her. "We met by chance. I had seen your
show, admired it, and you. That I later discovered
you came from a good family didn't displease me.
Naturally."

"Oh, God! I wondered why you picked me out of
the North Beach Players. There were several other
women, prettier, better dressed, more your style—"

"That's not true, believe me—"

"No, I don't believe you. You lie about everything.
Smoking, for instance, a stupid lie when I could
smell it on your breath. You knew who I was, all
right, before you made your move. You knew about
the Ryland house and the Ryland wealth, and my
dying grandfather—"

Tony slammed his cup into the saucer. "As God is
my witness, I did nothing wrong. All right, I was impressed with your background. I wouldn't choose
just anyone for a wife. In fact there were richer
women in San Francisco, and I resent your accusation. Especially since I've paid my way from the very
beginning. You were such a mouse when I met you. I
dressed you, taught you style. And I turned that
three hundred thousand dollars you inherited into
millions."

Jennifer was appalled. It was suddenly clear to her
that if she had been penniless Tony would not have
courted "such a mouse."

In spite of the way he had romanced her—the
flowers, the candlelight dinners, the attentive-
ness—he had never felt true passion for her.

Jennifer pushed her cup away. The coffee and
conversation had left a terrible taste in her mouth.
"Debra told me you want her to have the baby."

He didn't answer.

"She might as well. I can't go on with this mar
riage."

"Don't say that, *cara*, please. I won't accept it
You've had a shock. I'm sorry. But please, don
leave me."

"You and I think differently about everythin
that's important—"

"No, not about anything. We love each other."

"My love was built on lies, on misunderstandings
On a stranger. I could never trust you again."

"Don't look at me that way. I meant no harm, be
lieve me—"

"You may not have meant harm, Tony, but harn
was done. To Melissa. Yet, six years after her death
you picked up where you left off, with the sam
woman who . . . who . . . And every evening when
we drank a toast to our daughter . . . How could
you do it? And not feel like a hypocrite?" Jennife
couldn't go on, as tears choked her.

"*Dio mio,*" Tony muttered. "Why are you so inca
pable of understanding that the thing with Debra i
nothing more than animal lust? Something left ove
from our cavemen ancestors. It has nothing to d
with my love for you—"

"Stop saying that word! Love means nothing to m
if it doesn't include animal lust!"

Tony's eyes widened. He started to laugh and then
thought better of it. "Please, Jennifer. Don't be in
competition with Debra. It's no contest, believe
me."

"All these years," Jennifer said, "when I missed
real passion between us I thought that you simply
weren't that sort of man. Now I know how wrong I
was. What you withheld from me you gave to her."

"Never. I never took from you to give to Debra.

There was no need, since I have enough for two women."

"Oh, God!"

"It's true. Did I ever neglect you?"

"Yes! Yes! You neglected me sensually. You put me on a wifely pedestal, where I don't want to be, where I don't belong! I could have been as passionate with you as Debra if you'd just given me the chance."

"Jennifer, please." Tony put his hands to his head. "I don't want to argue with you."

"I don't want to argue with you either. Would you give Debra up?"

"Yes, of course." He averted his eyes. "Only now the situation is complicated. She could make a lot of trouble for me, *cara*. She could drag us through the courts, slap a paternity suit on me. I have to keep her happy for a while."

"How are you going to do that without divorcing me and marrying her?"

"There are other ways. I need time to think."

Jennifer looked at him coldly. "And in the meantime? I'm supposed to go on sharing you with her? Even if she were willing—which she's not—why should I be?"

"Don't compare yourself to her. Debra is a—how do you say it?—empty-head. She lives only for pleasure. You're intelligent, talented, a decent woman. You have your work. I haven't ever interfered, have I?"

"No, but you resent my work, you said so before. You're willing to let me have my career, but the *quid pro quo* is you're allowed to have a mistress, right?"

"Jennifer, don't say such things. I'm your hus-

band. I treat you with kindness and love. I protect you—"

"I don't need protection, I need openness. I need honest communication. And passion. God, how I need passion."

"What are you talking about? You want bright lights in the bedroom? Me, without a stitch on? If nothing were held back, we would soon grow tired of each other. A husband and wife can't be like a couple of rutting animals. Why can't you understand?"

"I understand what you're saying, but I don't agree. I'm not like you. I invest my love and passion in one person—"

"We are talking in circles."

"Yes, I think we are. This marriage is based on misunderstandings. It would be best to end it."

"*Cara—*"

"We have to end it, Tony. I won't take the fertility drug. I don't want your child. Every time I look at you now, all I can think of is how Melissa died." Her voice quavered.

Tony tried to take her hand, growing agitated when he realized that she was serious about leaving him. "Don't say things you will want to take back—"

"I don't want to take them back. It's not only your fault, it's mine too. We should have had this conversation before we got married."

"Jennifer, stop it. You are tearing out my heart. We have shared so many things—"

"Only superficial things," she cried. "Travel, meals, this overly luxurious apartment. We never shared our feelings. We never told the truth. You've lied and lied, and I've . . . I've held back too. The only thing we shared deeply was Melissa, and when

we lost her, we lost everything," she finished mournfully.

"We can have another child. I will change. I will learn. We can buy Debra off somehow. But don't say you're through with me, *cara*." His voice broke.

Jennifer felt a surge of tenderness for him when she saw that his anguish was real.

"Could you give up all other women in the future?"

"Yes." However, his deep sigh told her of his doubts.

"And if you couldn't," she continued softly, "would I have the same privilege? As long as I was devoted, considerate, discreet, would you mind if I had a lover?"

He stared at her. "You aren't serious."

"Yes. I am."

He held out his hands, palms up. "A little flirtation, that I can understand, but a lover, as you call it. Really, Jennifer, you aren't the type."

She felt herself flush with anger. "You're wrong about that," she said in a low voice. "Just because I'm not blatant about it doesn't mean that I'm not tempted. If someone really wants me, feels passion toward me, someone I can also admire . . . There are a lot of people out there. A lot of temptations. A man or a woman can always find someone else. Younger, smarter, richer, wittier. The point is that an adult can make a choice. To have an affair or to let the moment pass. It depends on how much the marriage matters—"

"Wait a moment," he broke in. "What are you saying to me, Jennifer? You haven't ever . . . I don't believe it."

She forced herself to meet his gaze. "Yes, I have."

Tony jumped up and grabbed her by the shoulders, wrenching her from her chair. "I cannot believe this of you! You're saying this to pay me back, aren't you?"

She squirmed out of his grasp. "I'm telling you the truth. I don't see why you're so angry. After you and Debra—"

"How dare you compare yourself to me! You think women are the same as men? Well, you're wrong. They try. God knows they try, in this stupid country, but it's all wrong! It's a man's nature to be able to love many women, but a woman's nature to love only one man. A woman makes a home, she cares for her children, her family comes first. Of course, when there are no children . . ."

He threw up his hands. "I was stupid. I see just how stupid I was to encourage you in your career. You blame me for Melissa's death? Well, I blame you! If you had been home where you belong, a mother full-time, it wouldn't have happened. The only thing your career did for you was introduce you to those disgusting people in the theater—dopetakers, homosexuals, people with no family feeling! Who was it? I demand to know the name of the man!"

Jennifer walked out of the kitchen and into their bedroom.

She put her suitcase on the unmade bed, opened it, and removed most of the things Tony had packed. She wasn't going to need three evening dresses.

Tony followed her into the room. "Do you love him?"

Jennifer carefully folded a sweater and put it into her suitcase. "Yes, I do." She knew that if she told the truth Tony would let her leave.

An expression of anger mixed with loathing passed
ver his features. "My first guess would be Patrick.
3ut when a man has a wife like Meredith . . . well,
ou wouldn't really be his cup of tea. It's more likely
hat Garcia fellow."

Jennifer felt a wave of pain, and then anger, but
eeing Tony's furious, uncomprehending face, she
it back a retort and continued to pack.

It was useless to retaliate. Tony was hopelessly un-
ble to understand her or view her as desirable. He
ad expressed himself clearly on the subject. To him
he was a nurturer, a maternal figure. He had chosen
er to be the mother of his children, not his lover.
)nly a voluptuous woman could play that role for
iim.

Tony had wounded her, but she would not wound
iim back. Not tell him how much she and Patrick
dored one another, and how mutually devouring
heir passion was. It was a love that was sacred, a trust,
iot to be cheapened in a vengeful moment that would
)ass.

Taking off her engagement and wedding rings,
ennifer put them on the dresser.

"I warn you, Jennifer, if you make a big court case
)ut of this, I will hound your seducer to the ends of
he earth."

"There'll be no court case," she said flintily. "I
lon't want anything. Keep the fortune you've made.
'll settle for the return of my . . . my dowry."

He took a deep breath and nodded.

The last look they exchanged was that of hostile
strangers.

* * *

Jennifer left her suitcases with the concierge and went outside to a pay phone.

As she reached for a quarter, her fingers closed over a key. The key to Patrick's studio.

She held it in her hand for a long time.

28

During the first week that Jennifer was gone, Patrick
missed her unbearably. Several times while walking
in the street he spotted a woman that resembled her.
Immediately he imagined her in London, in Rome,
in Paris. With Tony. And his chest would tighten
and a curtain of depression would descend.

At least he knew that she loved him. That belief
sustained him and enabled him to finish the music
for the television special.

On his way out of the studio, after delivering his
work, he ran into the producer, Mel Fox.

"So what's next on your agenda?" Mel asked. "I'll
bet you're hatching another musical."

Patrick sighed. "Yes. But just now my collaborator's in Europe."

"Uh-huh. Are you sure?"

"Of course I'm sure." Patrick stared at him.
"Shouldn't I be?"

"Listen, I may be talking out of turn, but for what
it's worth, I saw Jennifer getting out of a taxi yesterday on West Fifty-seventh Street."

"But that's impossible. She left last week—"

Mel shrugged. "I could be wrong, but she's a
pretty striking lady." He described her, from her
hairstyle to her black-and-white-tweed suit.

Patrick knew the suit. But how could she be in town? And if she was, why hadn't she told him?

He rushed to a telephone. The De Palmas' home phone was answered by a service. Mr. De Palma was in Europe. About Mrs. De Palma there was no information.

Patrick hung up, very uneasy. Something was definitely wrong. Had she quarreled with her husband?

At the Trump Tower the concierge repeated the same message as the answering service. Patrick pressed him. If Mrs. De Palma wasn't in Europe, where was she? The concierge hesitated, took the five he was handed, and consulted with someone else. Mrs. De Palma had gone to a hotel about a week ago, but he didn't know which. Another man had been on duty. Couldn't be reached until tomorrow.

Anxious and frustrated, Patrick went to a phone booth. No Yellow Pages. With the help of Information he phoned all the likely places: the Plaza, Helmsley Palace, Pierre, St. Regis, Carlyle, Stanhope. No Ryland or De Palma was registered. Nor at the Chelsea, the Barclay, the Algonquin, the Hilton.

Dammit, where was she? He simply had to find her.

Jennifer sat in a chair in the room of her small, sedate hotel, leaning her elbows on the windowsill and gazing out at the East River. After nine days of this she had become quite an expert on river traffic. She could estimate the wind velocity by how many boats were under sail, and judge whether a barge being pulled by a tugboat was full or empty by how low it sat in the water.

She went for an occasional walk, and at mealtimes

chose small, undistinguished places, not much concerned with what she ate.

She had told nobody anything. Left no forwarding address. After nine years as Mrs. Tony De Palma she needed this period of hibernation to think, to try to understand. So that her life could make sense once more.

Thinking produced memories. Living in San Francisco, tending to her ill grandfather. Meeting Tony. Handsome, attentive, giving her the confidence she needed and distracting her from her longing for Patrick.

Jennifer frowned. Why had she never bothered to find out what Tony expected in a wife? How could she have been so naive? Or lived in such a dream world? How could she have agreed to marry a man she hardly knew?

Then it came to her that at the beginning she hadn't considered Tony as a possible husband. She had liked him, yes. In the course of a month they had gone from dating acquaintances to lovers without quite being friends.

But Tony's proposal had stimulated her feelings for him. He treated her well, and she had gradually begun to love him. Yet, she had had doubts.

And then she had learned about Patrick and Meredith, and the new collaborator.

Suddenly the moment came back clearly. Dazed by the news, Jennifer had hung up after talking to Meredith, then lifted the phone and dialed Tony. *She* had been the one to say, "Let's get married. As soon as possible."

God. She hadn't remembered it quite that way. How she had fooled herself! She saw now that she had enmeshed herself with Tony as a way of up-

rooting Patrick from her heart, like a gardener digging up a weed.

Well, now her marriage was ended.

For the first time Jennifer was on her own. Free to do whatever she wished. Theoretically. During the first two excruciatingly lonely days in the hotel she had had fantasies of going to Patrick's studio. Of losing herself in his embraces, fiercely, passionately reaffirming that he was her true love, always.

But she wasn't able to do it. It would have been only a temporary respite. She had no right to throw herself at him and expect him to change his life just because she was changing hers.

In one way she was glad that he assumed she was in Europe with Tony. It gave her time, and time was what she needed.

But the nights were particularly hideous. She kept awaking from nightmares about Melissa. Never would she be able to forget how her daughter had died. All the pain had to be relived, in the face of her new knowledge, and she would never forgive Tony for having caused her this added anguish.

When her telephone rang, she jumped, her heart pounding. Nobody knew she was here.

But someone did: the rental agent she had seen on Fifty-seventh Street. He had an apartment sublet for her to look at. She told him she would be right there.

Patrick was glad that Lissa was going home with a friend that afternoon and would be sleeping over. He phoned Meredith in her dressing room after she had finished her Wednesday matinee, and told her he wouldn't be able to come to the theater that evening. Revisions on the TV special.

After that lie, he felt terrible. God, he was coming

unstuck. Frantic about Jennifer, imagining her somewhere in the city, not letting him know, for whatever reason. . . .

Where could she be?

He suddenly remembered something she had told him when they were in Cambridge, about staying at a hotel overlooking the river. But which river?

Patrick ran into the street and hailed a taxi. Handing the driver a twenty, Patrick had him cruise the West Side from the Eighties down to the Village, stopping at every hotel and motel with a river view.

Then they started up the East Side. Jennifer wasn't at the United Nations Plaza or the Beekman Towers. Not at the Waldorf, nor the Harley.

Just when he was getting discouraged, he had success. There was a J. Ryland registered at the Tudor, on East Forty-second. He smiled to himself. A modest hotel, so like Jennifer.

But she wasn't in her room, and the clerk couldn't say when she had gone out or when she would return.

Patrick waited for more than an hour, trying to read the *Times*, wrestling with the crossword puzzle, but mostly speculating on what had happened to prevent her from going to Europe as planned.

Suddenly he looked up, and there she was, coming into the hotel, not seeing him. She asked for her key at the desk.

One glance at her face, even in profile, told him she had been suffering.

"I'll be checking out tomorrow," Jennifer told the clerk.

When she turned from the desk and saw Patrick,

she caught her breath sharply. Her pulse was racing. "How did you find me?" she whispered.

"It wasn't easy." He looked tousled, worried.

"But . . . but how did you know I didn't go?"

He told her, adding, "Why in hell didn't you call me? Whatever's happened, I'm your friend, and you're very dear to me. Don't you know that?"

Jennifer suddenly dissolved in tears, hiding her face in her hands.

He put his arm around her and led her out of the hotel, stroking her hair, comforting her.

"Forgive me. I can see you've been through hell, and I'm making it worse just because I was hurt and worried. Tell me, darling, tell me everything."

Gradually she stopped crying. They found a coffee shop and sat at a booth facing one another.

As she calmed down, she was able to summarize her meeting with Debra and her confrontation with Tony.

When she got to the part relating to Melissa, Patrick put one hand over his face and shook his head incredulously.

Her voice faltered but she continued to the end.

Patrick looked pained. "Jesus. I can imagine what you've been going through. I wish you'd called me, let me help."

"I thought of it, but I really needed time to come to terms with it myself. And with my own responsibility," she said.

Patrick looked at her tenderly. "Jennifer, I'm so sorry."

She sighed. "Anyway, it's over now. I have to live with the memory but I don't have to live with him. I'm divorcing him, quietly. The gossips will dig up enough without my help."

She looked at Patrick with glistening eyes.

His face was full of compassion mingled with despair. "God, what a story. I can't even strike a righteous pose about your husband's mistress. I'm almost as bad, living a lie with my wife. Even if the facts are different, the deception's the same. And I hate it. God, how I hate it." Patrick pushed his hands through his hair. "Jennifer, I'm at the end of my rope. I don't know what to do anymore. If only Meredith didn't need me so much. After the last time I saw you, I was like a crazy man. My family thought I'd flipped out. Exploding for no reason. Except guilt. Frustration. Wanting you so much. . . . I stayed at the studio for a couple of days to spare them, to try to put the pieces of myself back together. Meredith kept calling me, begging me to be at the theater, worrying she wouldn't be able to perform, that her voice would give out again."

Jennifer was silent, finding Meredith's shakiness a little hard to believe, after all this time. She had seen the actress onstage, poised, playing her role beautifully, singing superbly, glorying in her curtain calls. Maybe she had her own reasons for wanting her husband to believe he was needed at the theater. And his guilt did the rest.

"Did you tell Tony about us?" Patrick asked.

"Yes. I didn't say who, of course. Tony was predictably furious." She smiled wanly. "Wanted the man's name. A question of honor, he said."

"I'd like to wring his neck for causing you so much pain."

"How would you feel, Patrick, if you learned that Meredith had a lover?"

"You want the truth? I'd welcome it. She'd be happier with someone else. She deserves to be loved

the way I love you," he added in a low voice. "If only I could get out of my marriage without hurting her and Lissa. But there's no way, no way at all. Not now, anyway."

Patrick ordered more coffee. "I'm surprised Tony didn't guess it was me."

"He did. I mean, it occurred to him, but he dismissed it. Couldn't imagine that anyone married to Meredith would give me a second look."

Patrick compressed his lips. "He's an idiot. I ought to know. I'm only a recent convert from idiocy myself."

Jennifer regarded her cup while Patrick regarded her.

"I'm terribly in love with you, Jennifer. So much that I can't stand to be without you. Especially now, with your situation changed."

"But your situation is the same,"

"That's true, for now. But it won't always be this way." He shook his head. "Jennifer, I can't lose you. Please, darling, please let's work something out."

As she looked at him, she loved him so acutely it brought on fresh tears. Mournfully she shook her head. "We can't. *I* can't. Don't ask me to be the other woman in your marriage. Love isn't excuse enough. Debra claims to love Tony, and saw nothing wrong in her actions. But I can't play that role, Patrick."

He looked devastated as he leaned forward tensely and reached for her hands. "But it's not the same! You're not just an amusement to me, Jennifer, you're the love of my life. But to tell Meredith about us now, when she's still so shaky—she'd be crushed. I'm almost like a father to her. I think that's why she asked me never to leave her. That's a promise that no

adult can reasonably expect another adult to keep.
Love has to be given freely, as I give it to you. I love
you with every breath in my body. I have never
loved anyone this way."

Neither had she. His words, describing her own
feelings, made her weak. She kept blinking back her
tears, trying not to give in.

"Please, we can work it out," he pleaded softly.

"How would you live with your guilt?"

"With difficulty. But nothing would be as difficult
as living without you."

Jennifer bit her lips. "Meredith is a friend. I can't.
I simply can't."

"Just for a while. Maybe only a few months."

A few months. Jennifer suddenly imagined Patrick
at her new apartment, his special, loving presence
lending it warmth. Doing things a couple in love
did: cooking meals together, bumping into each
other in the small kitchen. Reading the Sunday papers companionably while the rain fell outside and
the wind howled. Later, snuggling close under the
covers in bed. Feeling cozy and safe and secure. And
loved.

He saw her wavering, and his face lit up with
hope. "A love like ours comes along only once in a
lifetime, darling. We have to grab it, nurture it, and
never, ever let it go."

In spite of his words, her fantasy suddenly gave
way to reality. "How can we grab it? How would it
work?" she asked in a low voice. "We'd meet, work,
maybe have something to eat, to drink. Make love.
And then what? You'd have to leave," she finished,
her voice as miserable as the thought made her.
"You'd have to go to the theater, or home, or to pick
up Lissa."

"Not all the time. I'd find a way—"

"Patrick," she asked quietly, "would you be abl‹ to spend the night with me? The whole night?"

For a moment he stared at her. Then his eyes grew bright as he slowly shook his head.

"I couldn't bear it," she cried. "Couldn't bear t‹ know that you were going home, that it would b‹ another woman you'd hold in your arms all nigh‹ long. I'd feel so jealous and resentful. I can't do it Patrick, I simply can't."

"Oh, Christ!"

"I can't go on with the collaboration, either. I‹ won't work, under the circumstances."

"You're going to take even that away from me?"‹ His voice broke.

"I must," she insisted. "The only way we won'‹ give in to our feelings is if we don't see each other."‹

"Wait. Please. Don't throw me away altogether. ‹ promise—"

"No! Those are just words! I deal in words, remember? They can persuade and promise, but when‹ they come up against feelings, they're useless. Little puffs of nothing, like in comic strips. Words haven't kept us apart in the past and they won't in the future. Only distance will do that. Patrick, I'm not going to‹ tell you where I'm moving."

"It doesn't matter," he cried, his face almost frightening in its intensity. "I'll always find you. The‹ way I did this time." He told her how.

Jennifer listened as if to a fairy tale. She felt in the grip of a love so great, so transcendent, that it seemed to overcome every practical obstacle, no matter what. Incredible. A chance, throwaway remark about a hotel with a river view, a remark she had made months ago and forgotten, *he* had remem-

bered. He had searched Manhattan for her until he found her.

Again she wavered.

Again she forced herself not to give in.

Making a last supreme effort, she whispered, "If you love me, don't look for me. Let me go."

He shut his eyes for a moment. "Make it just a moratorium. You set the time and I'll stick to it. I give you my word. But at least . . . at least leave me some hope."

"All right," she agreed finally. "A couple of months. No phoning, no contact of any kind. We'll have to stall Sharon. Agreed?"

His eyes were smoky with pain. "Agreed."

They stood in the street and looked sadly at one another.

Patrick sighed deeply. "I don't know how this is going to end. I haven't any answers. I only know that I love you very much. And someday, somehow, we'll be together."

29

"Did you see that item about Jenny and Tony in today's *Post*?" Meredith asked her husband one evening when he arrived in her dressing room with Lissa.

His heart sank. "No," he said while his daughter went to the piano and began to play with one finger.

"They've split up. Did you know?"

"Yes," he sighed.

"You knew, and you didn't say a word!" Meredith turned and stared at him.

He fidgeted uncomfortably. "She was going to tell you herself when she's ready—"

"But she told you! When?"

He shrugged. "A few weeks ago. She had to tell me because we've postponed working on the show—"

"Thanks a lot! I tried to call Jenny today, as soon as I read the item, and the maid or someone told me she's not at the Trump Tower anymore. And you knew all the time and let me make a fool of myself—"

"Not now, please," Patrick said, nodding toward Lissa. His daughter was still picking out tunes on the piano.

"She's not listening. Anyway, busted marriages aren't news to her. Most of her friends' parents are

divorced. We can't keep her a baby forever." The phone rang, and Meredith answered.

Patrick sighed. The month since he had last seen Jennifer had felt like a year. Unable to work on the new musical, he had taken on more television projects. Meredith was so self-absorbed these days she hadn't once inquired about his progress on the musical.

Patrick had observed his end of the bargain with Jennifer. Didn't phone, didn't even know where she was.

He felt uncomfortable in his wife's dressing room amid the lilac walls and draperies, contrasting with deep purple carpeting and purple velvet sofa. There were also several matching upholstered chairs. Her dressing table was antique white and gold, as was the piano. All around the walls were pictures of Meredith in the different roles she had played, as well as a photo of Patrick and Lissa.

God, how he had grown to loathe the color purple.

"So how's she doing?"

Meredith's voice jolted him. "Who? Jennifer?"

"Of course, Jennifer. It can't be pleasant for her to know that the gossip is all over town. Listen to this." Meredith read from the newspaper: " 'It's splitsville for leather man Tony De Palma and his lyricist wife, Jennifer Ryland. The Italian charmer has been seen all over town snuggling up to gorgeous blond leg model Debra Dillon. I'll report on the gams when I can unglue my eyes from her luscious . . . shoulders.' "

Patrick squirmed. "I doubt that Jennifer reads that rubbish."

"Probably not." Meredith carefully positioned her

wig of Grecian curls. "I always thought there was something fishy about that marriage. He's got it made, so he found himself a model. No doubt young. It figures. But imagine Jenny moving out of Trump Tower. She should have made him get out."

Patrick didn't respond. His wife was assuming that Tony had left Jennifer and not the other way around.

"Where's she living?"

"I don't know."

Meredith studied his brooding reflection in the mirror. "You're worried, I can see that. Look, Partick, broken marriage or no broken marriage, you've got a show to do. If she's not up to it, maybe you should find somebody else. It's better than moping around here."

"At your invitation," he said moodily.

"Okay, okay. I just don't want you to get stuck with no collaborator, that's all."

"That's my lookout," he said tightly.

"It's my lookout too. I don't intend to stay in *Helen* forever, you know. A year from now—"

A knock at the door interrupted her.

"Oh, hi, Judy," Meredith said to the brisk, attractive young woman who was accompanied by a photographer.

"This is Patrick Lattimore, my husband, and Lissa, my daughter. Judy and Rod are with *People*. . . . Yes, I had my dressing room decorated by Fred Duncan, who did the sets for *Helen*. Well, I think of this as a home away from home. . . ."

Patrick declined to be photographed, but Lissa smile, excited that her picture would be in a magazine.

Patrick was feeling so depressed he could barely

rouse himself. He and Meredith had begun sniping at each other. He disliked exactly what she relished: the publicity, the show-business extravagance. Not that he didn't understand her feelings. She was a star. He was genuinely glad for her. If only she would leave him out of it. But she wouldn't relent. If he arrived at her dressing room ten minutes late, she threw a fit.

"Patrick, I'm speaking to you!"

He looked up in a daze. The journalists had left, and Meredith was dressed and ready for her first scene. "Sorry, dear, what did you say?"

"I asked you what's wrong. You seem very down."

He sighed and rose from his chair. "I'm okay. Come on, sweetie, time to go."

Meredith looked at him fearfully. "I'm afraid I'll make a mess of the show tonight. I'm not feeling up to it."

"You'll be fine," he assured her, walking up and putting his arms around her. He hugged her, rubbing her shoulders. "You look terrific, better than ever. Every night you go out there and knock their socks off. And you will tonight. Break a leg, baby," he murmured in her ear, kissing her cheek. "Pick you up at eleven."

"Break a leg, Mom," Lissa said, kissing her.

Patrick took his daughter by the hand, and they left the theater. "Now, how about a special treat? You pick it. What would you like to do?"

"Oh, could we go to Rumpelmeyer's for a hot-fudge sundae?"

"You've got it."

He enjoyed watching his daughter eating her ice cream.

"You know, Daddy, Jill's father takes her here

every Sunday. Without her mother. They're divorced. Hey, she gets a sundae on Sunday. Isn't that funny?"

"Yes, very funny." He sighed.

"Are you and Mom going to get divorced?"

He looked at her quickly. "What makes you ask a question like that?"

"I just wondered. I heard you and Mom talking about Jenny. And last week my teacher asked how many kids live with their real mother and father. Only four of us do. Out of about twenty. Just think, Daddy, if you and Mom were divorced, you'd always take me out on Sunday. And coming to Rumpelmeyer's wouldn't be a special treat at all."

Meredith took several curtain calls. Her dressing room afterward was a madhouse, with all sorts of people milling backstage.

Patrick did his best to be polite but he was near the breaking point. He felt like a rat in a maze, with no way out.

The one thing he wasn't up for tonight was supper with some members of the cast. "Go without me," he told Meredith. "Please, dear, enjoy yourself. I'm tired. I'd rather go home."

"Okay, if you're sure."

At home he drank a beer and went straight to bed. However, he was a light sleeper, and he heard his wife come in and get ready for bed.

When he stirred, she leaned over him. "You're awake, aren't you? Listen, what's the matter? You've been acting funny all evening."

Patrick wearily sat up. The beer had been a mistake. His head felt fuzzy.

"Are you worried about something, Patrick?"

"No. Not really. I'm just feeling a little . . . blah."
He sighed.

"Well, try to perk up, for God's sake. Everybody
noticed tonight."

Her tone annoyed him. "I don't care what 'everybody' thinks. It's hard for me to be at the theater
every single evening and twice on Wednesdays and
Saturdays. That's what's getting me down, if you
must know. I have to drop everything to come and
hold your hand—"

"Don't, then," she snapped.

"What do you mean, don't?"

"Don't come. I'll try to do without you, if that's
the way you feel. And if I fall apart before a performance, so be it."

"Oh, hell. Don't be a martyr, please, it's not necessary. I'm not saying I don't ever want to be there,
but could we cut back on it? Would you at least try?
Suppose I stand by, near the phone, either at home
or the studio. And if you need me I'll hop in a cab.
I'm thinking of Lissa, too. She's dropped her ballet
classes because she'd rather be with us than home
alone with Bridget—"

"That's not what she told me," Meredith said
shrilly. "She lost interest in ballet—"

"No, baby, she didn't."

"Oh, I see. The usual. Father and daughter, and
I'm the last to know. Don't think I don't see what
you have, you two. She's *your* child, looks like you,
thinks like you, and is closer to you. And you're
afraid that if she comes to the theater where *I* shine,
for a change, it might equal up the sides."

Patrick shut his eyes for a moment. "I wasn't
aware that there were sides. Lissa belongs to both of

us. And I think it's great for her to see you at the theater, but does it have to be every single night?"

Husband and wife looked at each other.

"I guess not," she finally relented. "I don't want
her giving up ballet. If only she'd told me the truth.
I'll speak to her about starting up her lessons again.
You tell her, too."

"Yes, all right."

The one thing they had always agreed on was to
present a united front to their daughter.

"I'll try things your way, Patrick. Just as long as I
can reach you by phone. And you'll come to the theater if I really need you."

"Of course." Patrick yawned. "I'm sorry, dear. I
really am dead tired."

Meredith sat at the edge of the bed, thinking,
while he fell asleep again.

Something was going on, something Patrick wasn't
telling her. She would have to find out what it was.
In the meantime, she had better not push him.

Sharon McEwell arranged a lunch at "21" to discuss
the forthcoming London production of *Helen, Hel-
en!* An exciting development, Jennifer felt. Sitting
next to Sharon, she was listening attentively to the
producer, but from the corner of her eye she kept
seeing Patrick on the other side of the large table.
Every once in a while their eyes met briefly.

Unfortunately, nine weeks of not being in touch
with Patrick hadn't altered Jennifer's feelings toward him. She was settled into her apartment in the
West Seventies. It was the first time she had lived
alone, and she was enjoying her new independence.
She saw friends and kept busy, trying her best not to
miss Patrick. Without succeeding.

Also present at the lunch were two Englishmen, Brian Witt, producer, and Sean Blayne, director.

They were discussing how they were going to mount the London show and which of the road-company actors would star initially, before British actors took over.

Sean said, "We want to expand several of the scenes, cut one or two, and add some entirely new ones. A battle scene, for instance. And of course we'll need some new numbers."

"We'd like you two to come to London and work with us for four or five weeks," Brian added. "Other adjustments have to be made for a London audience, and it will be easier if you're there on the spot through the previews."

Jennifer felt a surge of anticipation, which told her that she had been missing the collaboration terribly. All this time she had been readjusting herself, dealing with banks and accountants, and in effect stalling and not doing any work at all.

She glanced at Patrick and saw him looking at her with glittering eyes. He was silent, waiting for her to speak. Could she risk working with him for so long, and so far away, without Meredith there? And even if she felt she could not, did she have a right to mess up the London production by refusing?

She couldn't refuse, and she said she'd be able to go to London. Patrick echoed her acceptance.

While the others at the table talked animatedly, Lattimore and Ryland exchanged a burning glance.

Suddenly there was a commotion, as Meredith was led to their table. People at neighboring tables whispered to each other and smiled when they recognized the star of *Helen, Helen!*

Meredith flounced into the chair that was brought

for her and agreed to have coffee. "I've already eaten. I was in the neighborhood so I thought I'd drop in and say hello. I envy anyone going to London. Wish I could be in two places at once."

Something in Meredith's voice made Jennifer uneasy. Also, the actress had barely greeted her, and seemed to be ignoring Patrick altogether.

Meredith stayed less than five minutes, claiming she was off to an appointment.

As the party was breaking up, Patrick and Jennifer found themselves side by side. He looked at her with concern. "Will you be all right in London?"

She nodded, a look of determination in her eyes. "Yes, as long as we keep it strictly business. I need your promise."

"You have it," he said in a low voice, immediately moving away.

A few days later, as Jennifer was at home looking over the *Helen* libretto, her doorbell rang.

It was Meredith.

Surprised, Jennifer welcomed her. But Meredith looked distressed.

"What's wrong?" Jennifer asked, her heart pounding. "Please, sit down. Can I get you something to drink?"

"A Scotch on ice, a stiff one. You'd better have one too."

Jennifer's hands trembled as she made the drinks. All she could think of was that something had happened to Patrick or Lissa.

Meredith gulped half her drink and then said accusingly, "I know what's going on between you and Patrick."

Jennifer's heart stopped. She took a swallow of her Scotch.

The two women studied each other.

"What has Patrick told you?"

"Not a damn thing. He didn't have to. And I haven't asked, either. That would be too humiliating."

"Meredith, there's nothing—"

"Oh, Christ, don't play games with me, Jenny. You're in love with him."

Jennifer blinked but forced herself to meet Meredith's gaze.

"God, the way you look at him! It's infuriating. I saw it for the first time in Boston. But the idea seemed so preposterous I couldn't believe I'd seen right. I decided it was the usual Lattimore-and-Ryland stuff. I put it from my mind. But I can't do that anymore."

Agitated, Meredith walked stiffly to the living-room window. When she turned, her eyes were sparking with anger. "You must think I'm deaf, dumb, and blind. Think you played it smart, huh? You've lost your own husband and now you think you're going to get mine, don't you?"

"No. I—"

"Liar! Look at this place. A furnished apartment, as impersonal as a hotel room. Obviously you're not intending to live here for long. This London thing is just what you've been waiting for, isn't it? Being alone with my husband for a month or more, while I'm stuck over here—"

"No!" Jennifer broke in. "No, it's not true—"

"I don't believe you," Meredith shouted. "I know you, Jenny. I see it in your eyes. You love him. And

he's obviously tempted. The way he's been behaving lately is not to be believed."

Jennifer felt as if her insides had rearranged themselves.

"You know something? I've been onto you for a long time, Jenny. Haven't trusted you in years. Not since you and Patrick first began your collaboration. You always left me out, and now you want to cut me out altogether. Well, I won't let it happen."

Jennifer tried to speak, but Meredith refused to listen. She was talking herself into hysteria. "Patrick is my husband and Lissa's father. Just because you've messed up your own life doesn't mean you're going to mess up ours. Do you understand? I won't let you. I'll do anything I have to do, anything to keep you from breaking up my family. I know I lost a lot of ground with Patrick when my voice went. And I've sometimes been afraid of losing him the way you lost your husband—to someone younger. But for Christ's sake, it never occurred to me that I might lose him to you! Until the other day, in that restaurant, when I walked in thinking to surprise you all. Boy, the joke was on me! Jenny, you should have your eyes torn out to look at someone's husband like that. How do you have the crust to sit there and pretend you're not in love with him!"

Jennifer's mouth felt dry. She took a sip of her drink. "Yes, I am in love with him. I always have been, even before you were."

Not content to hear of Jennifer's early feelings toward Patrick, Meredith pulled the whole story from her. Including what had happened between Lattimore and Ryland on the night *Make Love, Not War* opened in New York.

"You dope," Meredith exclaimed. "In those days

'atrick was screwing everything that moved. You now why? He was waiting for me, that's why. Even fter I turned him down, he waited and hoped. After ou'd been gone for a while he was really with me, nstead of always joking with you. That private hing between you two used to make me want to cream. Without you there to make me feel stupid, I :ould relate to Patrick beautifully."

Jennifer looked at Meredith, her heart heavy. 'Was that why you told me on the phone that he'd ound another collaborator?"

"I guess so. I don't know, I didn't plan to say that. 3ut it must have hit me that if you came back and ou two started all over again . . ."

"I'm sorry you felt that way," Jennifer said,)ained. "I didn't want to love Patrick. I was in-volved with Tony."

"Sure you were," Meredith snapped bitterly. "And ie's terrific. Too bad you couldn't hold on to him. Didn't you ever realize that he could have anybody? Didn't you ever wonder why he picked *you*?"

Jennifer swallowed. "Naively, I . . . I accepted what he told me. Now I realize that . . . that my charms were less important than my grandfather's money."

"You'd better believe it! In fact, you've never loved Tony," Meredith accused her. "It's always been Patrick. I see that now."

"I did love Tony. I certainly believed I loved him and I married him in good faith. But I didn't know him very well. And . . . and after Melissa . . ." Jen-nifer bit her lip, trying to hold back her tears. She didn't succeed. Every time she thought of Tony and Debra in bed together while her little girl was chok-ing to death . . .

Meredith prodded Jennifer relentlessly until she got the whole story from her.

When Jennifer stopped speaking, she saw that Meredith's fury had been tempered by a modicum of sympathy.

For a long time both women were silent.

"Is there any more Scotch?" Meredith asked finally.

Jennifer made them each another drink.

"I'm sorry, Jenny. But my sympathy over your child doesn't change the fact that Patrick is mine and I intend to keep him."

Jennifer winced at Meredith's proprietary tone. As if Patrick had no will of his own. Yet she knew she must not reveal Patrick's love for her. No matter how difficult it was to withhold the information.

"I've tried my best not to come between you and Patrick, Meredith. I don't want to be the other woman in your marriage. I don't want that at all. I . . . I couldn't bear to do to you what Debra did to me."

"Sure, sure," Meredith said. "I suppose you'll deny you two have been in the sack together. Since the old days, I mean. No, don't answer that," she amended, suddenly looking devastated.

Jennifer's eyes glistened. "I love Patrick deeply. But you have my word that I've given him up."

Taking a troubled breath, Meredith studied Jennifer's face. "Has he given you up?"

Jennifer averted her eyes. "Don't ask me to answer for him."

"And the collaboration?"

"I honestly don't know. We haven't worked together for over two months. The meeting with Sharon was the first time we'd been in touch since

. . since Tony and I split. For professional reasons
'd like to continue the collaboration, but at this
point I don't know if I can. Whatever happens,
Meredith, I meant what I said. I will not have an af-
air with Patrick."

Meredith suddenly began to cry. "Oh, God, what
a mess! Why does life have to be so stupid? So complicated?"

To those questions Jennifer had no answer. Meredith's tears had brought on her own again.

After a while they wiped their eyes and regarded
each other sadly. They had come to a guarded but
compassionate understanding based on their love for
the same man.

30

Two days before they were to leave for London, Patrick phoned Jennifer.

"I can't go. Sorry. I'm late with a TV special, and something else is in the works . . ." His voice trailed off.

Jennifer, her heart pummeling her ribs, thought he sounded depressed. Was what he said the truth? Or was Meredith making it impossible for him to leave New York?

Whatever the explanation, Jennifer mustn't make things worse. She took a deep breath. "I'm sorry too, but if you can't, you can't. I guess we can manage on the phone." Keeping her voice as businesslike as possible, she began to discuss the work they had to do.

They spent almost half an hour clarifying a number of things for a new scene and talking of the additional songs they were going to need.

Then there was an awkward silence. Had Meredith told Patrick of her meeting with Jennifer? She doubted it. Anyway, she couldn't ask him. "I guess that about does it for now," she said. "You have my hotel number, and I'll let you know the number at the theater as soon as I get to London—"

"Jennifer, I miss you terribly," Patrick said in a low voice.

Her blood turned to fire. "Don't, please. Don't make it worse."

She heard him expel a long, aching sigh.

"I . . . I have to go," Jennifer said quickly. "I'll call you."

When she hung up she was shaking, and the tears simply poured out of her. It was just as well he wasn't coming to London.

Patrick heard the click of the phone, and then the dial tone. He was finding it difficult to breathe.

Meredith had been driving him up the wall during the last few days. Touching him constantly, kissing him, initiating lovemaking. He was so exhausted, physically and emotionally, that he had fled to his studio once again.

But even here he couldn't escape. Meredith kept calling him, as demanding as she had been a couple of months ago. She insisted he come to the theater nightly again, claiming that because of cast changes she was having new problems.

If he had been hoping that she was gaining strength and confidence, he now saw it was only wishful thinking. Not only had it been impossible for him to go to London, it was now out of the question to talk to her of their situation.

It had been bad enough when Jennifer was with her husband. But now she was free. Free to meet someone else, perhaps. And Patrick rued his selfishness in not wanting that to happen.

In despair, he threw himself on the futon. Remembering the wonderful afternoon he and Jennifer had spent here when they had suspended time, blocking out everything else and just rejoicing in their love, in being together.

He fell asleep and dreamed that they were on opposite sides of a river, with no way of getting across. And then a bridge materialized. They began to run toward each other. In slow motion, as in a film. He was so afraid she would disappear—but no, closer and closer she came, until she was in his arms. He held her, kissed her, murmured over and over that he loved her.

Patrick awoke with a start. It was dark, and his arms were empty.

Rolling onto his back, his hands beneath his head, he shut his eyes, feeling hot tears slowly moisten his cheeks.

Debra Dillon buttered a piece of toast and looked with satisfaction at her fresh fruit salad. "This is really fabulous," she said to Tony, sitting across from her.

They were having breakfast in the dining room of the Breakers at Palm Beach.

At last Debra was where she had always wanted to be, a guest at this elegant hotel, with handsome, rich Tony De Palma, her fiancé.

They had no sooner returned from Europe than she had begun to talk of Palm Beach, pointing out that she would soon be too gross to go anywhere, do anything exciting. And Tony had agreed to a little extra vacation. He had been perfectly wonderful, in fact.

Tony had never given her any of the details of the breakup with his wife. Debra could guess, of course. And was grateful that Tony hadn't been angry, hadn't even mentioned that she had snitched and set everything in motion.

He had simply called and told her without expla-

nation that she was going to Europe with him.
Debra hadn't asked any questions, either. Just did
her best to earn her trip. All through Paris, Rome,
Milan, London, she had tried to keep Tony in a constant state of sexual arousal.

Fortunately, his wife wasn't making a fuss. As far
as Debra could tell, the divorce was going to be
quiet, as long as Tony paid up. Well, Debra could
understand that. There was enough dirt already in
the gossip columns. No woman wanted to see in
print that her husband had dumped her for someone
younger, more beautiful. Although Debra suspected
that Jennifer had dumped Tony, the columns slanted
it the other way, and that was fine with her.

She was finding living in Palm Beach in style even
more thrilling than the European trip, maybe because it was an old dream come true. She played a
little golf, lounged at the pool, and went shopping
for beautiful maternity clothes. She knew she didn't
look her best, especially now that her pregnancy was
beginning to show. And she had never felt so tired in
her life. Still, the main thing was that she had gotten
her man.

It was far more exciting to be Tony's fiancée than
Arnold's. Arnold had been richer, but everyone had
heard of Tony De Palma, and he had a boutique
right in town. Debra became friendly with women
guests at the hotel, feeling, at last, equal in wealth
and stature to the kinds of people she had envied all
her childhood.

Tony stifled a yawn as Debra prattled on about
the baby. He had a brief moment of missing Jennifer, but it quickly passed. He had been left with a

feeling of cold hatred for his estranged wife, who had dared to give him horns.

Women were treacherous, untrustworthy, even the best of them. Never again was he going to be so foolish as in the past. No future wife of his would have a career. And whoever married him would have to sign a prenuptial agreement so that she wouldn't get her hands on his wealth if the marriage ended.

Tony glanced at his watch and hurried his breakfast. There was just so much he could take of Debra's inane talk. He was also finding it less than delightful to look at her these days. Unlike some women—Jennifer, for instance—who looked so beautiful pregnant, Debra had grown puffy, and her skin was blotchy.

Why in the world she had wanted to come to Palm Beach in May, he couldn't imagine. Well, at least it was out of season and nobody whose opinion he valued was here in this heat.

The trip to Europe had marked the last of his infatuation with his young mistress; ever since, her pregnancy got in the way. Not only didn't she look appealing, she was sleepy too much of the time. If he had really loved her . . . But he did not. And her performance as his mistress was badly below par.

"I must go to work now, *cara*," Tony said, getting up from the table. "And then I have a business lunch. I hope you can amuse yourself until this evening."

"Oh, yes. I'll have lunch with my friends." Debra smiled at him as he kissed her cheek.

He went in search of a public telephone.

While he and Debra had been in Europe, Tony had hired a private detective to look into her back-

ground. He wasn't really surprised to learn that she came from poor beginnings and that the woman she called her hairdresser was actually her sister. For Tony, family feeling was of great importance. His respect for Debra went down another notch.

He phoned the buyer for his Palm Beach shop. "Shall we have lunch, *amore*? No, noon won't be too early. I want every possible moment alone with you," he murmured, feeling his blood begin to heat up.

The buyer was a divorcée in her mid-thirties. Dark, attractive, and very lusty. He had been having discreet midday assignations with her ever since arriving in Palm Beach.

Tony had told Debra the divorce from his wife was going to be a long, drawn-out affair because Jennifer wanted an astronomical settlement. A lie. It was Tony who was stalling, waiting until Debra gave birth.

He wanted to have a good look at the child, have it tested and be sure it was sound in mind and body. And he wanted to establish paternity without a doubt.

Only then would Debra Dillon become the second Mrs. De Palma.

Jennifer walked slowly along the Victoria Embankment, next to the Thames, drawing her Burberry trenchcoat closer, as a chilly drizzle continued to fall, and her hair became as damp as her spirits.

She was coming from the Drury Lane Theatre, where the cast had begun rehearsals. Everyone was frantically trying to get the show in shape for the upcoming previews. New staging, scenery, costumes, lighting, and an expanded libretto had been

achieved in the course of the month Jennifer had been in London.

But the songs were a problem. Working by the phone, Lattimore and Ryland had managed to piece together three new numbers. As the actors rehearsed and sang them, however, the wrinkles became apparent. Jennifer could deal with the words, but Patrick had to be put on a conference line so he could alter the tunes on the spot. It was inefficient, and the orchestrator was threatening to quit, making producer Brian and director Sean extremely irritable. Jennifer kept intervening on Patrick's behalf, and would call him privately, hoping they could work out the problems without others listening.

Still, she felt discouraged, knowing that the new songs weren't up to the rest of their numbers. And only this morning Sean had sprung on her that he wanted an additional song in the first act. On her way to Troy with Paris, Helen misses Menelaus and laments how long she will have to wait until they are reunited.

It had been too early to phone Patrick, and Jennifer had volunteered to do so later in the day. She also rashly promised Sean that they would have the number in a day or two.

She stopped walking at her steady pace and lingered at the railing, looking out at the river. Its gunmetal hue blended with the smoky gray sky.

Jennifer sighed. The past month had seemed more like six. Her life with Tony had become remote, and it surprised her at times how little she remembered him. Maybe it was a measure of their lack of true intimacy. She wished she could so readily forget the way her child had died.

In previous trips to London, with Tony, Jennifer

had been on a whirlwind, going to business-related lunches and dinners, ending up in after-hours clubs. This time she had little opportunity for anything but work. On the evenings she wasn't revising the book or lyrics, she attended the theater, mostly with her colleagues.

No matter what she did, she couldn't stop brooding about Patrick and agonizing, especially during those difficult transatlantic calls. The magic of the collaboration seemed to dissipate over the phone wires. And sometimes the connection was so bad that Jennifer could hear an echo of her voice, repeating what she had just said, as if she were speaking underwater.

In any case, the tension of having to come up with the numbers quickly was enough to dispel their usual bantering. Even if the frustration of their thwarted love hadn't added to the pressure.

When Jennifer had inquired about his TV-series music, he had glumly admitted he had finished it. Still, he had made no mention of coming to London, and she suspected Meredith was standing in his way.

Now, gazing into the opaque Thames, Jennifer remembered another time, another river. She thought of the crazy canoe ride with Patrick during their marvelous weekend in Cambridge.

Her longing for him grew until her whole body ached.

Someday, somehow, we'll be together.

Patrick's words came back to haunt her.

The drizzle stopped, and Jennifer, reluctant to return to her hotel just yet, began to walk over the Waterloo Bridge.

Suddenly she made the connection between her feelings and those of Helen, who had been parted

from Menelaus. Despair, yes, but also faith in an enduring love, a love that would finally overcome all obstacles.

Jennifer stopped, took out her pen, and wrote in her notebook, "We'll Be Together." She walked on, stopped again, and wrote. By the time she had reached the South Bank she had the basis for a new song.

Excited, Jennifer hailed a taxi. She couldn't wait to get back to the Savoy and phone Patrick.

It was with disappointment that she heard his voice on the answering machine.

"Hello, this is Lattimore, not quite live but bursting with good intentions. If you leave your name, number, and day and time of your call, I'll get back to you as soon as possible."

Jennifer took a deep breath. "Lattimore, this is Ryland, live, I think. Sean wants a song for the new scene in Act I . . . ." She went on to recite her draft of "We'll Be Together," absurdly having to phone three times so she could get it all read before his tape ran out.

She thought of calling him at home but rejected it because she simply wasn't up to speaking to Meredith.

Jennifer hung around her hotel all afternoon and evening, hoping Patrick would return her call. But he did not.

She continued to work on the words; however, her progress was limited without music to guide her.

For the next two days rehearsals went badly, leading to frayed nerves and exploding tempers. Patrick couldn't be reached at home or at the studio, and subsequent messages weren't returned.

Throughout it all, Jennifer staunchly defended

him. She had realized that it was the July Fourth weekend. The Lattimores had probably gone away.

On Monday, July Fourth, the rehearsal was the worst ever. Jennifer grew hoarse trying to be heard above the shouting. She was still defending Patrick, although by this time she, too, was annoyed with him. He could have checked his messages. Surely he knew that Monday was a working day over here.

They rehearsed for hours, not breaking until six in the evening.

With her head aching and her throat tight, Jennifer returned to her room at the Savoy. She felt totally drained. Although it had turned warmer, she had a hot bath to soak away her troubles.

As she was slipping into her robe, the phone rang.

When she picked up the receiver she heard Patrick's voice singing "We'll Be Together" to a tune he had written. He hadn't even said hello, but she didn't care.

The melody was perfect, and she marveled at the way he had come up with something so exactly right. In that instant she forgave him for not having returned her calls sooner.

As he sang, his voice was husky, intimate, and Jennifer's heart pounded as a slow shiver worked its way up her backbone.

"That's wonderful, Patrick. Exactly right. It's uncanny how you've captured the mood so precisely."

" 'Uncanny' is just the word. You won't believe this, Jennifer, but I wrote the melody before I got your words, before I knew such a song was even wanted. Because I was thinking of you."

And I was thinking of you. No one but you.

But she didn't dare to say so to him. She stuck to

business, noting that the melody now showed up the bumpiness of the words.

"Never mind, Jennifer," he said confidently. "We'll smooth out all the bumps. Everything will be all right."

"I hope so. Today everything was all wrong. Sean's been frantic because we couldn't get in touch with you. And when I reminded him that it was a holiday, his mood didn't improve. You can imagine how the English feel about July Fourth."

She heard Patrick's appreciative laugh. The sound made her tremble, and she covered her nervousness by asking quickly, "Where are you, anyway? In Connecticut?"

"I'm downstairs in the lobby."

Jennifer caught her breath and shut her eyes. "In the lobby? Here? You don't mean it!"

"I do. I mean every word I say. Always. May I come up?" His voice was full of love.

"No! Wait. I . . . I'm not dressed."

"All the better," he said suggestively.

"Patrick, we can't."

"Oh, yes, we can," he contradicted huskily. "This is a special Independence Day, darling. Meredith has let me go."

31

Jennifer saw Patrick before he saw her. She had emerged from an elevator behind a group of people, and for a moment she remained off to the side, studying him. He was wearing a blue summer suit, dark blue shirt, and muted pastel-striped tie, and he looked tanned and achingly handsome.

She stood there feeling her emotional gears go into overdrive.

In an attempt to adjust to the bombshell he had dropped, she had stalled for time. She wouldn't let him come to her room, insisting they meet in neutral territory, have dinner, talk.

She knew too well that the moment they were alone their communication would cease to be verbal.

She now smoothed her beige linen suit, with matching silk shirt, and came up behind him. "Mr. Lattimore, I presume?"

He turned, his face coming alive with pleasure, and without a word held out his hands.

Jennifer took them, feeling the warmth of his flesh penetrate her own. She trembled slightly as his burning eyes regarded her.

"Oh, God, Jennifer!" He swept her into his arms and just held her, his face buried in her hair.

She wound her arms around him and experienced a moment of pure joy before breaking gently away.

"We have to honor our dinner reservation," she said, smiling at him.

"Hm. Too bad. Because I have no appetite for anything but you." His look of intensity was making her feel weak.

They were led to a table in the Savoy Grill, where they ordered drinks and greedily took in every detail of one another's features.

"You *are* telling me the truth? About you and Meredith, I mean," Jennifer said.

He nodded soberly.

When Patrick had begun talking of going to London, Meredith became very clingy again. His spirits sank, but he remained patient and understanding. He simply couldn't go when she was feeling so fragile, worrying every morning that her voice was weakening, claiming every night that she was exhausted.

"Take some time off, dear," Patrick suggested. "I don't want you to collapse from overwork."

"I won't. I'll be all right. I just need you to be here. I'd die if you went away now. You don't really have to go, do you? The way you and Jenny read each other's minds, there's no reason you can't work on the songs by phone."

Patrick finished his TV score, and for almost two weeks appeared dutifully in his wife's dressing room, night after night. Lissa was in Michigan, visiting with his parents.

Patrick's mood sank quickly. He was trying to work on the new material for *Helen* and finding it difficult to concentrate. Yet, Meredith's shakiness upset him, and he hesitated to stay at the studio overnight and leave her home alone.

Especially difficult for him were the conversations ith Jennifer. They usually came in the late morn-g, New York time, when the English cast was at re-arsal and he and Meredith were having a late reakfast together.

Whether he took the call in the kitchen or the bed-om, Meredith hovered around him, and he was ex-emely uncomfortable knowing she was listening to very word he said, every note he sang.

One morning she looked at him intently when he ot off the phone. "Would it help you to work in the udio for a couple of days?"

His glance was apologetic. "Well, it would, actu-lly, but if you're going to be upset . . ."

"No. I'm all right today." She threw him a brave mile. "Last night wasn't bad at all. I can manage lone tonight. Just be at the studio so if I get the jit-rs before curtaintime I can call you."

Patrick frowned at her inconsistency. Last night he had been nearly hysterical before the perfor-nance. And later in bed she had awakened him sev-ral times, asking him to hold her and never let her o.

But if she was willing to try to be on her own, he ad to encourage her. She had come out of her panic efore; with luck, she would again.

"Okay, if you're sure. I'll pick you up after the how."

But that wasn't necessary. She phoned to say that he performance was fine, and she was having sup-er with the cast.

In succeeding days, Meredith assured him he ould remain at the studio. She would be all right. In act, she welcomed some free time before Lissa came ome.

Although Patrick was relieved, he still felt restless and irritable. The music didn't come any more easily. He didn't really like being at the studio without Jennifer.

His downstairs neighbor, Penny, met him in the hall several times and one night invited him to dinner. Patrick accepted out of loneliness, and he insisted on paying for the food and providing the wine. What drew him especially, he had to admit, was her adorable little boy, whom he played with for a good part of the evening.

Patrick had the distinct feeling that Penny wanted him to spend the night. And he was almost tempted, but when he saw her sad, imploring eyes, he decided that an affair with her would be totally wrong. The only woman he wanted was Jennifer.

Patrick came home in time for Lissa's arrival. His daughter looked so much bigger, and seemed so much more grown up, after only ten days away, that he was overwhelmed. It was a happy reunion, and he had a great surge of family feeling. Meredith took three days off, and they spent them at the little house in Connecticut, swimming, hiking, and cooking out.

As long as Lissa was with them, Patrick felt all right. But then it was time for the child to leave for camp. That morning at the beginning of July when Patrick and Meredith saw her off on the bus, he nearly wept.

Meredith, no doubt feeling the wrench as much as he, proposed that they have lunch out, intimating that they could spend the afternoon in bed.

In the restaurant Meredith talked animatedly about the newest cast members and filled him in on the backstage gossip. She smiled a lot, her eyes dart-

g here and there, in acknowledgment of being re-
ognized.

But as soon as they left the restaurant, she grew
uiet.

The emptiness of the apartment hit Patrick like a
low to the stomach. Empty house, empty lives.
Vithout Lissa, he and Meredith were strained.

In silence she mixed a pitcher of martinis and
oured them drinks. He gulped his down, willing to
y anything to improve his mood.

Meredith threw him a seductive look and went to
1e bedroom carrying the pitcher.

Draining his glass, Patrick joined her in a few min-
tes.

To his surprise, she was sitting fully dressed on the
ed, drinking and staring into space.

"What's the matter?" he asked.

She glanced at him resentfully. "What do you
are?"

"Of course I care—"

"Like hell. You're in love with Jenny."

Patrick shut his eyes for a moment and sat down
ext to his wife. He sighed but didn't deny her accu-
ation.

She jumped up and walked unsteadily to her dress-
ng table, looking at herself reflected from three sides
n the mirror.

"What has she got that I don't? Jesus, every night I
;o out onstage and thousands of people cheer till
hey're hoarse. Men send me flowers, write me love
etters, wait for me outside the theater. Have you
iny idea of how many men I could have? How many
sroposals I've turned down in the last few months?"
:he queried, raising her voice. "How can you be so
;oddamn perverse? For years you mooned over me,

when I didn't even know you were alive. You coul[d] have had Jenny then, but did you want her? No! Yo[u] screwed her once and dropped her. All you wante[d] was me! Do you deny it?"

Patrick compressed his lips and blinked uncom[-]fortably.

"Say something, damn you! Do you deny it'[s] true?"

He shook his head miserably. "How long have you known—?"

"Not long enough," she spat at him. "The way yo[u] used to laugh at each other's dumb jokes, I shoul[d] have realized back then. I should never have give[n] you a second look. But I was stupid. After Jenny left[,] I forgot how you two used to carry on. When you told me you loved me, I believed you, like a fool. And while she was away, we were fine, weren't we? You were happy with me, I know you were. Unti[l] suddenly Jenny comes back and you go crazy. Just because she's married to a rich, handsome Italian and she's wearing good clothes for a change."

Meredith walked up and down, working herself into a frenzy. "I had a gut feeling it would be a mistake for you to collaborate with her again. But I couldn't believe it would be a love affair. Even when you began to call her Jennifer, even when I saw you two look at each other in Boston—even then I couldn't believe it. It's just the collaboration, I kept telling myself. Just Lattimore and Ryland doing their stuff. You were doing your stuff, all right, and rubbing my face in it!"

She stood in front of him, her fists clenched, more enraged than he had ever seen her.

Patrick swallowed, blinking. "I'm sorry, Meredith. I'm so sorry. I never meant to hurt you."

"Bullshit! I don't believe you! You'd be with her
ow if she'd have you. She's the one who won't go on
ith your affair. I know because I went to see her, to
ave it out with her."

Patrick took a swallow from his glass. This was
ideous, but at least everything was in the open at
st.

"When?" he asked softly.

With shaking hands Meredith poured herself an-
ther drink. "After I saw the two of you at that lunch
t "21." Because I couldn't fool myself any longer. I
anted to hate her but I just couldn't. She admitted
e loved you but swore she'd given you up. God, I
st don't understand how you could stop loving me
st like that." Tears prevented Meredith from con-
nuing, and she threw herself on the bed.

Patrick stood next to her awkwardly. "I still love
ou," he said softly. "It's just . . . different. My
ault, not yours. I'm the one who's changed." He re-
isted a strong impulse to put his arms around his
ife, to comfort her. Because the truth was anything
ut comforting.

Meredith rolled over onto her back and rubbed at
er eyes. "I was hoping that with Jenny in London,
nd . . . and if I could have you to myself, I could
in you back," she muttered.

As she told the rest of her story, slurring her words
ightly, he was dismayed to realize that her recur-
ing panic had been only a performance. Yet, in a
ay, he could sympathize. She had been trying to
ave their marriage.

"Anyway," she finished in a hard voice, "it didn't
vork. You've just gotten more unhappy every day.
And I don't want that, dammit. I don't need your

charity. I'm not just anybody, you know. I can d
very well for myself."

She sat up, put her legs over the edge of the bed
and laughed bitterly. "It's so ridiculous, all this
Christ. All those years ago, when I finally went t
bed with you on a whim, it was just my rotten luck t
get caught the very first time. That's right, I go
pregnant. And I thought, what the hell. It might a
well be you. After all, I believed in your love, foo
that I was."

Patrick stared at her. "You told me Lissa was pre
mature."

"She was, but only by two weeks, not six."

So Meredith had lied from the very beginning. She
had only married him because she was pregnant. *I
might as well be you.*

"Don't you dare look at me like that, you bastard!'
she yelled. "At least I was faithful to you. This is al
your fault, and I hate you! Oh, God, I hate you!"

He looked at her sadly. "If it makes you feel
better—"

"Well, it doesn't!" she cried. Her face suddenly
crumbled. "It doesn't help because . . . because I
loved you. Whatever that word means. I loved you
as much as I could love any man. My father aban-
doned me, never gave a damn what happened to
me. . . . Not even now, when I'm famous. . . . I always had a secret wish that if I made something of
myself, he'd come back, say how sorry he was, that it
was my mother he didn't like, not me. . . . Fickle
bastards, every one of you! Promise to love always,
and then you see another woman and . . . And I
don't need that. So you can just get the hell out of
here! I refuse to go on living with you when you love
another woman, God damn you!"

She threw herself against him and began to hit im with her fists.

Patrick grabbed her wrists and held her off, looking at her sadly, able to understand her rage.

"Oh, God!" she sobbed, breaking away and flinging herself facedown on the bed again. "I won't be ble to go on tonight. I'll never be able to sing gain!"

Patrick sat by her side, feeling helpless. Finally he aid softly, "I have a great tenderness for you, Meredith. And I won't abandon you. We've been through uch a lot together, had many wonderful times. And we're connected forever through our child. I still are, truly I do."

She lay motionless, facedown, and for a long time oth were silent.

When she turned over and looked at him, her ravaged face moved him greatly.

"We can't stay together," she sniffled. "I guess I wasn't really cut out for marriage. I tried, but I was always happier in the theater. Scared, but happier. There's always someone else out there ready to adore me. I don't need marriage. And I can do without the sex, too," she added sulkily.

If she had intended to wound him, she succeeded. Even though he had suspected her feelings, hearing her say such a thing was painful.

"When I hear the crowd applauding and cheering, that's love," Meredith said, a challenge in her tone.

"If you believe in the love of your audience, believe in my love, and count me among your most faithful admirers."

When his voice broke, she moved into his arms.

For some minutes they held each other tenderly. Patrick, stroking her hair, repeated, "I'll never aban-

don you. You'll be important to me always. And I can't imagine writing shows for anyone else."

Meredith's eyes glittered as she moved away from him and shook her head skeptically. "You and Jenny writing shows for me? I don't see how that could work, how I could stand it."

He sighed. "Maybe it wouldn't work. I hope it does, but I haven't any magic answers. I guess we have to take it one step at a time. I only know that I value you greatly, Meredith, and I want to keep you in my life."

Meredith eyed him suspiciously. "Don't think you're going to get Lissa away from me. That's out."

Patrick blinked, surprised. "It wouldn't occur to me. I love her too much to do anything to hurt her. Our separation will be bad enough."

"I know you love her," Meredith admitted. "Even though at times I've resented your closeness, I've also been glad. Because I remember how terrible it was to grow up without a father. But Lissa has to live with me. I'll never marry again, never have another child. I need her with me."

"Couldn't we have joint custody?" Patrick asked hopefully.

"No. I disapprove of joint custody. We'll work out an arrangement so that you can see her often, but I don't want her going back and forth like a tennis ball, not knowing where she lives. She's got to live with me."

They talked for hours, having much more to say when they were separating than when they were living together.

32

Jennifer and Patrick sat facing each other over the table, hardly touching a bite of their dinner and only sipping at their wine. They were too busy feasting on one another's eyes, smile, voice.

Several times Jennifer caught herself looking furtively at people passing their table, before remembering that there was no reason to fear being seen with Patrick.

She reached for his hand, smiling shyly. "I can't believe you're really here. That it's all right for you to be here. To think that I could have gone from such sadness this morning to such joy now."

"And the day isn't over yet," he murmured in his low voice that thrilled her through and through.

She felt her knees trembling under the table. As she looked at him, she was frightened by the intensity of her love for him. And although she was enjoying this moment, she couldn't wait to be in his arms.

Flustered, she lowered her eyes. "You must be tired, Patrick, from the trip, the time change—"

"Not in the least. I can hardly sit here, being civilized, when what I want to do is drag you upstairs."

"Yes, please," she said in her best English accent. And threw him a dazzling smile.

Patrick had booked a double room at the hotel and

filled it with flowers and champagne, an extravagance that pleased Jennifer greatly.

Taking her by the hand, he led her to the wide-open window facing the Thames. A warm, moist breeze blew off the river, which glittered like sequins under a full moon.

"That's the first time I've seen the moon in London," she whispered, awed, "at least for more than moments at a time. It's always hidden by clouds."

"Tonight there are no clouds," he assured her, pouring champagne for them. He lifted his glass, giving her a look that seared her with its love.

"No one but you, Jennifer."

"No one but you, Patrick."

"I have lived for this moment, darling, ever since Cambridge, when I realized just how much I loved you." He took the glass from her trembling hand and set it on the bureau with his, his eyes gleaming with a silvery light.

When they reached for each other, it was as if it were the first time. Taking her face in his hands, Patrick covered it with soft kisses. "I love you. God, how I love you."

"And I love you," she whispered fiercely, wishing she could invent a new way of expressing her feelings for him.

A boat passed by, music wafting from it, as people on a moonlight cruise danced on deck, their waving silhouettes faintly visible.

Jennifer and Patrick began to dance a two-step to the soft, slow music.

As the boat moved on, and the music grew fainter, their motions slowed, until they were swaying together in place.

He found her lips and pressed his mouth to them, tightening his arms around her.

She shut her eyes and surrendered utterly to him.

They explored one another with trembling, impatient hands, undoing buttons, snaps, and zippers, letting their garments drop at their feet.

Then Patrick lifted Jennifer and carried her to the bed.

Slowly they savored one another, interrupting to sip champagne and murmur words of love. Deliberately they held back, wanting to prolong as much as possible this precious renewal of their love.

They stroked, kissed, and caressed each other, building desire to an unbearable degree, exploring and defining each other's sensuality anew.

When they could no longer bear it, their bodies joined, rocked, and pulsated in climax, and for an exquisite few minutes two separate beings melted into one.

They slept, awakened, and made love again. Their feelings, shorn of guilt, were able to blossom and thrive, and the lovemaking was like nothing either had ever before experienced.

"I want you forever, Patrick," she cried, clinging tightly to him.

"You've got me forever, my darling Jennifer. Just try to let me go."

About the Author

Justine Valenti is a native New Yorker and former managing editor of *Gourmet* magazine. After spending several years in Europe, where she began writing novels, she returned to New York and now lives on Manhattan's West Side. Among her novels are *Lovemates* and *Twin Connections*.

World Renowned Authors from SIGNET

Buy them at your local

bookstore or use coupon

on next page for ordering.